The Gowrie Conspiracy

ALANNA KNIGHT has written more than forty novels, including twelve in the successful Inspector Faro series, plus a new crime series featuring his daughter, Rose McQuinn and four works of non-fiction on R L Stevenson, numerous short stories and two plays since the publication of her first book in 1969. Born and educated in Tyneside, she lives in Edinburgh. She is a founding member of the Scottish Association of Writers and Convener of the Scottish Chapter of the Crime Writers' Association.

For Barbara Wood
with my love and admiration

The Gowrie Conspiracy

A Tam Eildor Mystery

ALANNA KNIGHT

This edition first published in Great Britain in 2004 by
Allison & Busby Limited
Bon Marche Centre
241-251 Ferndale Road
London SW9 8BJ
http://www.allisonandbusby.com

Copyright © 2004 by ALANNA KNIGHT

A catalogue record for this book is available from
the British Library.

10 9 8 7 6 5 4 3 2 1

ISBN 0 7490 0699 4

Printed and bound in Great Britain by
Bookmarque Ltd, Croydon, Surrey

Acknowledgements

In the second of Tam Eildor's time-quests through history, from the many sources of research I should like to give particular mention to *The Making of a King and James VI of Scotland* (both by Caroline Bingham); *Anne of Denmark* by E. Carleton Williams; *Gold at Wolf's Crag* by Fred Douglas; *The Reign of James the Sixth* ed. by John Goodacre and Michael Lynch; *James VI and the Gowrie Conspiracy* by Andrew Lang; *Alexander Ruthven and the Gowrie Mystery* by Major and Mrs W. Ruthven-Finlayson; *Scotland's Last Royal Wedding, the marriage of James VI to Anne of Denmark* by D. Stevenson and *The Wisest Fool* by the late Nigel Tranter, a greatly missed friend.

My grateful thanks to the National Trust for Scotland at Falkland Palace and to the Scottish Library of Edinburgh Central Library, George IV Bridge, endlessly patient in providing obscure information. Finally to my husband Alistair for his tireless transporting of loads of reference books and his loyal support and encouragement.

Situation and Topography of Gowrie House

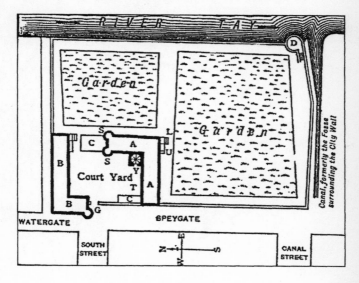

Interior

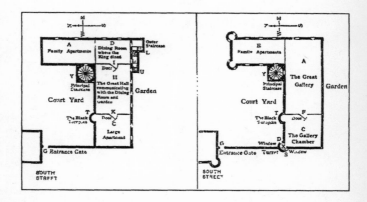

Prologue

From Lord Herries *Historical Memoirs of the Reign of Mary Queen of Scots and of King James the Sixth*

A contemporary account published by The Abbotsford Club, 1836.

...the kingdom and court was at quiet and the Queen, growing great with child retreated from Holyroodhouse unto the Castle of Edinburgh where, upon the nineteenth day of June she brought forth a son, betwixt nine and ten o'clock in the morning. This which follows is worth observing.

About two o'clock in the afternoon, the King [Darnley] came to visit the Queen and was desirous to see the child.

'My Lord,' says the Queen. 'God has given you and me a son, begotten by none but you!' At which words the King blushed and kissed the child.

The Queen took the child in her arms and discovering [uncovering] his face said, 'My Lord, here I protest to God, and as I shall answer to him at the great day of judgement, this is your son, and no other man's son! And I am desirous that all here, both ladies and others, bear witness; for he is so much your own son, that I fear it will be worse for him hereafter!'

Then she spoke to Sir William Stanley [Darnley's servant]. 'This,' says she, 'is the son, whom, I hope, shall first unite the two kingdom's of Scotland and England!'

Sir William answered, 'Why, madam? Shall he succeed before your majestie and his father?'

'Because,' says she, 'his father has broken with me,'

The King was by and heard all. 'Sweet Madam,' says he, 'is this your promise that you made to forgive and forget all?'

The Queen answered, 'I have forgiven all, but will never forget! What if Fawdonside's pistol had shot [referring to the killing of

David Riccio in her presence four months earlier and Darnley's plan to seize the throne] *'what would have become of the child and me both? Or what estate would you have been in? God only knows, but we may suspect!'*

'Madam,' answered the King, 'these things are all past.'

'Then,' says the Queen, 'let them go.'

Among the ladies were those closest to the Queen who had helped to deliver the child. After a long labour, difficult and painful, she lay also like one dead and two of the midwives signed a bond that was to cost many lives...

Chapter One

July 1600

Those who witnessed the sinister incident involving the King's runaway horse hinted at a miracle, that the presence of a humble fisherman on the bank had saved His Grace from a watery grave in the Falls of Earn.

Even an undignified drenching would have been disagreeable to a monarch who was not partial to bodily immersion at the best of times and considered that being the Lord's Anointed was quite enough in the way of ablutions. Warm water did not extend beyond his fingertips if he could avoid it.

When the identity of the fisherman became known however, 'Magic' was another word used to describe the incident. A word whispered with extreme caution in the King's presence, conjuring up as it did melancholy visions of His Grace's enthusiasm for witch-burnings and for personally attending and occasionally giving a helping hand in matters involving the thumbscrew and the iron boot.

The solitary fisherman was Tam Eildor, happy to escape the somewhat claustrophobic atmosphere of Her Grace the Queen's Household in Falkland Palace for a pleasant day by the Falls, a favourite leaping place for salmon. The fish were known to be plentiful but it was the joy of isolation with only muted birdsong, the swirling waters and an occasional fox barking that accompanied his meditation, the feel of warm July sunshine through the fine linen shirt.

King James had also been lured out that morning by the promise of a fine day's hunting, although he had little hope of the sun's rays penetrating the thick padding of his waistcoat and breeches, worn not as comfort against perfidious weather but as extra protection against the assassin's steel or bullet.

Nor did he share Tam's affinity with nature and the tranquil beauty of his surroundings. Such feelings of peace and meditation were unknown to him. A keen sportsman, he regarded the countryside as his killing arena, his sole purpose to bring down as many creatures great and small for the sheer pleasure of their destruction. What became of his trophies did not concern him. He noted only with gleeful satisfaction the growing number of carcasses signalling the day's success.

At the king's side, his retinue of fifteen courtiers included Ludovick Stewart, Duke of Lennox. Less striking in appearance and more sober in his apparel than the flamboyant young lords on whom the king bestowed fond glances and caresses, Ludovick owed his present elevation to boon companion as he was the son of King James's first boyhood love, his French cousin Esme Stewart.

The royal party had set out early that morning, their target the deer and wild boar. The huntsmen were not too proud to include any small creatures such as coneys and fowls unfortunate enough to be spotted going about their business in the royal forest.

The gentle river to which the runaway horse carried its royal rider was outwith His Grace's chosen area. The banks of its meandering course, too open for shy animals, were popular at court for rustic picnics and romantic dalliance. The only dangerous spot was a sudden rocky intrusion ten feet high where the smooth river changed course to become a reckless torrent, a picturesque waterfall popular with fishermen.

This was the spot Tam had chosen to set up his rod. Surprise and righteous indignation followed when peaceful birdsong vanished under a loud report which speedily erupted into shouts and the sound of a galloping horse.

Suddenly a magnificent white stallion bolted towards him from the clearing. With a yelling figure clinging for dear life to its flowing mane it was heading straight for the waterfall.

16

Tam leaped into immediate action. Without a thought for his personal safety he jumped into the path of the wild-eyed terrified animal and its even more wide-eyed terrified rider. They had reached the very brink of the Falls when Tam hurled himself into the fray and, seizing the reins with almost superhuman effort, dragged the beast to a standstill.

As he spoke words of command which the horse seemed to understand, it stood still, sweating and snorting, but respectful of the man who held its head in a firm grip, it pawed the ground as if in apology for its outrageous behaviour.

That matter settled, Tam went to the assistance of the rider who had lost reins and stirrups and whatever nerves he had started out with at the outset of the hunt that morning.

Tam had no difficulty in recognising the familiar brooding hooded eyes, the long melancholy face of the man still holding tightly on to the horse's mane. Bowing low, he said, 'I trust Your Grace has suffered no ill.'

And at that moment all indignation, all determination to make someone suffer for his indignity faded away from King James as he found himself staring down into the fine features and luminous dark eyes of his rescuer.

Ludovick Stewart had also reached the scene, reined in alongside to find the king oblivious to anxious questions regarding his safety.

James had fallen in love. Such a condition was not an unusual experience. It happened with alarming regularity over the years to the dismay of whoever occupied the enviable but tenuous position of his current favourite.

Queen Anne had learned to put up with the peculiarity of a husband who vastly preferred young men to bedding with a woman. She had long since resigned herself to the somewhat abrupt lovemaking regarded as the breeding necessity of a royal heir for the Stuart dynasty.

As for Ludovick Stewart, he had been around the royal court long enough to recognise the symptoms. But this was different; the young man was not of noble birth, just a simple

17

barefoot fisherman wearing a scanty white shirt and tight breeches. Perhaps it was only the novelty of his unadorned state which had instant appeal, Vicky hoped as James, suddenly aware of his presence, demanded,

'What kept ye, Vicky? Where were ye when this beast took off and almost killed your king?' Ignoring Vicky's spluttered reply, he raged, 'D'ye no' understand, ye glaikit wee mannie, we were almost drowned – dashed to bits on yon bit rocks down there,' he gulped, jabbing a trembling hand in the direction of the waterfall.

And then, rage abated, he bestowed a beaming smile on Tam. 'If it hadna' been for this gallant young gentleman –' he said softly, and pausing raised pious eyes heavenward, '– sent by the Good Lord's grace to save your king's life.'

Recognising his monarch's condition in the glowing eyes and tender expression, it was Vicky's turn to raise his eyes heavenward at the impertinence and the absurdity of the Duke of Lennox of the blood royal being described as a wee mannie and compared to a common fisherman elevated to the role of gallant gentleman.

Now both men took stock of Tam Eildor for their different reasons. The man holding the stallion's head was, whatever Vicky's reservations and cold appraisal, undoubtedly comely – strange looks indeed, but comely. Too dark for a Lowland Scot, a little over six feet tall and somewhere between mid- and late thirties – the king's own age. And cause for further caution, since this newcomer was also considerably older than the boys James usually chose to cuddle and coo over.

What did this portent? The man had an air of breeding, a touch of polished steel in his bearing, the wide shoulders and bare chest visible in the open shirt. A nobleman's bastard, perhaps.

And Vicky regarded James narrowly, noted that moon-struck expression. It was time to break the spell.

'Sire?' That was a question, since James seemed to have no notion of getting down from the saddle which Vicky rightly interpreted as awareness that on ground level his rescuer would tower over his royal person.

The remaining members of the retinue had halted a little distance away, an uneasy group wondering what was going on and blaming each other for the loud report that had caused such a catastrophe. Was the king at this moment considering retribution?

None had courage to approach where Tam awaited the king's instructions, the wild creature he had first encountered transformed into a contented animal quite happy to have its nose stroked while making several attempts to snort gently down Tam's bare neck, a familiarity which James regarded with considerable disgust.

Tam looked up at the king and smiled. 'He seems quiet enough now, sire. Something must have scared him.'

Remembering that explosion of noise, it was the king's turn to snort angrily, and when Tam added, 'Highly bred animals are often thus,' he shouted,

'Highly bred, did ye say? The loathsome beast almost killed me.' And, pausing to shriek at Vicky, 'Get me on to one of yon other beasts back there. As for this brute – we will have him destroyed. Now.'

Tam tried not to look appalled at such a hideous waste. He need not have done so. After all this was only a horse, a dumb animal. And King James was well-known to have as little respect for the human lives of those who earned his displeasure, high born or low. All were the same to executioner's axe or hangman's rope.

'Get ye gone, Vicky,' said James, slobbering a little. 'We havena' all day to stand here gossiping.' As Vicky continued to stare at him, he added angrily, 'Get me another beast, ony will do.'

Truth to tell, he was reluctant to descend from his high saddle and find his royal person reaching only – he did a quick assessment – his rescuer's shoulder. Another thought, a crafty motive. A sudden yearning to become better acquainted without Vicky's ill-concealed knowing look.

Watching him depart, James smiled down at Tam, demanded, 'Ye're no frae hereabouts?'

A difficult question for which Tam had no easy answer that anyone, least of all the king, could be expected to understand, so he ventured a vague, 'The Borders, sire.'

'Ye live nearby?' said James hopefully scanning the landscape for some humble habitation where he might dally a while and they might be private together.

'I am Tam Eildor, sire. A servant in Her Grace the Queen's Household.'

'H'mm.' All tenderness vanished in a glance of extreme distaste at the mention of his queen. Any mention of her household was not the best possible news for King James. As Tam and everyone else well knew, there was a constant state of war between the two.

One cause which united servants of both households in sympathy was that Queen Anne, by nature fastidious, found her royal husband's insanitary manners and unclean person displeasing. But of first importance to her was the fact that the baby Prince Henry Frederick, born after four anxious childless years, had been immediately whisked away from his mother's arms and removed to Stirling Castle to be fostered by its hereditary keepers the Erskine family.

James had tried in vain to placate and reason with his tearful wife. This was no reflection on her excellent qualities as a mother, he explained, but Stirling Castle had long been the Royal nursery for generations of Scotland's kings. Had not the Countess of Mar been foster-mother to himself when he was taken from his own mother, the unfortunate Queen Mary?

Anne's indignant snort as a reply would have clearly indicated to a less sensitive husband that this was no recommendation. That the same odious countess who now denied her access to her darling baby son had not made a very creditable job of his royal father. Anne had decided long ago that the

Erskines were not very refined. They had brought up James, the future king of Scots, to speak their own barbaric Doric, a coarse dialect which she, a Danish princess, had been forced to learn.

Now again almost six months pregnant, poor Anne's maternal feelings required that the young prince and her daughters, Elizabeth and Margaret, aged four and two, be close to her. She rightfully objected to the role of a brood mare obliged to provide princes and princesses and then fade once more into the background while James, his duty done, enjoyed a libertine's role with a series of dashing, disreputable young men. Life was so unfair.

'So yer wi' Annie, are ye?' James demanded. What advantage might be scored over his queen by this fortuitous meeting, he wondered, gazing down on Tam holding the stallion's head so firmly. And so simply attired, no concession to fashion, unlike any of his court; overblown, outrageously beribboned, strutting like peacocks with their jewels and ostrich-feathered hats, their slashed and padded breeches, their codpieces...

Why, this young mannie was almost indecently naked by comparison. The white shirt carelessly laced showed a great deal, aye, a very great deal, of warm-looking, healthily tanned naked flesh. His glance travelled downwards to the tight – aye, skin-tight – leather breeches. No need for codpieces there.

Suddenly tongue-tied as became a virgin lad and not a well-experienced king some thirty-four years old, James was aware of a certain quickening and found himself slobbering a little at the erotic picture. He was giving careful consideration as to how best he might carry on this promising acquaintance to his mutual benefit and smite Annie in the process, when Vicky reappeared. James sighed. He had almost forgotten Vicky's existence. But there he was leading a docile-looking brown mare, far less dashing than the white stallion which had introduced him to the infinite possibility of a rare new experience with a simple fisherman.

It was Ludovick Stewart's turn to study that simple fisherman again. He had been around James long enough to recognise the symptoms of royal infatuation, the challenge of sexual allurement offered by every new pretty boy's arrival in court. He did not share his royal master's taste for sodomy but the scene before him suggested that there was more to this young man than met the eye and that a careful scanning of his background would be enlightening. Especially in the interests of his own highly regarded position. Who was he? What had brought him into the Queen's Household and how long had he been there? Who were his friends and – more important since a favourite has no friends – who were his enemies?

These were the questions he longed to ask while helping the king transfer from one horse and quickly remount upon another. In the process, however, James could not resist getting a little closer to Tam. He held out a gloved hand and felt quite thrilled when Tam bowed, kissed it as he must.

After all, the grotesquely padded figure before him belonged to the King of Scotland who would within a few years, when the old harridan queen Elizabeth of England obligingly passed away, unite the two crowns of Scotland and England.

In the short time since his unexplained arrival in Falkland Palace, Tam had learned that kingship was the central fact of James's life. The obedience owed to it and the obligations which it imposed on him, were his deepest concerns. His lack of personal cleanliness, his slobbering, bad manners and vulgarity, his crude speech all hinted at the buffoon and disguised the "wisest fool in Christendom", scholar and poet who had already written two books on the practice of government and the divine right of kings.

Even the unhappy condition of his mother Queen Mary's long imprisonment and eventual execution had failed to weaken his resolve to be the future King of both Scotland and

England. He had played his cards well when he indicated in a letter to the Earl of Leicester that he would be a fool to prefer his mother's life to a throne.

His godmother, Queen Elizabeth, not known to be overburdened with sensitivity, was nonetheless appalled by such a response, having expected him to put up a fierce and vigorous battle to save his mother's life. That he did not raise a finger in protest, this cold lack of filial emotion and affection, branded him forever in her eyes as "that false Scotch urchin".

There were, however, extenuating circumstances. When Mary died beneath the executioner's axe at Fotheringay in February 1587, James was twenty years old and, in his defence, she was a stranger, not a mother, to him.

They had met only once for a few hours in the royal nursery at Stirling Castle before Mary's exile and imprisonment in England. James was ten months old. Subsequently he heard no good things of the late queen from anyone. In his early years the taunts of his tutor George Buchanan's description of his mother as a murderess and whore were consistent with sinister and ugly whispers concerning his birth.

Seeing the king settled on the brown mare, Tam bowed and waited to be dismissed.

James leaned down. 'No' so fast, ma mannie. Your king must give ye due reward. Aye, due reward,' he added rubbing his chin thoughtfully.

'I wish for nothing, sire. Only to serve you.'

It was a lie but James was delighted, he glowed. '*Aye, aye, ipsa quidium pretium virtis sibi.*'

The Latin tag belonged to a civilisation long lost to Tam's world. His blank stare, however, was not lost on the Duke of Lennox.

So the simple fisherman was not so well-bred after all if he did not recognise virtue as its own reward, a quotation known to every schoolboy.

James held out his hand and, without a glance in his royal cousin's direction, snapped his fingers in that singularly irritating fashion.

'You there, Vicky lad, have ye a purse on ye?'

Ludovick was shocked. 'Not on me, sire. Not at this moment.'

James glared, bit his lower lip and tut-tutted, as if carrying a weighty bag of coins for all occasions was a necessity at the royal hunt, where runaway horses were a daily occurrence with rescuers to be rewarded.

'Yer sword then, Vicky man.'

James had a phobia about naked steel and did not permit anyone in his court except the Duke of Lennox to carry a sword. For ceremonial purposes only, it was reassuringly blunt.

Vicky stared at him in alarm. 'Sire?'

James snorted impatiently. 'Aye, Vicky – yer sword.' And, pausing to beam at Tam, 'We are pleased to give our rescuer here a token of our gratitude.'

Vicky stared at him. A knighthood. Was that what James had in mind? But knighthoods cost money. A thousand pounds Scots was the usual price demanded of the grateful and favoured recipient.

So Vicky looked at Tam, did a quick calculation and was completely unable to imagine a poor serving man being able to produce, at most, more than a few hard-earned coins.

As for Tam, he had no such ambitions. The situation before him was poignant with future danger and he said quickly, 'Sire, I am grateful to Your Grace but I desire no such honour.' (Did he hear a small gasp of relief from the Duke of Lennox?)

Bowing, he continued, 'Sire, I would be well satisfied if I could be allowed to keep the horse here,' he said, patting the stallion's nose. No natural horseman, Tam had no wish to see the beast condemned to death and such a magnificent animal would be a very welcome addition to the Queen's stables.

James frowned, biting his lip, then he nodded enthusiastically. 'Aye, weel, laddie. Yer lack o' perspicacity does ye proud. A wee thing some men could tak a lesson by. Aye, it sits well on ye,' he added with a note of satisfaction and a sharp glance in the Duke's direction. 'Are we no right, Vicky?'

'Truly, sire,' said Lennox, his chilly bow managing to cancel his dutiful response.

At that moment, the situation was saved by the intervention of a sudden change in the weather. The hot summer day vanished under the menace of thundery clouds, unleashing what promised to be a deluge.

The king shuddered and sent a baleful glance heavenward. How he hated water, an abomination in any or all of its forms. If only his Divine Right included a clause to abolish rain...

Aware of lesser mortals, in the form of his retinue, regarding the approaching downpour with apprehension on account of fine feathers about to be ruined, James said to Tam,

'We are pleased to let ye have the beast as ye desire.' And turning the mare's head, he glanced back over his shoulder and repeated, 'So ye're wi' Annie, Master Eildor?'

'Yes, sire.'

'Aye, aye, nae doot then we will become better acquainted by and by.' Then James, with a final leer, spurred his horse leaving Tam to briefly acknowledge Lennox's cold glance.

Watching the two speedily join the waiting huntsmen who were trying in vain to avail themselves of the little shelter a thin copse of trees offered, Tam observed that the king had no trouble with the brown mare. His looks belied superb horsemanship; slumped in the saddle in his thickly padded clothes, the king closely resembled a badly packed parcel.

Angered by the rain, increasingly heavy as though in derision of the Lord's Anointed, James rode fast back to Falkland. Once in the royal stables, the grooms rushed forward while Lennox waited patiently to escort him to the royal apartments.

'Nay, Vicky. No' the day. We're awa' to see Annie.'

'Sire?' This was, again, a question. Unheard of that James should wish to rush straight from the stables to see his

Queen. In the middle of the day, without even taking time to remove his wet clothes. Without the due ceremony of announcement, like some hot-blooded lover unable to contain his lust rather than the jaded husband who regarded occasional consummation as a tedious necessity to beget the steady flow of princes and princesses required for a royal dynasty.

This new departure from customary procedure was vaguely threatening and Vicky repeated. 'That is your wish, sire?'

'Did ye no hear us the first time, Vicky? Are ye getting a wee bittee deaf,' was the irritable response.

Vicky bowed in mute apology as James continued, 'We have the notion for a cupbearer.'

As there was nothing wrong with the latest cupbearer, a pretty fifteen-year-old page who had recently taken the king's fancy, Vicky bowed mutely and waited, his lack of response taken for assent.

'Aye, Vicky,' James crowed. 'We thocht that mannie –' he jabbed a finger in the direction of the river and his rescuer, '– might be right suitable.'

Vicky said nothing. In truth he could think of no suitable reply, since the fisherman was at least twenty years too old for what was, in time-honoured tradition, a page's appointment.

'Aye, Vicky,' James continued with increasing enthusiasm for the idea. 'A cupbearer. Seeing the mannie wasna all that keen on a knighthood for rescuing us. *Traicit et fati litora magnus amor* – What d'ye think, eh, Vicky?'

Vicky was speechless, taken aback. James's tag regarding a great love that can cross even the bounds of fate clearly indicated the direction of his intentions regarding Tam Eildor.

'Well, then. Let's hear from ye, Vicky.'

Again Vicky took refuge in something uniting a bow and a nod which James accepted, with a happy sigh, as "yes".

Vicky, however, was busy mulling over that fortuitous meeting with an apparently well-bred fisherman who knew no Latin. A fellow who was going to need very close investigation. His own thoughts about James's plans for Tam Eildor were forming themselves in very large capital letters –

'NOT IF I CAN HELP IT!'

Chapter Two

Queen Anne was enjoying a gossip with her midwife, Margaret Agnew, a gossip that was more in the way of a regular consultation since Agnew would be present at her lying-in, for which event, in three months time, she was already making anxious preparations.

The queen had great faith in Agnew and trusted her implicitly; her practical advice and her knowledge of herbs were both helpful and soothing. Their conversation was limited to such matters.

That Agnew's mother had been one of the midwives present at James's birth in Edinburgh Castle had come as high recommendation to Anne. Any details of Margaret Agnew's private life were non-existent.

This was no drawback. One was not required to be on intimate terms with one's servants. Indeed, out of the royal presence they were obliged to fade into the woodwork and remain there until required.

Anne believed she knew all that was of use to her concerning Agnew. That she lodged close by, near the quarters of Tansy Scott, the Queen's Broiderer, who was in charge of robes for the new prince or princess whose christening, God willing, would take place in November or early December.

'Such a distance away,' the queen said wearily, her heavy body already something of a trial in this hot summer weather; she was a martyr to digestive upsets which only the midwife's potions could keep at bay.

Agnew's attention to her royal mistress's distress was interrupted by sounds from below the window. The clatter of horses' hooves indicated that the huntsmen had returned and the two women watched them, riding in at the gallop, with the day's trophies slung across the sumpter-horses.

Even at this distance, the king's angry countenance was visible under the drenched hat with its drooping feathers.

Anne sighed happily. Her husband's discomforts both great and small gave her immense pleasure. She was delighted that the weather had rained off the hunt and spared a few wild creatures to live and run until the next occasion.

A soft-hearted woman surrounded by her pet dogs, she had long since decided that she preferred animals with four feet to the men in her husband's court who had only two, but whose crude and lascivious behaviour was little better than the beasts they hunted.

Anne avoided bear-baiting which she considered a cruel and wicked sport, outraged by James's temerity to demand the pick of her larger dogs to supplement his own kennels. He explained that they were no longer able to breed fighting dogs fast enough to keep up with the rapid decrease in numbers. It appeared that the bear, even blind in one eye and chained to a post, took a hideous slaughter of up to four or five dogs each afternoon session.

The rain was heavier now. The royal party had hardly splashed across the cobbled courtyard for shelter when a page appeared and announced,

'His Grace the King.'

Anne was not pleased. She was not prepared for this, still in her nightrobe in the late afternoon. These days she rarely dressed apart from state occasions. Advanced pregnancy made formal robes a very tight squeeze and the tight corslet demanded by court fashion was cruelly uncomfortable and gave her another of those crippling digestive upsets which only Agnew's herbs made bearable.

Not that James would notice her lack of formality. However, since he was so slovenly in his attire, she disliked missing the opportunity of setting a fine example.

No matter. The sound of approaching footsteps indicated that it was too late now and she handed Agnew some pieces of satin and reels of silk.

'Take these across to Mistress Scott. Tell her these I have chosen.'

At the sight of the rain and Agnew's thin dress, she said, 'Here, take her cloak. She left it yesterday. Go along, wear it. That will keep you dry as you cross the courtyard.'

With her ladies-in-waiting clustered around her like a protective barrier, she firmly resolved that once again all her efforts would be devoted to a single-minded onslaught on her husband's conscience to restore their son and heir Prince Henry Frederick to his mother's side.

Weeping prayers did little, now she had only the hope that unrelenting nagging, like constant rain, would wear away even a royal stone.

Agnew's exit coincided with James's entrance. As she curtseyed briefly, he paused, looked after her thoughtfully and approaching Anne said abruptly,

'That lassie – Mistress Scott, is she no'?'

Anne curtseyed awkwardly. 'Nay, James. She is Margaret Agnew, bides with Mistress Tansy Scott of Ruthven.'

'Hmmph.' The king's frown delighted Anne as another small barb had found its mark. Any mention of Tansy Scott displeased James, since the girl was the granddaughter of Lady Janet Beaton of Buccleuch, whose unnatural powers in his mother's reign had earned her the title of the Wizard Lady of Branxton.

Early orphaned, Tansy had been adopted into the Ruthven family and as a child was living at Ruthven Castle near Perth when the Lords Enterprisers, led by the Earl of Gowrie, had kidnapped the boy king, sixteen-year-old James. There they held him captive until he would agree to suppress any suspected leanings towards Catholicism and secure the downfall and exile of his influential and adored cousin, Esme Stewart, of whom James later wrote, 'No winter's frost nor summer's heat can end Or stay the course of constant love in me.'

James had been very displeased to recognise Tansy once again as a close friend and adopted sister of Beatrix Ruthven, the Queen's Lady of the Bedchamber.

'It wasna' the Scott woman?' he demanded suspiciously.

Anne smiled. 'They are somewhat similar in looks.' So much was true. Both had striking red-gold hair but Agnew was stouter than Tansy. Now, regarding her husband's disgruntled expression with some satisfaction, Anne had another barb at hand. 'Perhaps you would care to meet Agnew, James,' she said sweetly.

James scowled. 'Would we now? And what makes ye think that the lassie would be of ony interest to us?'

'She is my midwife, sire. And what is more, she has a very personal link with your Grace,' she added with a sly glance at his dour expression.

James's frown deepened. 'And what would we be doing wi' such a craiter?'

Anne laughed lightly. 'Why, sire, her granddam helped bring you into the world. She was present at your birth.'

The royal frown became a scowl accompanied by some gnawing of his lower lip as James glared out of the window as though at a loss for words.

Anne, immensely pleased, knew she had won a small victory. For some odd reason she had never been able to discover, James hated any mention or reference to his birth.

'One would imagine he wished it to be considered as an Immaculate Conception,' she once confided in Tansy Scott in a moment of indiscretion when they had taken a little too much wine at Beatrix's birthday celebration.

The two ladies had laughed and shrugged off any significance, suggesting that perhaps it was his late lamented mother's improper behaviour with the Earl of Bothwell afterwards, followed by her exile and imprisonment, that angered the king so.

Beatrix and Tansy had exchanged glances. Court gossip had long since decreed that James's strange reactions to any mention of his mother were more from guilt than sorrow.

Such were Anne's thoughts as the unexpected meeting

31

with the woman Agnew had temporarily put out of James's mind his reason for this visit.

'You have business to discuss with us, sire?' she asked, restraining a yawn.

James withdrew his brooding glance from the window. 'Aye, madam. We have decided to... er, that is, it is our wish to have one of your servants – Tam – Master Tam Eildor, as our cupbearer.'

It was Anne's turn to be astonished. 'Surely there is some mistake, sire.'

'We dinna mak mistakes, Annie,' the king reminded her firmly.

'But Master Eildor is – is quite unsuitable –'

'And by what measure d'ye come to that reasoning, eh?'

'He is – he is – well, far too old,' Anne said in bewilderment as James smiled almost tenderly, she thought, at some elusive memory. 'Where ... how did this come about?' she added, knowing as had Lennox that the honoured role of cupbearer belonged to a noble boy, not a mature man of James's own age.

Again James smiled. 'Ah weel, Annie. It was like this. Our horse, that damned stallion your brother Christian was pleased to send us from Denmark, bolted wi' us. This – Eildor – was fishing at the time. He saved us, by God's Grace, from a watery grave and being dashed to pieces by yon waterfall at the river.'

He paused expectantly and was surprised to observe that her expression had not changed. Nothing of wifely concern, no cries or tearful expressions of horror at her royal husband's narrow escape from death. No pious exclamation thanking the Good Lord for his mercy.

James looked away from her in distaste. Never a beauty at the best of times, pregnancy ill-became her. He averted his eyes from the long thin face and pale hair that seemed to shrink into oblivion above the monstrous huge belly and blue-veined breasts hardly concealed by her nightrobe.

'Weel, weel, no matter.' Another Latin tag which left Anne bewildered. Speaking only French and her mother tongue, she had had to learn to interpret the Doric dialect of the Scots.

Noting her confusion, James obligingly translated, 'All's well that ends well.'

She wished he would go away and not just stand there. 'We thought you had a cupbearer, James,' she said weakly.

A cough this time. 'Aye, that is so,' he said trying not to sound impatient at her temerity in bringing this fact to his royal notice and thus involving him in lengthy explanations. 'We thocht it a suitable reward for Master Eildor saving our life.' He paused. 'And as it seems he is a servant of yours – '

Anne knowing Tam Eildor – well, as much as any did – shook her head. 'Alas, sire, you are misinformed.'

'He serves in your household,' James insisted.

'Only indirectly, in as much as Mistress Scott's apartments are under our jurisdiction.'

James bristled at the mention of the woman Scott. 'Surely ye have the right to command – '

Anne shook her head stubbornly. 'Nay, sire. Mistress Scott's servants are her own concern. You must take it up with her.' And so saying, she gave a great yawn, closed her eyes wearily and patted her large stomach in a clear indication that the interview was over and it was her time to rest.

James glared at her. 'We will that – aye, indeed we will,' and, thwarted once more, he stormed out of the room.

Unaware of the great honour that the king wished to confer upon him, Tam gathered together his fishing rod and basket and, in some trepidation, mounted the white stallion the king had graciously bequeathed to him.

As they headed towards the Castle in the heavy rain the horse, much to Tam's surprise, did not make any resistance to his inexpert horsemanship and behaved in an agreeably docile manner. Almost as if he knew that his rider had saved him from the king's vengeance and was suitably grateful.

Relieved by the sight of the Queen's stables, Tam saw the stallion settled and handed over the somewhat meagre results of his morning's catch to the royal kitchens.

Changed into dry clothes he was soon comfortably seated in Tansy Scott's lodging overlooking the Queen's apartment, regaling her with the tale of the king and the runaway horse.

Tansy sat in the windowseat, surrounded by a great spill of silks and satins. Laying aside her embroidery frame, she laughed. 'Her Grace will be delighted. Another score settled.'

Tam nodded. 'I suspect that the mares will be overjoyed at the presence of such a handsome newcomer too.'

Tansy smiled. 'And talking of handsome newcomers, we must find you some wedding clothes.' At his surprised expression, she said, 'I have just had a message that we are to go to Gowrie House. There is a wedding – one of my husband's kin – in Perth next week. This will be an opportunity for you to get acquainted with my adopted family – my mother and brothers – John the eldest is the present Earl, then Alexander, Master of Gowrie. You still have to meet Beatrix, she has been given leave to visit Dirleton Castle in East Lothian –' And Tam, listening to her, found it difficult, as she did also, to think that he had been part of her life for such a brief period.

*****

It had been a hot afternoon in late July when Tansy had found a strange young man seated in one of the secluded arbours in the Queen's garden. He was fast asleep.

At her approach, he opened his eyes and smiled as if this was no first meeting but a continuation of an encounter begun long ago.

Even as he rose to his feet and bowed over her hand, murmuring apologies, she smiled and said,

'You are welcome, Tam Eildor.'

A bewildered glance, another bow. 'You have the advantage over me, madam.'

Her smile was triumphant. 'But I have been expecting you, Master Eildor.' And, indicating the place beside him, 'May I?'

Once seated, she introduced herself and said, 'Lady Janet Beaton was my granddam. She told me to look out for you.'

Tam frowned. Janet Beaton. The name was familiar. A distant echo of some other time...

'How did you know my name?'

Tansy laughed. 'That was easy. I recognised you instantly from her description. She told me all about you just before she died.'

'So?' he asked cautiously.

'She said that one day you would come back and that I was to be ready to look after you.'

'What else did she tell you?'

Tansy looked around sharply as if fearing they might be overheard. 'You met her, you must have known she was a witch. I have always believed in her magic powers.'

At that she stood up and smiling down at him, she held out her hand. 'Now that you are here, you must be hungry,' and pausing, she gave him a candid glance and added softly, 'I suspect that you have come a long way, that this is end of a long journey.'

Following her across the garden, Tam asked the date. The question did not surprise her. 'It is the year 1600, the end of July and you are in the grounds of Falkland Palace in Fife.'

As she led him up the turnpike stair into her lodging, Tam was relieved that he had found someone well prepared for his unexpected arrival. Especially a young woman as attractive as Tansy Scott. Tall and slender, with red-gold hair and sparkling blue eyes. As he tried in vain to recall her grandmother, a Janet Beaton whom he had obviously encountered some years ago, Tansy asked,

'Can you tell me anything – about yourself, where you came from?'

Tam shook his head. How could he begin to tell her that the rules for time-travellers were inviolate. Access to memories relating to earlier quests or any memory of the present that he had temporarily abandoned was forbidden to him.

'My granddam hinted that you were from the future, oh – hundreds of years hence,' Tansy said helpfully, 'when machines and men flew in the air like birds and carriages moved without horses. When men, by the turn of a switch, could see what was happening in other lands and planets. See and talk to people across time and space through a tiny box held in the palm of their hand –'

She paused as if waiting for confirmation and, when there was none, she added triumphantly, 'Even your name – Tam Eildor – by rearranging the letters Janet Beaton worked out that it spelt "a time lord".'

Tam could not tell her a great deal more than that. How to explain that he did indeed come from a future where men had not only conquered space travel but also time itself?

There were no longer any unsolved mysteries except those of ancient history, but once on a mission a time-detective was bound by the laws and methods available in the Earth-time of his chosen period. In effect Tam had only his own wits and resources with no more facilities than were available to the persons and criminals he was investigating. Nor could any action of his change the course of recorded history. Since Tam was similarly cut off from the present he had just left, he was unable to provide Tansy with any useful information. His only certainty was that he was on the threshold of some momentous event that had baffled historians. An event about which he was in total ignorance – as much as those living in Falkland Palace at the end of July 1600. He must wait and see, be vigilant, and patient.

Before the episode of the runaway horse and his first meeting with King James, Tam had a chance to familiarise himself with his surroundings and get to know Tansy Scott and, through her, become acquainted with Queen Anne and the trying conditions of her royal marriage.

He found favour immediately in the Queen's eyes as an agreeable young man who was kin to her broiderer Mistress Tansy Scott, the latter having quickly invented a cousin from the Borders to explain his presence there.

The queen, never one to be curious about those who served her, accepted this fiction and merely agreed that there was indeed a strong family resemblance. 'Cousins, indeed,' she said. 'You could be brother and sister – twins even.'

Out of Her Grace's presence, Tansy laughed and standing with Tam before a looking-glass they could see sense in the royal observation.

Apart from one having red hair and the other black, their features were undoubtedly alike. The same bone structure, firm chin and wide eyes, the same mouth, especially as Tam was beardless unlike the court fashion of the time.

They were also of a similar age. Tam, regardless of his travels, remained in his mid-thirties. Tansy born in December 1567 was eighteen months younger than the king and had been married at fifteen, a dynastic marriage to a Ruthven neighbour.

Walter Murray of Tullibardine had been twice Tansy's age. Childless, she had rebelled against his cruelty and the privations of her life, relieved when estate interests took him across the Borders. There he found a mistress who presented him with a son and heir and where he was presumably content.

'If only he would divorce me – as a barren wife, he would have just cause,' said Tansy, 'then Will and I could marry.' And Tam learned that Tansy had a lover, the natural son of James Hepburn, Earl of Bothwell, who was briefly Mary Queen of Scot's third husband.

Tam hoped he would have a chance to meet William Hepburn who had been raised by his paternal grandmother Lady Morham and, on her death, inherited a small estate in Perthshire, neighbour to Ruthven Castle. Unmarried, approaching forty, Tansy Scott had for many years been the one and only love of Will's life.

Hoping Will was worthy of so great a prize, Tam also encouraged Tansy to talk about her granddam – the remarkable woman and witch Janet Beaton, aunt of Marie Beaton, maid-in-waiting to the Queen of Scots who had followed her into exile.

'My granddam was the trusted friend of His Grace's mother, you know, she was present at his birth,' Tansy said proudly. 'The queen had great faith in her herbs and, I do not doubt, in some of her magic spells,' she added in a matter-of-fact manner, as if such knowledge was readily available to all.

Tam regarded her anxiously. Aware of the king's merciless treatment of witches, he felt that Tansy, having already exhibited some of her granddam's powers, should be more discreet.

*****

Even as Tansy was informing Tam of Will's imminent arrival to escort them to Perth, and in the Queen's apartments the royal couple argued over King James's wish to elevate Tam to the role of cupbearer, Mistress Agnew, huddled in her borrowed cloak against the rain, was hurrying across the courtyard on her way to Tansy's lodging.

From her vantage point in the windowseat, Tansy paused to wave to her.

'At last,' she sighed. 'Her Grace has made up her mind about the right colours. That has been delaying me.'

And studying him she frowned. 'But what shall you wear for the queen's Masque, Tam?'

Tam shuddered. 'None of these slashed and padded breeches, if you please, Tansy. I am not a man of fashion.'

Tansy regarded him shrewdly. 'I agree. I cannot for the life of me see you in such a role. I think a scholar's gown would best become you,' and, eyeing him narrowly, 'yes, a good velvet cloak and a modest cap – black perhaps.'

'Have I then to visit the royal wardrobe?' asked Tam, having already decided to keep as much distance as would be acceptable without suspicion between himself and any future contact with King James.

Tansy smiled. 'I shall put you into Will's capable hands. He has an excellent wardrobe but shares your scorn for the fripperies of court fashion. I am sure he will provide you with something suitable for grand occasions, especially as he is much of your height and complexion.'

Pausing, she frowned. 'But where is Agnew? What has become of her? She is taking a very long time to climb the stair –'

Tansy opened the door where only the top of the spiral was visible. 'Margaret,' she called. And again, 'Margaret!'

Her answer was a banging door left open out of sight at the foot of the stair, a sound like a moan...

She gave Tam a startled glance and together they ran down the stair. At the base lay a crumpled shape wreathed in a rain-blackened cloak.

'Margaret, my dear, are you hurt? What has happened?'

As Tansy put her hand on the cloak, it came away with a sticky wetness. Not of rain but of blood. Gently, Tam turned the woman over. Her eyes opened and flickered for the last time as her head rolled back and he saw the dagger, the knife thrust to her heart –

Even as Tansy screamed her name they saw how she had met her death. Mistress Margaret Agnew had been murdered.

And for Tam the wheel had begun to turn.

Chapter Three

In the dim recess of the turnpike stair, Tam and Tansy bent over the dead woman.

'Who could have done such a thing,' whispered Tansy. 'Agnew never harmed anyone. She was such a sweet person; everyone trusted her, came to her for her herbs –'

Tam said nothing. This was the usual response on discovery of a murder victim. Only to reveal, as investigations proceeded, at least one person, more often than not a member of the family circle or a close and trusted friend, with a secret motive for murder.

'What shall we do, Tam?'

'I presume the Captain of the King's guard is the man to deal with this,' said Tam, moving into the light.

Tansy jumped to her feet. 'Then I am coming with you.'

Tam hesitated. The dead woman had just drawn her last breath as they arrived. Someone ought to remain with her still warm body in case her killer returned with the grim intention of making certain that she was dead.

As if Tansy interpreted his glance at the crumpled form of Mistress Agnew, she shook her head, shivered. 'Please, Tam. Do not ask me to … to stay here. I could not –'

Tam took her arm. 'I would not permit you to do so.'

He did not add that it might be dangerous. Considering his logical conclusion that the killer was still lurking nearby, Tansy might well become the next victim.

'Come then, we will go together,' he said allowing Tansy to lead him in the direction of the royal stables.

Tracking down Lord Fotheringham was more difficult than they had imagined.

The Captain was not in the guardroom. It was deserted

apart from a bored young groom yawning and hastily concealing a flagon of wine under the table.

Somewhat reluctant to rise to his feet and salute the newcomers, slurring a little he informed them that the royal guards were out on their inspection of the Palace. They should be returning within the hour.

'Exactly where might they be located at this moment? This is a matter of some urgency.'

Tam's stern demand penetrated the groom's somewhat wine-ridden haze.

He shook his head. 'This is a routine inspection, sir. Twice a day around the royal apartments and the gardens.' And, tapping the side of his nose in a gesture of confidence, 'The Palace is under constant guard against strangers and interlopers.'

Pausing, he darted a sudden suspicious look at Tam as if he might well be slotted into either or both categories.

Interlopers but not apparently killers, thought Tam grimly. Whoever killed Mistress Agnew had by now slipped their particular net.

'Your business with the Captain is urgent then, sir?' said the groom, anxious to be rid of them as he darted a fond glance in the direction of his wine-flagon.

'I have already said so,' Tam responded shortly.

'Of the utmost urgency,' Tansy added.

The groom, suddenly aware of her pale face and agitated manner, recognised the pretty lady who was obviously a close confidant of the Queen, since he often saw them walking together in the gardens.

'A woman has been killed at the door of Mistress Scott's lodging,' said Tam. 'One of Her Grace's servants, Mistress Agnew.'

The groom whistled softly. 'I ken her well, sir. We all do, she will be sorely missed. Her herbs have cured many a sore head from an excess of wine-bibbing here in the guardroom —'

41

And other less pleasant excesses common in the guard-room too, thought Tam, interpreting his doleful expression. Doubtless Mistress Agnew's popularity arose from her confidential cures for the pox, much in demand among the courtiers and lesser mortals.

Tam sighed. Here was another complication. As many visited the midwife secretly, both highborn and low, tracking down her killer was going to be even more difficult. Mysterious and unexplained deaths were not all that uncommon in the court where King James was known to be a dangerous man to cross. Offences were dealt with swiftly and terminated with unpleasant and often fatal results for the misguided wrongdoer.

On the other hand, Mistress Agnew's death might be related to a marital disorder, since women who were midwives had skills in bringing about convenient abortions or miscarriages.

'An accident, was it, sir?' the groom was asking.

'I think not. She died violently.'

Clearing his throat, remembering his manners, the groom struggled to his feet, dragged on his bonnet and came to attention. 'A servant of Her Grace's household too. This is an official matter for Lord Fotheringham himself to investigate,' he said sternly.

'Then go in search of him, tell him to proceed immediately to Mistress Scott's lodging where I will await him.'

The groom bowed and set off purposely, staggering only a very little in the direction of the gardens where the distant sound of trotting horses indicated the imminent return of the king's guard.

Queen Anne was upset by the sudden death of her midwife, although Tansy had tried to break it to her as gently as possible, saying only that Mistress Agnew had met with a fatal accident outside her lodging.

There was nothing personal in the queen's distress. It was

not for the unfortunate woman's sad demise but for the inconvenience of her absence, the loss of her soothing hands and the healing herbs that she had come to rely on.

Tansy preferred to evade such questions as she could see forming on Her Grace's lips. Curtseying, she said quickly that she must return to her lodging where she had left Master Eildor to deal with the situation.

Her royal mistress would not allow her to leave immediately. She had urgent matters to discuss regarding the forthcoming Masque and the silks she had entrusted to Agnew for safe delivery.

'I trust they were suitable colours?'

Tansy could think of no appropriate response, since she had not seen them. Such trivial matters were the last thing she would have looked for when they found the dead woman.

'My main concern, Your Grace, was for Mistress Agnew,' she said apologetically.

The queen gave her a hard look, pursed her lips and sighed. 'Surely Mistress Scott's first concern should be for ourselves, is that not so?' she asked her ladies-in-waiting who, having heard the shocking news, had gathered nearby. Thus appealed to, they nodded vaguely and directed, as was expected of them, stern glances at Tansy.

'I am disappointed in you, Mistress Scott,' said the queen with a sad shake of her head. 'The information concerning the silks as well as our costume for my Masque is of the utmost importance to us,' she added in wounded tones.

'They are indeed, Your Grace.' The queen's increasing pregnancy was a delicate matter. For decency's sake alterations were necessary to accommodate a rapidly expanding figure in the costume of a scantily-clad goddess.

The queen's frown boded ill and Tansy said hastily, 'I do apologise, Your Grace. It was thoughtless of me not to have given the silks due consideration. I will look into it immediately.' Curtseying, she was about to withdraw.

'A moment, Mistress Scott, we have not yet dismissed you,'

came the stern reminder. 'Where is the cloak we entrusted to Agnew to restore to you? We trust since it was a gift from us – very recently,' she emphasised, 'that it has not suffered during this unfortunate accident.'

'I did not notice, Your Grace,' Tansy stammered, which was solid truth.

The queen considered this information for a moment and sighed deeply. 'We believed that, having forgotten to take it with you, you would wish to have it safely restored to you immediately.' And with a sigh she gestured towards her ladies. 'See what trouble a good-hearted gesture gets one into, how carelessly received.'

The ladies exchanged glances. Murmurs of sympathy directed at their royal mistress reached Tansy's ears. But she was well aware of their understanding regarding Her Grace's much vaunted generosity in the matter of gowns and jewels she no longer cared for. Her apparent benevolence contained an unwritten clause; the gift was to be visible constantly and admired frequently.

If the new owner failed in this respect, she would soon fall victim to the queen's remarkable recollection of every item distributed from the royal wardrobe and jewel box. The recipient of her bountiful gesture would be mercilessly questioned as to its present whereabouts. Sad realisation swiftly followed. No matter how small or insignificant their worth, gifts were not bestowed at all, but rather released on permanent loan.

'The cloak, Mistress Scott?' the queen persisted.

'I am deeply grateful to Your Grace,' said Tansy, evading the question and, as she withdrew from the royal presence, adding to herself, 'And for sure, I will never wear it again.'

Outside the rain had ceased, the sun shone through a cloudless sky raising clouds of steam from the Palace's grey walls and reflecting bright mirrors of light across pools of water among the cobbles of the courtyard.

As Tansy hurried across and reached her lodging, she expected to see Tam and, with considerable dread, the body of Margaret Agnew. To her surprise the turnpike recess was deserted. Only a dark pool – of blood fast drying – remained to show that a body had lain there.

A scattering of the bright silks that were the queen's main concern lay in a corner under the stair. Completely overlooked and completely ruined.

Hoping that Tam had removed the key that Agnew wore on her chatelaine, Tansy ran quickly up the stairs and along the corridor to the servants' quarters.

The midwife's door was locked. Tam was not in evidence.

With some misgivings Tansy returned to her lodging to sit by the window and anxiously await his return. Distressed and sickened by Agnew's murder she had also remembered with fast-beating heart the one significant fact that had been overlooked.

The midwife had been wearing her cloak.

At last she saw Tam emerge across the courtyard in deep conversation with Lord Fotheringham. The two men parted outside and Tam hurried towards the turnpike.

Eagerly, Tansy listened to his footsteps on the stair. In his presence she felt safe. Opening the door she asked, 'What has happened? Have you found out who killed Agnew? And did you remove the key she carries?'

Tam shook his head and as Tansy quickly explained, he interrupted to say, 'It appears that we were mistaken. In fact she was not killed at all.'

As Tansy began to protest, Tam held up a hand wearily and sat down on the windowseat beside her.

'Listen, Tansy. I met the Captain and he insisted that several of his men accompany us to the scene of the crime. When we got here –' He paused and looked at her grimly, 'Mistress Agnew was certainly dead, but there was no dagger. And no chatelaine or key that I could see.'

'Someone took it. No dagger! But that cannot be. We saw it –'

45

'We did indeed. But it had undergone a transformation during our short absence.'

'It cannot have done so – a dagger is a dagger.'

'I agree. But this one had turned very conveniently into shears.'

'Shears?' said Tansy, regarding him wide-eyed.

'Indeed, shears. The dagger had been removed from the scene and replaced by shears, the kind you use here –' Pausing he indicated the overspill of bright materials on the huge sewing table, 'shears thin-bladed, very sharp.'

Even as he spoke Tansy had rushed across the room and was searching among her rolls of silks and satins.

'Tam,' she cried turning to face him. 'They have disappeared!'

'Not really, my dear Tansy. They are not very far off. They were discovered lying beneath your poor friend's body. The apparent cause of her death. And they have been carried off as evidence of her unfortunate accident.'

'Accident – murder I think you mean,' said Tansy indignantly.

Tam nodded grimly. 'But the new evidence points to the fact that Mistress Agnew tripped on the stairs and fell on the shears she was carrying –'

'Surely you told them about the dagger – protested that was a lie,' Tansy interrupted angrily.

'No, I did not. Think about it, Tansy, I beg you. It was on the tip of my tongue to do so, then I thought better of it and decided to remain silent.'

'How could you remain silent?' Tansy demanded.

'With excellent reason,' Tam said grimly. 'I am a stranger here, remember? And I live in your lodging, only yards away from where Agnew was discovered.' He allowed that to sink in before adding slowly, 'Nor would I raise too much of an issue about your shears having disappeared.'

'Why not? Someone stole them – they are valuable,' was the short reply.

'Exactly. But think carefully. Realise that fact could be used in evidence – if anyone should insist that this was no accident but murder.' He paused. 'Now do you understand – that the weapon used was yours.'

Tansy was silent as the full implications were suddenly apparent. 'But the dagger –'

'Ah yes, the dagger. I suspect that the killer was lurking nearby when we rushed downstairs. When we were bending over Agnew, I had this uneasy feeling, almost as if I could hear him breathing, see his shadow.'

Tansy shivered as Tam paused and looked at her soberly. 'I realise now that although there was probably only one of him, that we were fortunate to be together,' and picturing the scene, he added slowly, 'Waiting for us to leave, he – yes, I presume it was a man – he quickly withdrew his dagger.'

'He was clever about that. Daggers can be identified,' said Tansy.

Tam nodded. 'He ran upstairs and took your shears, rearranged the scene to look like an unfortunate accident, as the Captain said and believed. It could happen to anyone tripping on the stairs in dim light.'

'How horrible – how wicked,' said Tansy.

Wicked indeed, thought Tam grimly. And knowledgeable too, trying not to recognise that the midwife's killing suggested premeditation, since the assassin was quick-witted and knew exactly where to lay his hands on Tansy's shears.

'Tam, there is worse to come, I am afraid,' said Tansy hesitantly.

'What could be worse,' said Tam lightly for her sake.

'She was wearing my cloak,' was the faint reply.

'Your cloak?'

'Yes, I had left it in the royal apartments and the queen gave it to her – out of the kindness of her heart – to come across in the rain. To protect the silks she was carrying, more than her own person,' she added glumly.

It was Tam's turn to look shocked. 'This indeed is even

worse. If you are thinking the same as I am...'

Tansy nodded miserably. She shivered. 'What if he thought it was me rushing in from the rain with the hood down over my face?'

And suddenly she hugged his arm, her face pale. 'Oh Tam, I am so glad that you were here.'

Tam nodded grimly. 'Had you gone down alone and had it not been raining, then he might have realised too late his mistake.'

'And there might have been two corpses to explain away,' was Tansy's horrified whisper.

Instead of one fatal accident to be explained away so smoothly and dealt with so efficiently, thought Tam grimly.

'But why should anyone want to kill me, Tam?' Tansy demanded. 'I have no enemies. I have never quarrelled with anyone and Her Grace is devoted to me – ' She shrugged. 'As devoted as she can be to anyone.'

Tansy's innocent reasoning did nothing to console Tam. A devoted confidante of the queen was reason enough for some jealous member of the household to wish to get rid of Mistress Tansy Scott.

The speed with which the murder weapon had been replaced by Tansy's shears and the body swiftly removed by the Captain's guards suggested careful planning. Thrusting aside the enormity of his thoughts, Tam said, 'Let us leave Mistress Agnew aside for the moment and concentrate on you.'

Pouring out a goblet of wine for Tansy who was visibly shaken by the dreadful implications of the borrowed cloak, he asked,

'How many persons have access to your lodging?'

'I have no idea how many. There are messengers from the queen, pages, other servants. All sorts of people call upon my services for repairs and alterations to costumes for the Masque on Saturday. My door is always open.'

Taking a sip of wine, she said slowly, 'What you are suggesting is … is monstrous.'

The rearrangement of Agnew's body to pass it off as an accident suggested to Tam that several people had been involved. When the mistake of the victim's identity was discovered, they had had to work fast.

Not mere guards under the Captain's orders but a keener brain issued by a higher authority. Tam would have sworn that Fotheringham, unless he was a very good actor, was innocent of the deception.

'I even told Her Grace that it was an accident,' Tansy said miserably. 'I did not care to upset her with a violent crime to one of her servants, especially Agnew who she relies on. Her Grace is in a particularly delicate condition just now. And although it is unlikely that the death of her midwife would cause her to miscarry, we all are doing our best to keep her as calm as possible – and that is far from easy, I can assure you. At the best of times, she is of a volatile humour.'

Tam asked 'You say you have no enemies. Are you absolutely certain that there is no one in the court who wishes you ill? Think carefully.'

Tansy looked preoccupied and then shook her head. When she spoke it was with reluctance. 'The only person is His Grace himself. I have long been aware that he is not enamoured of my presence in the court.'

'For what reason, pray?'

Tansy shrugged. 'He cares not for me, but he has no authority in the queen's household to have me removed.'

Except on a permanent basis, thought Tam grimly.

'Only once did he storm out in a fury,' she said thoughtfully. 'Agnew and I were with the queen who happened to remark upon the odd coincidence that we were both orphans, brought up by our granddams who were midwives at his birth. His Grace's sensitivity on that subject is well-known but I assure you I can think of nothing I have done personally to upset him.'

Tansy thought for a moment, then spoke again. 'The

offence, I am afraid, goes further back than that. As I told you I was fostered by the Gowries after Janet Beaton died. And His Grace hates the Gowries. Their grandfather, Lord Ruthven, was the first to dagger Davy Riccio in the Queen Mary's presence, three months before James was born. His son, the Earl of Gowrie, led the Lords Enterprisers in the Raid of Ruthven. His Grace was sixteen when they kidnapped him and held him hostage for ten months in Ruthven Castle. Freed the following year, he had the Earl tried and executed for treason.'

Pausing she sighed. 'His Grace never refers to my adopted family. Alexander Ruthven, my young foster-brother, was Gentleman of the Bedchamber but something happened – I can only guess. He was a favourite with the queen too. Ever since, I am well aware of His Grace's black looks whenever he meets me in her company.'

This information was a new slant on an old grievance. Court relationships were transient and fragile in nature. The king's displeasure was enough excuse – perhaps a grim remark about Mistress Scott when the king had taken a little too much wine – for any who wished for royal favour to take it into their own hands and despatch her.

As though interpreting his thoughts, Tansy said, 'His Grace is well-known to have cultivated a neat habit of disposing of people against whom he bears a grudge. I dare say he would like to have me out of his sight permanently.'

She sighed. ''Tis only because of the queen's high regard that I have survived so long and not been packed off in disgrace back to Ruthven on some trumped-up excuse.'

'Regarding grudges and absent kin,' said Tam. 'Has Mistress Agnew any kin here in Falkland? They would need to be informed.'

Tansy shook her head. 'There was a man in the village I suspect that she visited as often as the queen allowed her leisure. I once met her leaving a house with a pretty garden…'

'Where was this exactly?' asked Tam, his mind racing

ahead.

'Across the road from the smithy. She was not exactly pleased to see me and said she had been visiting her brother. But she seemed very embarrassed at our meeting.'

Tam's immediate reaction was that the man was not a brother but a lover.

'We know so little about her,' said Tansy, bringing to mind a kind and gentle manner always eager to please, but the smiling face remained that of a stranger. 'I imagined somehow that she had been married briefly and widowed. There may be documents in her room,' she added hopefully.

'Did she ever talk about what brought her into the realm of midwifery?' Tam asked.

'Usually it is a skill handed down from mother to daughter. She never talked about herself, all she ever boasted about was that our granddams had been close friends in their Edinburgh days. Since she arrived in the queen's household that was the only real conversation we ever had. A bond – an interesting coincidence.'

Tam's thoughts on any significance that interesting fact might have had were interrupted by the sound of footsteps on the stair.

Footsteps that Tansy recognized, it seemed. All else forgotten, her face suddenly glowed with delight.

'Why, it is Will,' she said with a gurgling laugh and rushing to the door she threw it open to welcome him.

Chapter Four

In the king's apartments, Lord Fotheringham was making his routine report on the royal guards' tour of duty which was to be delivered by him in person twice each day. As befitted a king by nature devious and suspicious, James listened carefully to every detail, occasionally interrupting with a question or the flourish of a Latin quotation.

Lord Fotheringham seldom found his royal master alone. Most frequently he was in his bedchamber indulging in a bout of heavy wine imbibing with one or more of his favourite pages, sitting up in bed and wearing his monstrous ostrich-feathered tall hat from which, it seemed, he was rarely parted.

On this occasion, as luck would have it, his sole companion was the Duke of Lennox listening to a tale of woe about Annie's misdoings. Vicky listened dutifully, stifling a yawn with some difficulty. He found this regular tirade against the queen exceedingly boring and had long since run short of the sympathetic exclamations required of him.

Now he was preparing for another stern exercise on his patience from the pompous Captain of the Guard's narrative. A simple report that all was well, drawn out into several minutes of probing question and long-winded answer.

Not today, however. Today's account promised to be refreshingly different.

'I have to report, Your Grace, that there has been an accident – to one of Her Grace's servants.'

A royal frown. His Grace did not care to be bothered with matters relating to his wife's household and accidents to servants could be very tedious.

'Aye, man. Get on wi' it,' he said impatiently.

'Her Grace's midwife, sire.'

The king nodded, took another gulp of wine. Tales of accidents were not unfamiliar or, in certain cases, unexpected. The deed done, the details did not interest him.

Lennox was even more bored.

'Mistress Agnew was found dead. At Mistress Scott's.'

Ah, that was better. Now this item of news was of extreme interest to Vicky. Tansy Scott was distant kin to Tam Eildor who shared her lodging. Here the face of opportunity beckoned. Perhaps an excellent way of ridding himself of the king's latest infatuation.

Lennox had not wasted any time since the king's remarkable rescue by Master Eildor. Enquiries were already well under way and had yielded a means by which this interloper might be despatched. In his own employ, he was fortunate to have Sandy Kay, one-time body servant to Walt Murray, Tansy's legal husband, who was paying Kay to keep him informed of any matters concerning his estranged wife.

Divorces were tricky, difficult and costly even when a wife was barren, and Kay hinted that something more urgent and permanent engaged Murray's thoughts. How to rid himself of his unwanted spouse so that he could marry his present mistress and declare their son his legitimate heir?

That any connection between the dead woman Agnew and Tansy Scott might lead to destroying Tam Eildor loomed large in Lennox's mind. With the interesting possibility that several scores might be satisfactorily settled;Tansy Scott and Eildor both obliterated with one well-aimed stone.

In Tansy's apartment and awaiting a supper of soup, roast meat, bread and ale that was being prepared by Tansy's servant, Will Hepburn informed them that this was but a fleeting visit. Before escorting Tansy to Perth he had business to attend to and was heading to Edinburgh to visit his lawyer, an elderly cousin.

Tam observed the newcomer closely. Tall, good-looking, Will's forty years sat lightly upon him. From his father James,

Earl of Bothwell, he had inherited dark auburn hair and fox-brown eyes, but other than colouring he had none of the tough aggression that characterised the Border warrior breed.

His fine features were the inheritance from his Norwegian mother, Anna Throndsen, who had returned to her own country when she realised that the bastard son she had borne the Earl of Bothwell did not guarantee her marriage as his betrothed, or the right to be received in royal society as his Countess.

With no place in court circles, Will had eventually assumed the role of a gentleman of good estate, enjoying the leisurely pursuits of hunting, riding and the cultured social attributes of a peaceful country life.

Tam had watched Will and Tansy embrace. This was no lovers' meeting but the continuation of a long-standing relationship for a couple who should have been settled down with a family had Fate not decreed otherwise.

In his growing affection and attraction to Tansy, Tam recognised there was need for Will Hepburn, whose love would endure long after his own transient appearance in their lives. Introduced, Will turned to him, smiling. His handshake firm and warm, his friendly expression indicated that he was prepared to be well-disposed towards the mysterious Master Eildor.

As Tansy led the way to the little parlour where they were to sup, Will said, 'Tansy has written of you. That she had a visitor from the Borders – distant kin,' he added with a curious look that invited explanation.

There was none forthcoming from either.

Will smiled. 'I have been looking forward to meeting you.'

Truth to tell he had been apprehensive. Although Tansy had told him nothing that should give rise to alarm, conscious of his good fortune, Will's fears were always that his adored and vulnerable mistress might be snatched from him by some handsome rival. And the extremely comely young man before him who now shared her lodging, however distant kin, suggested ample grounds for anxiety and suspicion.

Except for one remarkable factor.

Releasing Tam's hand, Will looked across at Tansy and smiled, his relief evident. 'Master Eildor is no stranger to me.' And turning back to Tam he bowed. 'We have met before, sir.'

Tam shook his head, bewildered. 'That cannot be, Master Hepburn.'

'I assure you it is,' said Will, who continued to regard him intently. Nodding vigorously, he continued, 'Do you not remember? It was at Lady Morham's – my granddam's – home in East Lothian. I was four years old and you were on your way to Branxton Castle. I recall that you were steward there – to the household of Tansy's granddam, Lady Janet Beaton.'

And at Tam's confused expression, 'Marie Seton was with you. Surely you remember? Marie Fleming was visiting kin and about to be married.' He waited for Tam to say something. There was no response.

Will sighed, disappointed. 'I remember it perfectly in every detail. We had so few visitors at Morham,' he added with a touch of melancholy.

And something stirred in Tam's mind, a sudden flash like a scene he had witnessed as an onlooker.

Will as a small child sitting on an old lady's knee. There was a woman in the background, a young woman. Fleeting pain and heartbreak. The agony of loss.

A half-forgotten dream.

Except that when Tam slept out of his own time, there were no dreams. He merely opened his eyes again on another day in one continuous pattern.

In that instant the vision of the small child was lost.

Although Tam was allowed neither dreams nor the indulgence of memory, Will Hepburn had somehow slipped through the eradication procedure of a mind wiped clean of previous encounters before the next quest began. Not so Janet Beaton, despite Tansy's intriguing suggestion that they had

55

met before. If only he could recall something of that occasion.

Now Will was regarding him curiously. 'You do not remember?' he insisted. 'It is quite extraordinary.' Pausing he regarded Tam with a puzzled frown. 'Obviously I have made a mistake.'

And to Tansy, who was listening intently, her gentle smile offering no attempt at explanation. 'That must be so.'

Then again to Tam. 'You look exactly as I remember you, sir, thirty-six years ago, when I was four years old and you were a grown man.' And shaking his head, bewildered, 'May I ask how old you are now, sir?'

'I am thirty-six.'

Another pause. 'Are you then some kind of a wizard, sir?'

Although his voice was gentle and mocking, his glance at the silent Tam held anxiety and demanded explanation. There was none forthcoming. Will's sharp look at Tansy held an element of warning, for such creatures were dangerous associates for his beloved.

Aware of his bewildered concern, Tansy touched his arm and said lightly, 'Perhaps you were mistaken, Will. That was a very long time ago and maybe it was someone who looked like Master Eildor. After all, doubles are not impossible, especially when one lives in the Borders where gentlemen as well as the steel bonnets spread themselves somewhat freely.'

Will eagerly seized upon this possibility. 'Your father, sir. Could it have been he that I met that day?'

Tam shook his head, thought fast and said, 'I think not, my father did not come from England.'

Aware of the tangled web Tam was getting into, Tansy said, 'We are very glad to see you, Will. You have come at a most opportune time. We need your help. Something terrible has happened –'

'How terrible?' Will demanded anxiously.

'Mistress Agnew, the queen's midwife has been killed.'

'Killed – how so?'

'Murdered, Will. Murdered. We found her just hours ago –'

Tansy had changed the subject so swiftly Tam realised that, for her own reasons, she had not told Will about Janet Beaton's prediction that one day Tam Eildor would return. Lovers did not always tell one another everything and presumably Will was to be excluded from that information.

Listening to Tansy relating the details of the tragedy they had witnessed, Tam knew that the fewer who shared the secret of his identity, the better. Such knowledge was indeed dangerous in the court of a king who had an obsession about witches and warlocks. He did not want to burn should James's infatuation for him be distorted by jealous enemies into suspicions of witchcraft and sorcery.

'So they removed the body,' said Will at the end of Tansy's dramatic disclosure. 'They would presumably take her to the guardroom and will keep her body until they find kin to bury her.'

'That will be no easy matter, Will,' said Tansy. 'Very little is known about Margaret Agnew or her kin.' And in a horrified whisper, 'What think you of the fact that the dagger was replaced and dismissed as a tragic accident? When Lord Fotheringham found her it was not a dagger but shears in her breast. My shears,' she added grimly.

Will put a consoling arm around her shoulders. 'Tansy, my dear Tansy,' he said soberly. 'There is certainly a mystery here, but it is my most earnest desire – indeed I implore you – that you do not involve yourself in this matter, even knowing the unfortunate woman as you did.'

Shaking his head, he glanced over at Tam. 'I feel that there is much more in this unhappy story than we will ever be allowed to know about. If you have any ideas about what goes on here in Falkland, then you must realise that the king's authority is final – and dangerous to those who unwittingly offend him.'

Again he gave a sad shake of his head. 'I cannot explain why but I suspect a sinister reason behind it all. A reason which goes deeper than the poor woman's death. In these circumstances, it would be well for all of us to look the other way.'

'Look the other way!' Tansy exclaimed. 'That I will never do, Will Hepburn. Agnew never harmed anyone. She was a good kind soul – a friend to many in this court and to me – '

'A friend, dear Tansy. Could you really claim her as a friend, this woman about whom you know nothing?' Will interrupted shrewdly and, including Tam in his sharp glance he added desperately, 'I beg you, sir, if you know any means of dissuading Mistress Scott from interfering in this matter –.'

'Interfering!' Tansy was furious. 'I will not be told what to do, Will Hepburn, not even by you.'

Will's arm about her tightened. 'Indeed you will, my dear,' he said his voice soft but stern. 'Listen to me, both of you. Realise there are dangerous forces at work. Someone wanted Margaret Agnew dead and it would be better for all of us if we did not know why and did not try to find out. If we remained silent,' he added emphasising the words.

Turning again to Tansy, he said sternly, 'I have warned you. I like it not your being close to the queen and I want you kept clear of court intrigues, so step aside and do not become involved.'

To Tam, he said earnestly, 'I do not care for Mistress Scott's relationship with the Gowrie family either. The king hates them. He bears a long grudge – '

'Master Eildor knows all about that,' Tansy put in shortly.

'Very well,' said Will. 'But do not imagine that King James has forgotten – or forgiven – the Gowries or anyone related to them.'

'This is old history,' said Tansy impatiently.

'Old history perhaps, but by no means forgotten or forgiven. If there is one thing certain sure, the king has a remarkable memory for those who abuse him. He is prepared to wait patiently, years if necessary, to have his revenge. And I do not doubt that his day will come.'

Tansy darted a frightened glance at Tam as Will continued

solemnly, 'As a close neighbour to Ruthven, I have heard much that disturbs me and one day, sooner or later, James will strike at them. When he does so, Master Eildor, I do not want my Tansy to be involved. Because he will not spare her. Or any who have associations with the Gowries.'

Will's words had a sombre echo for Tam. He knew instinctively that there was a grain of truth, of deadly foreboding, that Mistress Agnew's death and the careful efforts to mark it as an accident were only the prologue to a greater tragedy. Yet even if he knew the nature of the imminent danger to Tansy Scott, he was helpless to avert it, with no power to change the course of recorded history.

As Tansy once again changed the subject to more general remarks about Will's visit to Edinburgh, a page came in and announced that Her Grace wished Mistress Scott to wait upon her immediately.

'This will be more about her costume for the Masque,' groaned Tansy. To Will she said, 'Is it possible that you might be back with us by Saturday, then you could escort me.'

'I cannot be sure,' said Will, 'but if I fail to return in time, perhaps Master Eildor?'

'I will do so gladly, sir.'

Will smiled his thanks. 'Meanwhile I will escort you, my dear, to the queen's apartments.' And taking Tansy's hand, he turned again to Tam. 'May I ask you, sir, in my absence from Falkland to watch well over my lady?'

As Tam bowed his assent, Tansy's eyes raised heavenward and her lips tightened perceptibly, indicating that she felt she needed no man to guard her and that she was well able to take care of herself.

Preparing to depart, Will looked out of the window. 'It rains again, I see. You will need your cloak.'

Tansy avoided his eyes. 'Oh, I left it in the queen's chamber.'

As Will shook his head and said, 'Have mine, then,' Tansy's swift glance in Tam's direction held mute appeal. It warned him not to mention that Mistress Agnew had been wearing it when she was murdered.

Taking their leave of Tam, as they walked across the courtyard, Will said, 'I am not convinced.'

'Convinced about what?' asked Tansy, knowing perfectly well.

'About Master Eildor. I am certain that we have met before.'

'That you cannot be, love. You were just a child.' Even though she said the words, Tansy knew that Will had an exceptional memory. Conscious of his intent gaze, she asked, 'What is amiss, love?'

He laughed. 'Do you ever look in your mirror, my Tansy?'

She frowned. 'Indeed I do.'

'Then has it not occurred to you that there is a very close resemblance between you and Master Eildor. You could be siblings.'

Tansy shook her head. 'Alas, I had neither brother nor sister,' she said sadly.

Will smiled. 'Distant kin, you said.'

'Remote cousins,' said Tansy abruptly, not wishing to continue this conversation. Unhappy to deceive Will she had nevertheless sworn to Janet Beaton never to reveal Tam's origins and she was determined to remain true to her word.

Will's arm tightened about her. He looked down into her lovely face for a moment. 'Distant kin, eh?' and stroking his chin thoughtfully, he smiled wryly. 'And we are not unaware of what goes on in those wild Border strongholds.'

Tansy smiled, relieved that Will had found his own solution to her likeness to Tam.

'The Tam Eildor I met had some connection with your granddam, Lady Beaton. Perhaps that is the link. She was a very strange woman.'

Pausing he looked at Tansy, hopeful for an explanation.

He waited in vain. Tansy remained silent and he asked,

'What do you know of his early life?'

'Only what Granddam told me before she died. And that was very little. But she told me I could trust him.'

'And do you – trust him?'

'With my life, Will,' said Tansy firmly.

'Then let it be so.' And kissing her fondly at the entrance to the queen's apartments, he held her close for a moment.

'I will not be long, love,' she whispered. 'You will stay?'

'I will, but I must be on my way by early morn.'

She stroked his cheek gently. 'There is a whole night before that.'

Leaving her, he realised that this had always been the story of their lives together. From the very first, only a few stolen days and nights together. Even for that, they must be grateful, he thought.

Returning to her lodging, Will was already framing some searching questions for Master Eildor about what circumstances had brought him to Falkland Palace to visit a remote cousin. And in particular, how long he intended to stay.

Chapter Five

Anticipating Will's return and doubtless some probing questions about his background, Tam conveniently absented himself. He had no wish to be interrogated or have to deal out unnecessary lies to Tansy's lover.

Avoiding direct lies for the complications they caused, one lie begetting others, to tell the truth would be incredulous to those living in the sixteenth century. As well as an invitation to disaster in an age dominated by a king whose obsession was with witchcraft and who had already written a learned treatise on the subject.

Tam guessed shrewdly the need to take great care and walk warily. Suspecting that through the king's evident infatuation he had made a powerful enemy in the Duke of Lennox, he was certain there would be others who had witnessed the incident of the runaway horse and his rescue of the king.

Certain that no stone would be left unturned in their efforts to poison the king against him, he was in little doubt about the result and what would be his fate. To be dismissed as a sorcerer, thrown into prison – or burnt as a warlock.

His immediate plan after Tansy departed was to set off in search of the man Mistress Agnew had visited in the village. However, as he walked across the courtyard darkness was falling, the heavy dusk of a hot summer's day had settled across lawns white with dew, and trees heavily burdened with summer leaves seemed ready to droop into exhausted sleep.

Not everyone slept. From the king's apartment came raucous sounds of merriment, laughter mixed with the sound of music inexpertly performed. Candles were lit in the windows and he could well picture the scene within.

It was peaceful in the gardens. Time for the wild creatures

who lurked in woods nearby to live out their short lives. Night-time insects too were on the move. Bats fluttered before his face and large moths danced in his path to the tune of an owl's melancholy hoot from a branch above his head.

Such peace. But twilight was fast fading into the dark side of the moon, lying like a cloak enveloping the huddle of thatched roofs that made up the royal burgh of Falkland.

A watchman on his rounds called out the hour. 'Nine o' the clock and all is well.'

Was it really, thought Tam? He would hazard a guess that he had lost his opportunity and it was already too late to call on the unknown man who had been brother – or lover – to the murdered woman. Most probably the latter, which accounted for her embarrassment at meeting Tansy outside his door.

Ordinary folk had only rush-lights to see by and without the luxury of wax candles retired with the dark and arose with the dawn. Mistress Agnew's lover would doubtless have long been abed.

With a sigh, for it would need daylight for him to identify the house he sought, Tam reluctantly decided that his visit must wait until morning, despite the gnawing sense of urgency that time was not on his side.

The sooner he made contact and warned the man of Mistress Agnew's death the better. He could not shake off an ominous feeling that if, as he suspected, her murder had been premeditated, then he might already be too late and the man himself in dire peril.

He reached his room in Tansy's lodging only seconds before he heard Will ascending the turnpike stair. Relieved that he had been spared the encounter, as always Tam slept without dreaming and awoke refreshed to birdsong early next morning.

Hearing the murmur of voices from Tansy's parlour and Will's deep voice, he decided that the only way to avoid a meeting was to remain where he was until Will departed.

Turning on his side, he slept again and awoke to silence to

find himself alone in the lodging. Breaking his fast on bread, cheese and ale which had been left out for him, Tam reflected that Will would be heading for Edinburgh and Tansy, no doubt, about the queen's business.

As it was a fine morning with the promise of another pleasant summer day, Tam decided to take the short cut across the gardens. As he strolled he began to recognise again the sense of antiquity that stretched well beyond the palace; the sense of a land settled by an ancient race long-forgotten, nestling at the base of the Lomond Hill. On the distant horizon, blue-hazed to the west of the prehistoric hill fort of East Lomond, with the Pictish slab Tansy had pointed out to him on one of their walks to the Maiden Castle, stood another hill fort with cup and ring marks whose interpretation was lost long ago.

The site of the palace had been granted to the Macduff Earls of Fife in the 12th century and passed to Robert Stewart, later Duke of Albany in 1371. Gazing up at its lofty grey walls untouched by sunlight, its windows deep and dark in cold morning shadow held secret tales of savage cruelty and treachery not unknown in royal palaces. Here, on the site of the present magnificent Palace, David, Duke of Rothesay, eldest son of King Robert III, was kept prisoner and starved to death by his uncle Albany in 1402.

The 15th century saw the lands reverted to the Crown and the modest castle had become the favourite hunting seat of the Scottish kings who were James's ancestors. A hundred years ago in 1500, the king's great-grandfather, James IV, began construction of Falkland Palace. Completed by his grandfather James V as a royal residence, it was made up of buildings which formed three sides of an informal quadrangle. The great south range with its twin-storeyed gatehouse, built in the style of the French Renaissance and containing the chapel royal, faced on to the burgh's main street.

Tam crossed the inner courtyard of the east range with its royal lodgings and emerged into the gardens whose shaded walks and high hedges afforded privacy for dalliance and for conspiracy.

His head down deep in thought, too late he became aware of voices and found himself in the path of King James, who was accompanied by several of his courtiers and leaning on the arm of the Duke of Lennox.

Tam bowed low and stepped aside for them to pass, hoping that he would be invisible as the king, clutching his beribboned staff, talked loudly to Lennox.

Tam was unlucky. James saw him, stopped and said, 'Bide a wee, Vicky.' And beaming in Tam's direction. 'Weel now, if it isna the fisherman again. What brings ye here, Master Eildor?'

Without waiting for the reply which Tam was already framing, he went on, 'Are ye here to rescue your king from a matter as dire as yon runaway horse?' and put his hand to his lips in a conspiratorial manner.

Tam bowed. Some response was expected of him. 'What would that be, sire?' he asked cautiously.

'Being bored to death – by idle chatter, aye, that's it, the company o' fools,' said James. Slapping his thigh and doubling up with mirth at his own wit, he darted hard looks at the courtiers who were obliged to fall about with suitable exclamations of merriment.

James gave a satisfied grunt and said, 'We are on our way to the tennis court, Master Eildor, and we would have you accompany us.'

That was a command and Tam bowed again.

'Walk with us,' said James. 'Here at your king's side,' he added. Giving Tam an appreciative glance, 'We will lean on Master Eildor. He looks as if he might bear his monarch's weight,' he added with a faint leer and, pushing Lennox unceremoniously aside, he gestured to Tam to take his place.

Although Lennox bowed out gracefully enough, Tam was aware of the venomous look that boded ill for him.

'And does our simple fisherman play the game?' James demanded.

Tam thought quickly. He knew something of ancient games and was interested enough to meet the challenge. Realising that to refuse would displease the king, he hoped that his bow and accompanying smile conveyed sufficient enthusiasm. As well as curiosity to see the royal court in action, the occasion promised a rare opportunity to enjoy some serious exercise.

On one of their walks Tansy had told him that the game was introduced into Scotland and built at Falkland by the king's grandfather, a great enthusiast for all things French, in the year before his death in 1492.

Its origins were as "*jes des paume*", *game of the palm*, some 300 years earlier by monks playing handball against the monastery walls.

'The word "tennis" is from the French "tenez" – "take this" – as one player served to another across a rope in the courtyard,' Tansy told him. 'Bare hands at first became a glove with webbing between the fingers, succeeded by a solid paddle. Now they use a long handled racket with a ball of hair, wool or cork, wrapped in string or leather.

'His Grace restored the court neglected for many years and plays regularly. For a man who seems often clumsy in his movements, his game – according to his courtiers – is like his horsemanship, quite excellent.'

Tansy had smiled wryly and added, 'Sometimes I suspect that they let him win.'

Tam was remembering Tansy's words as they entered the court. A stone floor surrounded by four high walls with a service and hazard end, open to the sky. The net was a simple cord made visible by the addition of tassels, five feet at either end dipping to three feet in the centre. The onlookers were protected by a partition on the right hand side of the court.

At the king's request, Lennox explained the rules and method of scoring to Tam, very fast and somewhat incomprehensibly and giving him no opportunity for questions. Then without further ado a racket was thrust into his hands and Lennox announced to James that they were ready to begin.

James shuffled forward to Tam's side and, showing slightly more consideration, asked, 'D'ye ken fine all Vicky's instructions, Master Eildor?'

'I believe so, Your Grace,' said Tam, bewildered and sounding considerably more confident than he felt at that moment.

'Then we are ready, sire,' said Lennox taking up his racket and looking steadily at Tam.

'No' you, Vicky. Step aside,' said James shortly and sucking in his lips, he said slowly, 'We wish to set Master Eildor against Johnnie here.' And to Tam, 'The lad is a fine player, best in our court.' With a sly shake of his head, he added, 'Aye, Johnnie Ramsay will be able to teach our simple fisherman a thing or twa, nae doot.'

Tam groaned inwardly. He did not doubt that either for John Ramsay at sixteen had the face of an angel combined, according to rumour, with a waspish tongue and a cruel and vicious streak.

Ramsay squared his shoulders, smiled and bowed to James before eyeing Tam with an expression of contempt, certain that this man twice his age would be an easy opponent.

Although Lennox had no liking for Ramsay he was similarly pleased, certain that Tam defeated and looking foolish would go down several notches in James's estimation. And that was splendid news, he decided, watching the two men strip off their outer garments.

For Tam it was a simple matter of removing his leather jerkin, leaving him in breeches and shirt. For Ramsay, however, it was a very different ritual, clad in heavy doublet, padded breeches and thigh boots.

But it appeared that fashion set by the king must be followed in court, regardless of the weather, which indicated that there was already heat in the sun despite the early hour.

James had not yet retired behind the partition and stood alongside the two men eagerly watching Tam who said, 'If

67

your Grace permits, I would also remove my boots. I prefer to play in bare feet.'

'Aye, ye do that, mannie, ye do just that,' said the king excitedly, lingering to gaze with delight at Tam's well-shaped feet and ankles while Ramsay looked on with disgust at such a common man's vulgar notion.

He would soon show this upstart the error of his ways. His supercilious smile towards the onlookers indicated that he was already confident of the result, a victory that was also a waste of his precious time and talent on such an unworthy opponent.

James addressed the courtiers waiting to escort him to his seat, 'A wager – gentlemen. A wager – ma siller on Master Eildor,' and so saying he took from his pocket a purse which he handed to Vicky Stewart who, after a swift glance at the contents, sighed with relief.

James was known to be cautious about his silver as well as frequently and conveniently forgetful to pay up when he lost a wager.

'Tis a warm day,' the king said, 'we believe ye'd play better were ye bare-chested,' and to Ramsay, 'Johnnie lad, ye'd better strip down also, then ye'll be evenly matched.'

An expression of distaste hastily concealed twisted Ramsay's mouth at having to obey this royal command.

As Tam removed his shirt, the king glanced from one to the other and noted with considerable pleasure and excitement that Master Eildor was, as he had expected, a fine well-set up figure o' a man, broad in chest and shoulders.

Alongside him, James and the assembled courtiers, some who were jealous rivals, could not help but observe with considerable satisfaction, that Ramsay looked what he was, a mere boy who had not yet reached manhood's maturity.

With a gamesman to keep the score, the king took his seat and gave the signal for play to begin. As each sent the volley of balls across the net, Tam, who had an excellent eye and was well co-ordinated, was soon ahead of Ramsay who, although the more experienced player, had his speed of movement considerably hampered by the heat and his unwieldy attire.

Used to having the king as his opponent, whose enthusiasm was greater than his skill, Ramsay soon discovered that he was being beaten by Eildor. And the more James applauded the score, the angrier and more flustered Ramsay became which did little for his prowess.

At last James held up his hand. 'Enough. The game is over.'

Ramsay stared at him defiantly, since he had scored that last two points and was still hopeful of victory. 'Sire?' he pleaded.

James shook his head. 'Nay, I have seen enough. *Da locum melioribus* – give way to your betters.'

Ramsay's bow failed to hide his furious countenance which delighted his rivals for the king's favours, gratified to witness the young upstart's humiliation at the hands of a common man – and one old enough to be his father.

The score was counted. Tam had won by twelve points and the king applauded.

'I have won my wager,' he said eagerly, snatching his purse back from Lennox.

Meanwhile Tam approached Ramsay to gallantly offer his hand to a defeated opponent whereupon the boy turned his back rudely and strode off the court. Watching him, Tam realised sadly that he had made an enemy; an unforgivable insult for a king's favourite to lose face by defeat.

He was surprised when the king came forward humbly carrying his shirt and jerkin over his arm. Smiling broadly he came close enough to touch Tam.

'Well done, Master Eildor, well done. And ye won our wager for us. Here, put it on,' he said holding out the shirt. 'Ye'll catch a fever,' he added anxiously. 'Ye're too heated.'

Not as heated as Your Grace, thought Tam wryly, regarding James's flushed countenance. The brooding eyes misted with excitement and Tam tried not to wince as his bare arm was gently caressed by the royal hand as it emerged from the sleeve of his shirt.

'Good strong muscles there, Master Eildor. Aye, fine indeed,' James added with a sigh, smacking his lips. 'But what have we here – this mark? Have ye been hurt?' he said anxiously, touching a dark triangle on Tam's forearm.

'A mere bruise, your Grace,' said Tam, thinking quickly.

'A bruise, is it?' James asked doubtfully. 'It looks ugly.'

'It will soon heal, your Grace,' was the consoling reply.

James continued to look concerned. 'We trust so, Master Eildor. We would not wish for you to take ill from such a bruise. We could have our physician bleed you, just to make certain.'

Tam shook his head. 'That will not be necessary, your Grace. Please rest assured it is nothing.'

But the king's discovery was calamitous for Tam. The crystal charmstone formerly worn around his neck had been superseded, as too obvious and potentially dangerous, by a tiny microchip under the skin marked by a triangle, his sole connection with the life he had temporarily abandoned.

His first instinct had been to inform the king that this was a birthmark. But thinking quickly, he had thought better of it. Mention of birthmarks might have aroused thoughts of witchcraft in King James's mind.

Tam looked around anxiously. He did not think that any had witnessed the scene but he could not be sure about Lennox who hovered nearby within earshot.

Although Lennox gave no indication that he had overheard or had been interested in the king's concern, Tam realised that he must take care to keep his arms covered in future.

James was gesturing to the courtiers. 'Go you ahead. Master Eildor will escort us.' And leaning heavily on Tam's arm, Tam was very conscious of the angry looks in his direction by both Lennox and Ramsay, united for once in their distaste for the king's obvious infatuation.

'Still bide wi' Mistress Scott, d'ye?' the king asked conversationally.

'I am, sire.'

James frowned. 'That will no' do. We would wish to see you in better lodging.'

'Sire?'

'Aye, Master Eildor. In our royal apartments yonder. There is room enough.'

'As Your Grace wishes.' Tam hoped that his bow indicated gratitude and his voice expressed enthusiasm for this honour but he was secretly dismayed.

To be in close and convenient daily contact with the king and under the watchful jealous eyes of his court was the last thing he desired. As well as unpleasant and embarrassing, it could be extremely dangerous.

James delighted, beamed on him. 'We will arrange it forthwith.'

And that will not add any to my popularity either, thought Tam grimly. Being courted by King James when one thing was certain. In the life that was temporarily lost to him, sodomy had not played a role, since in his quest period he remained true to his nature, a young man who was susceptible to females.

Especially to Tansy Scott, to whom he was irresistibly drawn, but who, sadly for him had a happy and long-term relationship with Will Hepburn.

He wished them both well. And he cursed the evil chance that had made him irresistible to the amorous King who stared up into his face with such adoration.

Chapter Six

King James did not relinquish his grip on Tam's arm as they reached the entrance to the royal apartments and Tam realised that his hopes for a speedy release from the company were to be thwarted.

Accompanied by the courtiers a short distance behind them, the king led the way through saluting guards and bowing servants up a handsome staircase and along a corridor into the royal bedchamber, where servants awaited to remove his outer garments and dress him in a less restricting robe.

Tam, feeling the king's eyes resting upon him during this procedure, turned his attention to the contents of the ornate furnishing of the vast room, dominated by the king's bed on a raised dais, ornamented with the royal coat of arms and curtained in crimson velvet.

The bedchamber was also King James's informal room of state and this throne-like object of furniture provided the acme of royal comfort. His bed was also the centre of his kingdom; in whichever royal palace he lived the massive bed accompanied him. And from its depths of floating pillows, James wearing his high hat with its ostrich feathers, held audience and received ambassadors from England, France and Spain.

Here he planned his days, read and wrote learned works and poems and in moments of leisure commanded entertainment by the court jester whose bawdy jokes and suggestive contortions were very much to James's taste.

When the candles of evenings were lit, it became a background for more intimate scenes of carousings and caressings accompanied by considerable amounts of food and wine. Music was provided by a small orchestra of frustrated musicians, whose flutes and fiddles were seldom audible above the raucous sounds of merriment.

Tam was anxious to be gone, exceedingly embarrassed and out of place under the glaring, resentful eyes of James's courtiers while trying to remain oblivious to their behindhand whispers concerning this shabby interloper.

How had such a wretched man managed to worm his way into His Grace's affections? Such poor, unfashionable clothes, with breeches and shirt as the poorest peasants wore. Not even the meanest of royal servants would have been seen in public in such attire.

That such a lowly ill-dressed creature was capable of attracting His Grace's attention. Most of the courtiers were of royal blood or young noblemen and all were swift to recognise this newcomer as a threat to their personal futures, their jewels and favours, not to mention their security at court and ultimate honours and estates. In that moment they were united and John Ramsay's injured pride was soothed as they gathered protectively around him.

For his part, Tam would have been only too delighted to give the courtiers reassurance that, much as they wanted rid of him, he would be glad to be relieved of the king's favour.

With some misgivings as to what was coming next, he watched servants bring wine, fill two goblets and silently withdraw. A royal gesture signalled dismissal for the courtiers who bowed out of the room.

Last to leave were Lennox and Ramsay. If looks could have killed then Tam Eildor would have been spread out at their feet. Instead, what was almost equally as unnerving as sudden death was for Tam to know that he was now alone with James.

He took a great gulp of air as he was handed a goblet of wine.

Here was a situation out of nightmare, Tam thought, as James indicated a seat at the window by his side.

'Sit ye doon, Master Eildor. Nae need for formal manners when we are alone. Ah now – here's health to you.'

Tam inclined his head. 'And to you, sire.'

James drank deeply, put down his goblet and regarded Tam thoughtfully. 'We have a thocht to invest ye as our cup-bearer, Master Eildor. What think ye to that?'

Tam could not think of anything that terrified him more than such an unexpected honour and it was certainly the last thing, or almost the very last thing, he wanted in this world.

Conscious of James awaiting an answer, Tam smiled vaguely. 'Sire?'

This was taken as assent. 'Aye, that would please us might-ily.'

As James proceeded to explain the duties involved, Tam hardly listened. The prospect of close confinement with James was unbearable. This new honour would not please him nor fit in with his plans. His mind in turmoil, for he had no idea how long the quest would last and could only pre-sume that it was not only the murder of Mistress Agnew – which he suspected was merely a curtain-raiser, the prologue to some bigger ploy – that had been selected as his challenge to solve.

He realised that if faced with the matter of satisfying the king's lust for him then he would have to abandon the quest and seek an emergency recall. He had never done so willing-ly, but his present predicament added another dimension, a moral dilemma.

He considered the king, a man of his own age who looked considerably older. Had he been more attractive and cleaner in his person, for he smelt abominably at close quarters on a hot day, Tam wondered if he could have abandoned his own scruples for the sake of finding the solution to an event that had baffled historians.

At last James paused with a flourish of Latin quotations none of which Tam understood, to ask again, 'Weel, Master Eildor, what think you? Are ye no' pleased to serve your king?'

As Tam had not been paying attention, he could only

respond with, 'I am glad to serve Your Grace, but alas, this honour is too great for me – '

'That is for your king to decide,' James interrupted sternly.

Tam bowed his head. 'Sire, I have no noble background. I am …I am only a humble scholar.'

James's narrowed glance, sharp and shrewd, told Tam that he had made a mistake.

'Humble, indeed, ye may well be, Master Eildor, and sich-like modesty becomes ye well. But a scholar who kens no Latin taught to every lad in the village school?' he added softly. 'An erudite man ye are, your origins well-bred too, oh aye.' A pause for comment which Tam chose to ignore. Rubbing his chin, James frowned. 'So whereabouts was it you came by your learning? Was it in some place beyond our realm?'

'I had a learned tutor, near Peebles,' said Tam and went on hurriedly. 'To where I must imminently return – '

At that moment there was an interruption in the shape of Vicky Stewart. Tam greeted his appearance with a profound sigh of relief. Never had he imagined that he would have occasion to bless the Duke of Lennox for deliverance.

'Sire,' Lennox bowed.

James made an irritated gesture. 'No' this meenit. Later, Vicky.'

'Sire, there are messengers waiting.'

'Aye, then let them wait,' said James huffily, turning back to Tam with an encouraging smile.

'Sire,' Lennox persisted, 'they are from Elizabeth of England, Your Grace's godmother.' And with a sour look at Tam, he came between them leaned over to James and whispered, 'Her Majesty has been unwell this fortnight and there are matters serious and urgent concerning the succession which they must discuss with Your Grace.'

James sighed. This was one matter certain to receive all of his attention. Nothing on earth was more important than the fact that when Elizabeth died he was her sole heir and stood to inherit the throne of England. His one dream, his every scheme since boyhood, led to the fulfilment of the burning ambition which obsessed him. To be king of Scotland and England, to unite the two countries.

He sighed, nodded. 'Ah, weel, let it be so. We will see them.' To Tam, 'We will talk again when we have prepared a place for you, Master Eildor,' he said, holding out a grubby hand for Tam to kiss.

That act of submission performed, Tam bowed and hurried away reeling from the scene, with the nearest he had ever suffered to a blinding headache of mammoth proportions. The heavy wine so early in the day was only partly to blame.

Walking quickly towards the gatehouse, he had more pressing matters to concern him than how he was to deal with the king's invitation – nay, command – to be the royal cupbearer.

For instance there was the urgent matter of why Mistress Agnew had been murdered and of tracking down her killer as soon as possible. What troubled him most was Tansy's revelation that the cloak Agnew was wearing had belonged to her, a gift from Queen Anne. And that suggested to even the most unintelligent that the assassin had made a mistake. He had killed the wrong woman. In the dim light of the turnpike stair, his dagger's deathblow had been intended for Mistress Tansy Scott.

Tam sighed deeply. However he resolved the situation of the king's infatuation he could not quit while Tansy was in any danger. And at the back of his mind something he had heard but which he could not quite get into focus. Tansy's story of the king's bitter reaction to any reference to his birth.

Was it possible, could the fatal connecting link between Agnew and Tansy be that both their grandmothers had been in attendance on Queen Mary during the period of her lying-in and delivery?

From Tansy's directions, Tam had little difficulty in finding the house Mistress Agnew had visited. He knocked on the door, which was slightly ajar. There was no reply.

'Is someone there?'

Still no response, so cautiously he pushed open the door and found himself inside a large room, its gloomy depths only faintly livened by thin sunlight from one window.

As his eyes adjusted to the dim light he recognised the outline of a bed with straw mattress, a pillow and rough blankets, recently slept in for it was unmade. At a wooden table, two chairs sprawled at untidy angles.

An empty hearth. He went close, put out his hand. The ashes still gave out heat, adding to the significance of the unmade bed, that the occupant of the house had left recently and in some haste.

Tam set to right the chairs which uneasily suggested a struggle and that the occupant might have had unexpected and unwelcome visitors. It was then he became aware that the door of the press was open and some parchments lay scattered on the floor nearby.

As he picked them up, he felt sure that a searcher had been at work. The name on them was David Rose. They were legal documents, bills of sale relating to property.

Tam's conclusions, based on this evidence, were not difficult to reach. The man he sought had fled, or been taken, but more important as far as he was concerned, the vital opportunity of extracting information from him regarding the possible reasons for Mistress Agnew's death was also lost.

He considered the scene and again what the rifled documents suggested. That whoever induced the man to leave, willingly or not, it was the documents themselves which had concerned them. The state of the room also told Tam that they had been interrupted and had left in great haste.

Tam looked around carefully. The signs were that Mistress Agnew's man, David Rose, was the owner of the house and most certainly an educated man who could read and write.

Closing the door behind him, he crossed the road to where a blacksmith of enormous dimensions was hammering at his forge. He had observed Tam leaving the house and his look posed a question.

'Is it Davy you seek, sir?'

'It is.'

'He's no' home at this hour o' the morning.' And as if Tam should be aware of this he said, 'Ye're no' from these parts, sir.'

Tam hoped his vague nod was sufficient as the blacksmith said, 'Ye'll most like find him ower there,' and pointing to the church, 'He helps the minister wi' his garden and sichlike'.

Tam would have liked to ask more questions but the man had already turned his attention back to his forge's glowing iron.

Walking quickly through the kirkyard, Tam already had an ominous feeling that he would not find David Rose at work there.

The signs he had left at the house were sinister hints at an unexpected and violent departure rather than a man casually off to a day's work.

The church was considerably older than Falkland Palace. A place of worship poorer and much less ornate than the chapel royal and serving only a small parish, it was overshadowed by the wealth and magnificence of the royal court, most of whom Tam suspected had never set foot in so humble a church.

The interior was cold and gloomy, but showed evidence of having seen better days. Niches that had once held holy water and sacred images were empty, sternly set aside when Scotland's old Catholic religion had given way to the Reformation and the Protestant faith.

As for the minister, who approached Tam with faltering steps from the dim recess near the altar, his rusty black hat and robe with unstarched curling white linen bands implied, as did his church, that he had also seen more prosperous days.

78

Peering at him short-sightedly, so close that, despite the spectacles he wore, Tam suspected that the old man was almost blind, was confirmed by his question, 'Davy, is that you?'

'Nay, sir. It is Davy I search for,' said Tam. 'I was told I would find him here.'

The minister shook his head. 'Alas, he failed to arrive this morning. A matter of great inconvenience for he was to help me with some parish affairs, accounts and so forth.'

Sounding rather cross and put out, he added, 'Davy writes a fair hand, a fair hand indeed.'

His firm statement led Tam to speculate further that the minister also relied on the absent Davy's superior eyesight.

However there were more important issues suggested by the man's failure to put in an appearance which implied that Davy Rose was no simple crofter who could not read and write but a man of some education. A fact that further intrigued Tam regarding his connection with Mistress Agnew.

'I cannot imagine what has happened to him,' said the minister. 'He is usually so reliable,' and with a sigh, 'Shall I inform him of your visit, sir?'

'No need for that, minister. I will look in again.'

'It is no trouble, sir,' the minister urged. 'If you leave me your name I will tell him.'

Aware of the minister's curiosity regarding his identity, Tam thanked him kindly and left before any further questions were put to him.

As he walked quickly towards the Palace he was full of foreboding and a growing certainty that the killer of the queen's midwife had also cut short the life of the minister's scribe.

He had been too late. Tam was certain that David Rose would never be seen alive again.

Chapter Seven

Tansy had returned and was in her sewing-room surrounded by bright silks, satins and velvets; costumes for the queen's Masque.

At the end of Tam's account of his visit to David Rose's home in the village she frowned. ''Tis curious about those parchments. As you know, Mistress Agnew kept her door locked. She was a very private person and her herbarium was part of the royal apartments.'

She paused. 'I spent evenings with her sometimes and she had a press where she kept goblets and so forth. There were also rolls of parchment, books which she said contained her recipes. I went to her room, expecting the door to be locked.' She paused. 'It was open.'

'So someone had removed the key from her body,' said Tam.

Tansy nodded. 'It seems so. All her possessions, the contents of the press, had vanished. The room was so empty, as if she had never existed.'

Again she paused. 'What do you think, Tam? Is it not strange that the man she visited in the village has also disappeared?'

'And his house has also been searched, his documents carefully examined,' said Tam grimly. 'All this is too much of a coincidence.'

Tansy looked fearful. 'A very sinister connection by the sound of it.'

'I am certain that the link, the key to this mystery, lies in the missing documents. Documents, we can conclude, that were the object of their search.'

'But we do not know who,' Tansy whispered.

Tam shook his head. The speed with which matters had

been carried out pointed to some person who had an effective and very efficient organisation at his command.

King James fitted that category admirably.

Sounds of mirth outside erupted into the arrival of six young women who were very interested in seeing the breeches they were to wear at the queen's Masque. Tansy laughed at Tam's puzzled expression. 'The queen has commanded that ladies wear men's attire and the gentlemen wear court dresses.'

'That should create some problems,' said Tam drily.

'And a lot of merriment,' said Tansy.

One of the ladies, introduced as Matilda, held up a pair of padded breeches and sighed. Such a style would do her ample hips no favours.

'Is it not a comical sight? Quilted doublets, so unwieldy and uncomfortable – stuffed, bombasted so that men can neither work nor yet play in them.' And to Tansy, 'Who on earth invented such an absurdity?'

'The Italians, about a hundred years ago,' said Tansy. 'The slashings were meant to display to the world the wearer's ability to obtain undergarments of fine linen, by cutting slits in the outer costume and pulling a contrasting colour through. Like so,' she demonstrated, on the garment being held up for examination.

'But the custom was thought to have begun with the mercenary soldiers who kept their good clothes under their fighting rig. Sleeves and doublet were first, colours ran riot and, as slashing became more popular in other regions, the tops of breeches were literally cut to ribbons. Huge padded sleeves to give balance across the shoulders, then the codpiece – cod meaning bag, as you know– a flamboyant addition in dress whose emphasis is masculine virility.'

'Men,' said Matilda contemptuously, handing the breeches back to Tansy with a sigh, her sad shake of the head echoed by her companions.

Then, looking approvingly towards Tam, a silent listener in

modest unadorned garb, she asked, 'What think you, sir?'

'I agree with you. It is certainly not the garb in which one can comfortably play – and win – a game of tennis.'

'Tell us more, Master Eildor.'

But at that moment, the door opened again to admit a maid who staggered in and set down on the table an armful of ruffs, a fashion that had evolved in France from frills formed by the drawstrings fastening men's shirts and ladies' shifts at the neck.

'And every one of those to be starched!, groaned Tansy. 'For that we have to thank Mistress Dinghem, wife of Queen Elizabeth's Dutch coachman who brought the art of starching over to England in the '60s.'

Tam listened fascinated, as Tansy continued: 'Made her fortune by taking in pupils and charging five pounds sterling each to teach them the secrets of white and yellow starches, the additional stiffening provided by silk-covered wire.'

Tam laughed. 'Which accounts for that look of hauteur.'

'As well as very long and painfully aching necks!' said Tansy and leaving the ladies privacy to try on the various garments she ushered Tam into the parlour. 'What did you think about the royal game of tennis?'

'I did more than think. I took part – at His Grace's insistence.'

'You played with him?' asked Tansy wide-eyed.

'No. My opponent was John Ramsay.'

'You mean that the king matched you against his favourite, his star player! How embarrassing. Did you lose?'

'On the contrary. I won. By twelve points.' At her shriek of delight, Tam added modestly, 'But Ramsay, I fear, was hindered by his padded breeches and boots.'

Tansy shuddered. 'On such a day. In all this heat. Tell me what happened.'

Briefly Tam described the match and then added, 'But that was not the end of it. His Grace now commands that I move into the royal apartment.'

Tansy stared at him. 'Your game must have been very impressive, since it would appear that you have usurped John Ramsay in the royal favour.'

'And if I accept, then I fear the next step will be up into His Grace's bed,' said Tam dolefully.

Tansy shuddered. 'Poor Tam, what a very unwholesome predicament.'

'It is indeed, especially as I have no taste for kings who seldom wash, or for young lords and ambitious pages.'

Tansy smiled sadly. 'Fashionable in the royal court, I am afraid, like the absurdity of slashed breeches and codpieces.' And regarding his solemn expression, she asked softly, 'So where does your taste lie, Tam Eildor?'

'I thought you had guessed that already, Mistress Tansy Scott.' His voice was gentle, his tender smile held her eyes.

She blushed and shook he head sadly. 'No, Tam, you must not love me – I beg you – it could never – '

Tam leaned over, put a restraining finger to her lips. 'Do not say it.' And a stern warning. 'Even had you been free, I cannot commit myself. I know nothing of what your grand-dam told you about me...'

He paused awkwardly and she touched his hand, whis-pered, 'The man without a memory of – from whence you came – ' Then looking at him curiously, she said lightly, 'You have no memory at all of Janet Beaton?'

'None whatever.'

'Oh Tam, that is so sad. Such a waste. And each day I see you, I wonder if this will be our last day together. And if you will remember me.'

Tam laughed. 'Have no fear, Tansy. I suspect you will have me for some time yet. I will know when it is time to go and I promise to give you as much warning as I can.'

They were interrupted by sounds of giggling from the sewing-room.

Matilda's face appeared around the door. 'We are ready, Mistress Tansy. I think we will make interesting and pretty young men. As for our court dresses, I long to see what the courtiers will make of them.'

'They will no doubt enjoy the experience,' said Tansy as Tam indicated that he was leaving.

As for Matilda, she curtseyed and took the opportunity to quiz them both. In hushed tones, she confided, 'There are whispers about the court that you are brother and sister.'

Tansy exchanged an amused glance with Tam. 'You must put an end to that rumour, Matilda.'

'But you are so alike,' Matilda protested, disappointed at having anticipated some rare piece of gossip of brother and sister separated at birth in tragic circumstances, or some such romantic nonsense.

Tam merely shook his head, bowed and left Tansy to deal with the situation, anxious to return to the village and continue his search for the missing David Rose.

Tam hurried across the courtyard, carefully skirting the area overlooked by the windows of the royal bedchamber. Determined to take avoiding action at all times, he resolved that the less he encountered King James during his quest, the better he would be pleased. So taking a longer more circuitous route through the gardens, thinking he would be safe, he was soon cursing his choice and ill-luck.

Danger was close at hand. The sound of loud male voices and a jester's raucous singing indicated that the king and his courtiers were walking on the other side of the high hedge.

Doubling back on his tracks and hastening through the gatehouse, once again Tam emerged on the main street. Praying that he would find David Rose at home or in the minister's realm, against all the evidence of his earlier exploration, he hoped that he was not too late, his gloomy misgivings the product of an overwrought imagination.

Once again the door was ajar. As he remembered closing it behind him he had an ominous feeling that in the interval there had been a second visitor.

There was no answer to his summons and, belief in finding Davy fast dwindling, his fears were confirmed when he cautiously opened the door.

The room was empty. The documents still scattered on the floor beside the open press were enough to convince him that Davy had not returned. And that he never would.

The one link that might have led him to the reason for Mistress Agnew's murder, and the apprehension of her killer, was gone forever.

He took a final look around the room then, about to leave, he had reached the door when he heard a noise.

Another sound, a stifled sneeze. And again, louder.

'Hello, who is there?'

There was no reply, no sign of anyone lurking in the room's darker corners.

But there was someone in the vicinity. The only place to hide could be the bed. Not in it but underneath where another sneeze confirmed a human presence.

Realising that it must be a very small person to take cover in such a small space he said, 'Come out. I will not harm you.'

A childlike hand, tiny and very dirty appeared, then a head of curls, two bright but terrified eyes.

Their owner was a small girl who wriggled her way out with some difficulty, puffing and panting with the exertion of having been confined in such a tiny space.

She remained kneeling on the ground beside the bed and, her thin body trembling, gazed imploringly up at Tam.

'Please, sir, do not hurt me, I beg you. Uncle Davy will kill you if any harm comes to me,' she added in solemn warning.

'Stand up, child,' said Tam, helping her to her feet, so thin and waif-like, he felt that if the door had been opened she might have been blown away like thistledown.

'I mean you no harm. Come sit by me – ' he patted the bed '– and tell me about your Uncle Davy. Where is he – was he expecting you?'

Still trembling, the child shook her head. 'He was not

expecting me, and I do not know where he is. I thought to find him here – I came all the way from Edinburgh.'

As she paused and took a gulp of air, Tam said, 'That is a very long way for a little girl.'

'Oh I wasna feart,' she said bravely, 'an' I got lifts from tinkers and their carts. And – and – ' But, suddenly overwhelmed by fatigue, hunger and fearful memories of that long journey, courage faded and tears flowed.

Such a sorry spectacle, such a tiny creature to have travelled such a distance alone, Tam's heart was touched.

He put a gentle arm around her thin shoulders and said, 'There there now. Don't cry, child. You are quite safe. No one is going to harm you.'

Still sobbing, she nestled against his shoulder and gazed up at him tearfully.

'What is your name?' Tam asked.

'Jane, sir.'

'How old are you, Jane?'

'Thirteen come Martinmas.'

Tam smiled. She looked no more than ten, but he continued, 'Have you no family, Jane?'

She shook her head, her eyes flooded with tears. 'No one now. Only Uncle Davy. After my ma died I bided wi' a neighbour in St Mary's Close but her man – he – he – ' Shuddering she took a deep breath.

'He quarrelled with you?'

'Nay, mister. He wanted – he liked – to touch me. I was feart, I didna' like him, but there wasna' ony place to hide from him. Six other lassies in the hoose, but it was me he wanted. And Ma's friend, who was so guid to her when she was sick, loved her man Bart and would have thocht that I was telling lies. I would have been beaten for that, so I ran away.'

A sorry tale, thought Tam. And he could not leave her here.

'Come with me.'

'Where are you taking me, mister?'

'To a very kind lady who will give you something to eat and some clean clothes. And she will know what to do for you.'

The child hesitated. 'She willna' sent me back to Bart?'

'I can assure you that she will never do that.'

Again she hesitated. 'You – you will no' be like him. Wi' me, I mean?'

'That I do promise, Jane. Mistress Scott will look after you until we can see you safely back with your Uncle Davy.'

As they left the house, she asked where they were going.

'Just across the street. There.' He pointed across at the palace.

'Is that where you live?' she whispered in considerable awe as they approached the gatehouse.

'For the moment,' Tam said. Once he got her settled with Tansy, his hopes resurged that she might throw some light on the relationship between David Rose and Mistress Agnew.

And whatever document it was that those who searched his house had failed to find.

Chapter Eight

In Edinburgh's Lawnmarket, Will Hepburn was enjoying a glass of excellent claret with Martin Hailes, once Lady Morham's lawyer.

After death terminated her guardianship, Will was content to let affairs relating to income and estate remain in his elderly cousin's hands. True, it would have been more convenient to employ a Perth lawyer when Martin Hailes retired at seventy and was reluctant to make the long journey from Edinburgh. Will, however, disliked changes and despite Martin's urging was too lethargic to take his affairs elsewhere. Besides he had another reason, the excuse for an enjoyable visit to the bustling city.

In good weather he made an occasional nostalgic visit to Morham Castle, his home for many years. Despite James Hepburn's lamentable failings as his father, Will was proud of being a Borderer. Without having ever struck a blow or raised a sword in anger, ballads from his childhood roused memories of steel-bonneted warriors who called at Morham and stirred the pride of race that was in his blood.

'Somewhat unruly and very had to take,
I would have none think that I call them thieves.
The freebooter ventures life and limb,
Good wife and bairn and everything.
He must do so, or else must starve and die,
For all his living comes of the enemy.'

Morham had passed to other hands long ago, to other cousins who he hardly knew and none who would care to meet him. But the old lawyer, aware of William's remarkable recollection of his childhood, the way he could recall events in precise detail, always encouraged him to reminisce, as well as enjoying in return the latest gossip about Falkland Palace.

Unfailingly polite, his first question to William was, 'And how is Mistress Scott?'

'She is well, sir.'

Martin nodded. 'Excellent, excellent,' was the correct reply, having striven through the years to hide his disappointment in young William's choice of the woman with whom he wished to share his life.

Not that Martin had anything personal against Tansy Scott. On the several occasions when they had met, he had been agreeably surprised by her charm, her kindness and outstanding good looks. His reason was more practical. Simply that her presence in William's life had put an end to him ever marrying and raising a family of his own.

He could never quite understand why the lad, the bastard son of an infamous but undoubtedly attractive father, had chosen from all the women who would have made excellent wives, the estranged wife of a Fife laird. Estranged for the reason that she was barren, the shaming and unforgivable curse of womanhood, the death knell of queens.

The years had passed since Martin raised the subject of a suitable wife. If Walter Murray divorced Tansy, he knew that William would marry her at once. But still no bairns, a sterile marriage. The thought aggravated Martin, since forty was still an age of virility for men. Recently a widower, with eight living children, Martin had already been a grandfather at that age.

Sighing, he remembered his efforts to produce expensive supper parties through the years, inviting eligible Edinburgh young ladies for William's benefit and seduction. Ladies, he suspected, who would have been more than eager for his amorous attentions, with parents who would have rejoiced and welcomed an eligible bachelor, bastard son of Queen Mary's notorious third husband.

Martin's secret but scandalous hope was still that the lad might be compromised and forced into marriage. Sadly for him, William obviously had not inherited James Hepburn's

89

promiscuous and irresponsible attitudes toward women either.

Nor did Martin's plan deceive him. 'You are a poor matchmaker, cousin Hailes,' Will laughed, with a stubborn shake of his auburn curls. 'You are wasting your time and money on lining up prospective brides for me. If I cannot have Tansy Scott, then I will remain unwed for the rest of my life. And that is my final word on the subject.'

Today however, William's next words afforded his cousin a small gleam of hope. 'Tansy has a distant cousin staying, from the Borders.'

'And what is this lady like?' Martin asked, daring to hope.

Will laughed. 'You never give up, do you! This lady, cousin, is a bachelor, young and very handsome,' he added with a teasing glance.

'How old is he?'

'Thirty-six.' Again Martin's hopes soared for a very different reason. A handsome cousin, thirty-six. Perhaps his prayers had been answered, and he had come to sweep Tansy Scott off her feet.

'His name is Tam Eildor,' William was saying. He frowned. 'Do you know, something very strange happened when we first met.'

He hesitated for a moment and Martin asked, 'Indeed. How so?'

William looked at him, bewildered. 'You see, I thought I remembered him. From a visit at Morham long ago – '

As he went on to describe that meeting in some detail, Eildor with two of the queen's Maries, Seton and Fleming, himself sitting on his grandmother's knee, aged four, Martin shook his head.

'You must be mistaken. The man you met would now be as old as I am.'

Will shook his head. 'However old he is, he looks exactly as he did thirty-six years ago.'

Martin studied him for a moment. 'You must be mistaken,

William. Border families often have a strong likeness. Inbreeding, you know, and the wrong side of the blanket.'

'That is what Tansy is saying.'

'I am sure she is correct in that.' Pausing he glanced at Will. 'But you are not convinced.'

Will frowned, shook his head, and Martin hoping to change the subject asked, 'How goes it in the royal palace? Any new scandals?'

'Only a new murder.'

'A murder!' Martin whispered, waiting for details.

'The day I arrived, Tansy was very upset. There had been a serious accident – the queen's midwife and constant attendant had been killed. She lodged with Tansy.'

'Where was her cousin when all this happened?' Martin demanded suspiciously, his mind racing ahead.

Tam smiled. 'He was with Tansy. They discovered the woman dying – of a stab wound – on the turnpike stair. Mistress Agnew was a friend of Tansy. Similar backgrounds. As you know, Tansy was orphaned early and brought up by her granddam, Lady Beaton.'

Martin suppressed a grimace. This was another connection he would have preferred William's chosen partner to be without. Janet Beaton, Lady Buccleuch, had been a powerful and remarkable woman suspected of witchcraft.

'Mistress Agnew had also been orphaned and brought up by her granddam, who, like Lady Beaton, was also in attendance at James's birth.' Pausing, he added, 'I expect you remember that, cousin.'

Martin nodded. 'I remember hearing about it. It was a bad time for Scotland and there were ugly rumours concerning his birth. As he grew older rough townsfolk used to shout after him; "Ye son of Davy Riccio"'

'Was it true, do you think?'

Martin shook his head. 'Who knows what murky deeds the past conceals. Certainly on the rare occasions when I have observed King James riding past in Edinburgh, he has not inherited the outstanding good looks of either his father or mother. But I cannot imagine the lovely young queen with her ugly little secretary who I saw only once.' With a sigh, he continued, 'She preferred stronger men – '

'Like my father,' said Will bitterly.

'Indeed. That was the tragedy of both their lives.' Martin frowned, stroking his beard. 'Rumour whispered another explanation concerning James's birth. Concerning a document – '

'Tell me,' Will insisted.

At Falkland, the minister hurrying past on his way to church observed Tam leaving David Rose's house accompanied by a beggar's child.

He stopped, blinking in astonishment as this ragged apparition was introduced as David Rose's niece. 'Come to visit him, minister. Should he return imminently, tell him Jane awaits him at Mistress Scott's lodging, by the queen's apartments.'

And bowing, Tam marched the small girl firmly across the road before any further questions could be raised, leaving the minister staring open-mouthed after them.

Tansy Scott's reactions were identical at the sight of Tam with a ragged small girl clinging to his hand.

Quickly he explained, while Jane, wide-eyed, clutched his arm like the lifeline to a drowning mariner.

Taken aback, Tansy surveying the terrified child and hoping that a benevolent smile was assurance of a warm welcome, rang the bell that summoned Martha, her serving-woman, who was instructed to bathe, feed and provide the child with some suitable garment.

The latter suggested a problem, then, with a moment of inspiration, Tansy scooped up a small gown of satin and lace from the sewing-table.

'The very thing,' she said to Tam. 'This is a court dress for one of Her Grace's female dwarfs.' And holding it up against

Jane, she smiled. 'A little inappropriate, but adequate.'

Warm-hearted, kindly Martha, quite unfazed, put a protective arm around Jane who, even in the presence of such friendly people, continued to tremble and look apprehensive.

Martha had encountered and endured great poverty in her time and the child before her was not the most advanced example of suffering and neglect.

Examining the elaborate garment with its low cut neckline, she frowned.

'This will have to do for the moment, Mistress Scott.' And smiling down at Jane she went on, 'My lassie has a bairn about your age, my pet. She will find you something more comfortable, never fear.'

But only the promise of good things to eat in Martha's kitchen overcame Jane's reluctance to be parted from Tam.

Watching the door close on them, Tam explained the circumstances of his rescue.

'I thought you might give her a home until the situation is resolved.'

As Tansy nodded agreement, there was no doubt in her mind or in Tam's that Jane had little hope of a happy outcome and of being reunited with her uncle.

'I was hoping that she might provide us with some information about Mistress Agnew,' said Tam.

'A forlorn hope, I fear,' was the reply. 'Surely you do not imagine that her uncle would confide in a child seldom seen any details of an illicit relationship?' And always practical, Tansy continued, 'Have you considered having taken her into your care, what is to become of her if her uncle does not return? – if he is dead, as you fear.'

Tam sighed. 'We cannot send her back to Edinburgh, orphaned and friendless.'

Tansy glanced at him sharply. 'I think you mean that I cannot – or more correctly, will not – send her back to a brutal foster-father, orphaned and friendless.'

When Tam smiled, she said wryly, 'How well you know me

in our short acquaintance, Tam Eildor.' And with a sigh, 'We shall see what talents she has, if any, perhaps find her suitable employment in the palace here.'

But Tansy had few hopes regarding the success of introducing the waifish child Tam had deposited on her charity into the queen's household.

Aware of her reluctance to be involved, he said in Jane's defence, 'She must have been very brave to venture all that way from Edinburgh alone to find her uncle.'

'Very brave or scared out of her wits,' was Tansy's contribution.

An hour later they were taken aback when the door opened to admit a tiny figure, at first glance a dwarf in an elaborate court dress, followed by a proudly smiling Martha.

Tam laughed delightedly. He had no idea that the dirt and grime of a long arduous journey could have concealed such a pretty creature. Her pinched, wan appearance had been merely the result of hunger and fatigue for her exhausted pale face now blossomed into rosy cheeks, her freshly washed hair a mass of damp curls.

Plainly delighted to find herself in such a splendid gown, touching its satin skirts in wonderment, she looked at the sewing table and turning to Tansy she curtseyed and said:

'If it please you, madam, I can handle a needle and my stitches have been greatly sought after – even by Edinburgh gentlefolk,' she added proudly.

'Excellent. You will be earning your keep,' said Tansy with a laugh. 'You could not have arrived at a better moment for I need all the help I can get, every pair of hands that can handle needle and thread for the Masque.'

The royal palace, quite suddenly, had turned into a human beehive of buzzing, hurrying, scurrying servants. A seething mass of men moving tables and chairs, carrying backdrops of Arcadian painted scenery, all of them shouting and cursing each other as well as the women who got in their way with their armsful of curtains and furnishings.

The Queen's Masque was imminent.

Tam joined this bustling force of humanity, helpfully fetching and carrying and arranging scenery. Having refused Tansy's pleas to be fitted out with a suitable costume, he decided that curiosity might well drive him to attend the masque but the only costume he would wear would be his own.

'The theme is mythology: will you not be persuaded to appear as a Greek god?' asked Tansy wistfully, considering the man regarded by the court as her handsome remote cousin or bastard brother. And thinking to herself that she had the very costume that would turn him into a sensational Adonis.

'Never,' said Tam firmly. 'If I go at all, I go as myself, and that is final,' he added, keeping well away from Tansy's sewing-room and steering clear of the royal tennis court, and any possible encounters with the amorous king.

Meanwhile Jane had settled down happily with Tansy, busy with her needle all day. Her nights undisturbed by a predatory foster-father she slept on a dormitory floor with the female servants, unaware that Tam conscientiously rose early and visited her uncle's house on the off-chance of finding some evidence of his return. But each day closed the door once again on his fast diminishing hopes.

Taking advantage of yet another perfect day, Tam headed towards the wooded banks of the Maspie burn; less exposed than its parent river. Settling down with fishing rod and basket, he was ready to dive out of sight behind the nearest tree should any sound reach his ears to indicate the approach of any unwelcome visitor, in particular King James and his retinue.

On the day before the Masque, the body of Margaret Agnew was laid to rest in the kirkyard. In the absence of any kin, her plain wooden coffin was followed by Tam, Tansy and a few of the queen's serving-maids.

Cautious mention of her name to little Jane had aroused no recognition. Clearly her uncle's liaison was unknown to her, but during the minister's short service of committal, Tam looked around wondering whether Davy Rose knew of her death or if her killer lurked out of sight, watching the scene.

If so, then Tam concluded that he must be doing so with some satisfaction, certain that he was safe from discovery.

The motive for her murder was being buried in the grave with her, the mystery forever unsolved by Tam Eildor.

There were more pressing mysteries in the court, concerning Tam Eildor himself, under serious investigation by Sandy Kay, on behalf of Ludovick Stewart, Duke of Lennox. His efforts had led him as far as the Peebles area where heads were shaken. None had ever heard of the family of Eildor, or of Tam of that ilk. With his riders, Kay had travelled two days and nights and returned to Falkland exhausted and frustrated by his lack of success.

Lennox, however, willingly handed over the promised purse not, as Kay had feared, angry or concerned at this failure. He was in fact quietly triumphant and hastened to tactfully warn James that Tam Eildor should be arrested immediately and thrown into prison as impostor and spy.

James was not grateful. He did not command Eildor's arrest forthwith. Glaring balefully at Lennox, he shouted, 'A spy, ye say, Vicky. On what grounds d' ye come by that assumption?'

'He is unknown in Peebles, whence he informed Your Grace was his home. Nor is there any family by the name of Eildor. My men have searched high and low.'

'Have they now, Vicky. On whose orders?' James's voice was soft but Lennox recognised the danger signals.

'On my orders, sire,' he blustered. 'But for the good cause of Your Grace's safety and the well-being of your kingdom,' he added piously.

'Is that so? Our safety eh?' And James stabbed a grubby finger in Lennox's chest. 'Then let us be the one to decide such matters – who is for our good cause.'

'But, Your Grace, this man is unknown … I beseech you – '

'A meenit, if you please, Vicky,' said the king sternly. 'Let us consider this a wee meenit. Master Eildor is unknown, we grant ye that. But so are most of our subjects.' And, wagging a finger at him, 'No' everyone has the advantage o' your own high breeding, Vicky. Master Eildor is a fisherman, a humble but loyal citizen, honest – aye, honest.' Pausing he sighed, smiled a little, and added sternly, 'That is why we are drawn to him.'

Lennox bit back queries on that subject as James went on, 'Why should one o' my humble but loyal subjects be kenned in the castles on the Tweed with which our nobler subjects are acquainted, eh?'

This was a question to which Lennox had no quick answer as James shrugged huffily and continued in a tone of extreme irritation, 'Use what sense the Guid Lord gied ye, Vicky – and dinna weary us wi' your nonsense.'

'But, sire, this Eildor is no ordinary humble citizen. He is – educated. He speaks well. He is possibly in the pay of your enemies, sent to spy on you.'

'Then bring those enemies to us and we will know how to deal with them,' said James wearily.

Such an irrational statement was beyond Lennox but the king's grinning signal to John Ramsay lurking nearby indicated that the audience was over and that he was dismissed.

Bowing, he withdrew, his mind working rapidly, considering what to do next in the face of the king's lamentable infatuation with Tam Eildor.

Lennox was not finished, not by any means.

Nor, it happened, was Sandy Kay, who had some plans of his own for the queen's Masque, lured by the promise of a handsome purse once he dealt with Tansy Scott, the burdensome estranged wife of Walt Murray.

Chapter Nine

On the day before the queen's Masque, Tam awoke with the first light of dawn a tiny grey square in the high window of his room. Fully awake and aware that he would not sleep again, he dressed and went quickly down the spiral stair and out into the gardens where mist clung to trees and lay like a white shroud across the widespread lawns.

The sundial proclaimed the day but a few hours old and the sun's red orb rising above the hills forecast another hot day. Very soon these peaceful stretches of smooth grass would be a mass of servants preparing the stage for tomorrow evening.

Meanwhile, barring a few birds on early morning forage who paused to give him wary looks and a few inquisitive squirrels, it seemed Tam had the gardens and the peaceful scene to himself.

Not quite. The sound of girlish laughter nearby. Tam looked round. Could this be some of the village children having a very early rehearsal for their roles in the pageant?

At this hour, he thought bitterly, resentful of his lost moments of tranquility. Deciding to keep well out of sight and move to another part of the garden, the little girls suddenly emerged from the mist just a dozen yards away.

Five of them; the tallest in front, the other four behind her. They were playing with a ball, throwing it to each other and dressed for the evening pageant in the costume and headdress of an earlier reign.

The tall one saw him first. A movement of her hand. Her companions stopped, the ball thrust guiltily out of sight.

Their leader, for such she must be, smiled at him and the four girls curtseyed, a pretty flower-like assembly of spreading skirts across the dewy grass.

Tam bowed. When he raised his gaze, they had disappeared.

Shaking his head, Tam made his way back to his lodging. Tansy would know why the children had been sent for so early, dragged out of bed before dawn.

However Tansy was in no mood to discuss anything so trivial. A rider had arrived late last night with a letter from Will who was now at Dirleton Castle in East Lothian with Lady Gowrie. Her daughter, Beatrix, had been given special permission from Queen Anne to attend a wedding and her mother had taken ill soon afterwards. Good-hearted Will had immediately offered to escort them back to Perth and he had persuaded Martin Hailes to accompany them for a short visit to his home at Kirktillo.

'I feel certain that the old gentleman's health will benefit greatly from a change of air and there are estate matters which would do better from his personal attention.'

Will had observed that Martin was looking older and more tired since they last met in Edinburgh and had not recovered from the loss of his beloved wife of many years. Aware of his reluctance to travel, Will was agreeably surprised that no persuasion was needed. Indeed, Martin appeared eager and grateful for the suggestion.

Had Will been of a suspicious nature, he would have regarded this with surprise. For if truth were told, Tam Eildor was the main reason for Martin's visit. His object: to find some answer to Will's extraordinary insistence that this was the same man who had visited his granddam at Morham yet did not look a day older than at their first meeting more than thirty years ago.

In conclusion, the letter begged Tansy's forgiveness for his unavoidable absence from the Masque and assured her of his boundless devotion.

Tansy threw down Will's letter. She had another reason for anger. Earlier that day she had received another letter, borne by a former servant of her husband Walt Murray, that "our cousin at Tullibardine is to wed in early August." The letter went on that Tansy's presence was her wifely duty on this occasion, hinting that whatever the differences between them, it was essential that they present an agreeable appearance of marital harmony before the assembled family.

Tansy scowled angrily. The suggestion hinted obliquely at a public reconciliation and little as she cared for that odious idea, she realised that she had very little option but to obey her estranged but legal husband's command.

If Walt decided to reclaim his conjugal rights, even for one night under his family's roof and before their friends, then the law was on his side. If Tansy refused her wifely duty then she was trapped indeed.

And if Walt had King James's ear on the matter, His Grace, eager to be rid of her, would doubtless find some loophole by which she might find herself imprisoned for the rest of her life.

Tansy would have been even less happy had she known that the messenger bearing the letter, Sandy Kay – a servant of the Duke of Lennox who was no friend of Tam's either – was also being paid by her husband to spy on her.

All unknowing, she was the fly in the centre of a particularly nasty spider's web.

Tam, returning depressed from another useless visit to David Rose's empty house, the mystery of Mistress Agnew's murder still weighing heavily upon his mind, found Tansy very despondent indeed.

Questioned, her annoyance at Will's failure to return in time for the Masque had first place. 'You heard him, Tam. You must realise that any excuse would serve his purpose.'

Tam, having decided to tactfully absent himself from that event, found that it was his turn to be faced with opposition.

'Since Will cannot be present, then you must escort me.'

'Not I, Tansy,' said Tam. 'It is my firm intention to keep well out of His Grace's way.'

He hated refusing and letting her down but the whole business of the royal orgy, which he had already guessed would be the climax of the queen's Masque, had no appeal for him. Especially if this included the attentions of a lustful king. In that respect he had reasons of his own for depression, having just heard by royal command that he was to prepare to take up residence in His Grace's apartments within the next few days.

Passing this information on to Tansy, he expected more concern but, preoccupied with her own troubles, she merely murmured sympathetically.

Determined that Tam should accompany her to the sewing-room, he gave in, weakly eager to depart. 'Very well, if you insist. But I go as myself or not at all.'

Opening the door, all hands were busily engaged on assembling costumes and gathering pleated ruffs, where the smell of hot irons gave rise to less pleasant visions associated with the torture chamber.

From the table, Tansy took a fine linen shirt and a pair of new breeches.

Thanking her as she laid them across his arm, she pointed to the diminutive figure who smiled at them from her seat at the far end of the table. 'For the shirt you have Jane to thank.'

And as Tam bowed and blew her a kiss, Tansy laughed, 'You could not find a better or a faster seamstress anywhere.'

Matilda came in the door flourishing a doublet and looking anxious.

'Mistress Scott, I cannot wear this. The colour – the shape –'

'A moment, Lady Matilda, and you will have my full attention,' said Tansy leading Tam into the parlour.

'Matilda is but one of many this morning. Like a huge tidal wave they sweep through the sewing-room all day with their complaints, their alarms and skirmishes. Little Jane has been a treasure. A great find – she sews neatly and quickly and I have no doubt that a place will be found for her. Her future is assured.'

Tam was relieved to be free of that responsibility at least, as Tansy continued enthusiastically, 'She has a natural flair for designing new garments and adornments. Now I must leave you…' and she hurried back to her work.

The court held their breaths as the hot spell continued. Would it hold for two more days? Prayers were said in the royal chapel. Elsewhere, however, the weather's pastoral perfection did not have echoes in the queen's apartments.

King James was affronted by his wife's decision to hold the event outdoors, having decided on the Long Gallery as a setting. The queen knew of this and had taken advantage of his aversion to the elements of nature, over which he had no control.

'Twill rain, that's certain sure, Annie. We will all be drowned, the costumes ruined, the food spoiled.'

Anne's pleasant gentle smile masked the knowledge that her royal husband's nervous humour was ever alert to the impossibility of securing every corner of the royal gardens. In particular against assassins lurking in the dusk, awaiting their chance to strike, screened by high hedges and the branches of tall stout trees.

'Think a wee meenit on all yon fireworks, Annie. Costly, aye, verra costly to our royal purse. An unnecessary expense to be doused in water – '

Most of all James hated fireworks. Their brilliant display he regarded as his precious treasury going up in flames while their loud noises completely unnerved him, suggesting an assassin's pistol at his ear.

The queen listened impatiently, quite unmoved by his pleas. His Grace was forced to gloomily remember that pregnancy always made her more peevish than usual.

'We have planned our Masque to the last detail, sire. We cannot change one item of it now, regardless of the weather. Which we are assured will last for another week.'

As James continued to argue, bombarding her with his odious Latin quotations about wifely obedience and so forth, which floated over her head and out beyond the palace windows, she was secretly delighted. Once again she had succeeded in paying him back for keeping her dear children from her in the royal nursery at Stirling Castle under the protection of the formidable and utterly heartless Countess of Mar.

There was more to come.

This was not the sole reason for James's informal morning visit.

Observing his tendency to linger, Anne inclined her head and turned away, a gesture indicating dismissal.

'Aye, there is another wee matter, Annie.' When he remained firmly seated, staring at her and biting his lip, she hoped that this was not the preliminary to one of their rare copulations.

Her apprehensive expression invited explanation and clearing his throat rather noisily, James said, 'We have arranged for Master Eildor to take up lodging in our apartment.'

Relief gave way to anger. So Master Eildor was still the object of his most recent interest. Coldly, she decided he would get no help from her in this matter either.

'As Gentleman of the Bedchamber?' she said acidly.

'Aye, mebbe that,' was the careful reply.

Anne gave him a look of thinly disused disgust as both remembered the incident involving Alexander, Master of Ruthven. Two years ago he had been elevated from the Queen's Household to just such an appointment, with disastrous results.

James shifted uncomfortably under his wife's gaze as, turning away, she said coldly, 'We cannot allow that to happen again. Master Eildor is one of our most trusted and valued servants.'

'Is he now?' James banged his fists together. 'Our word upon yours, Annie, is that it?'

'We must remind you, James, that our authority in our household over our servants is absolute,' was the smooth reply, with emphasis on the word "our".

James jumped to his feet and pointed a grubby finger at her. 'Ye defy us, madam, is that the way of it?'

Anne stared stolidly towards the window as he continued: 'Are ye telling us that ye will no' release Master Eildor?'

'That is so,' she said coldly but firmly.

James continued to stare at her biting his lip. 'And for why, Annie?' He paused giving her a crafty glance. 'This servant – ye're no' surely intending taking him as a lover – as well.'

His mocking tone infuriated her. How dare he make such a suggestion! Suddenly a bellow of laughter, coarse and lewd. Looking at her he could hardly believe that any man would find this ungainly creature, never at her best in pregnancy, bedworthy. Especially a man of such splendid calibre and infinite delights as Tam Eildor.

The queen did not rise to his taunt, the slow movement of her head, the enigmatic fixed smile enraging him further.

Had she? Could she…

James had a sudden vision of Alexander Ruthven, a lad of sixteen, an enchanting face under a mass of red curls. His rival for the lad's affection in this instance, none other than the queen herself. The lad had been found asleep in her garden, brazenly wearing as token of esteem the silk scarf James had given her.

Her sudden change of countenance told him that the shaft had gone home. Taking advantage of that, he said in solemn warning, 'May we remind you, madam, that queens have lost their heads for less.'

It was Anne's turn to laugh. 'We think you would have some difficulty proving any such allegation against our virtue, James.'

Rising to her feet, she curtseyed awkwardly, 'Sire, we beg leave to bid you good day.' And without further word, she summoned her ladies who sat at a discreet distance. Now gathering around her protectively, curtseying to the king, they ushered the queen into her bedchamber, leaving His Grace staring after them before stamping out in a fury.

In her bedchamber with the door closed safely behind her, Anne decided that James's interest was not reciprocated by Master Eildor. Now that James wanted him she was more determined than ever that he should not have him.

Having sentimentally decided that Tam was enamoured of Tansy Scott, she frowned. That remarkable resemblance hinted at some strange bond. Perhaps they were long-lost brother and sister as her ladies suggested. How very tragic, the complications of an incestuous relationship.

Summoning Tam to her presence, she said, 'His Grace wishes you to take lodging in the royal apartment. As Gentleman of the Bedchamber perhaps,' she added, straight-faced.

Tam's barely suppressed shudder was all the confirmation she needed.

He bowed. 'Madam, His Grace is too kind but as I have told him, I am a humble fellow.' Pausing to give her an understanding smile, 'I am no cupbearer, quite unworthy of the honours His Grace wishes to bestow upon me. The idea overwhelms me.' He shook his head and looked at her in mute appeal. 'I do not know how to respond.'

The queen held out her hand for Tam to kiss; he dropped on one knee before her. 'Do not be alarmed, Master Eildor. We have responded for you. You are to stay with us.'

Tam knelt before her, kissing her outstretched hand. 'Madam, I am so grateful – there are no words – '

The queen patted his head, gazed for a moment into those strange luminous eyes and indulged herself for a delicious instant that she was no longer pregnant with a child she did not want by a husband she despised. Imagining herself young and carefree as she had once been, beautiful as she had been never, then such a man as this might be her lover.

Yet men *had* loved her. Francis Stewart, Earl of Bothwell,

nephew of Queen Mary's third husband and suspected dealer in witchcraft, was no friend of King James and his irrational exploits, scaring and taunting the king, had led to his exile.

Then there was Alexander Ruthven, appalled by James's treatment of her. Disgusted by what went on behind those closed doors of the royal bedchamber, and refusing what was expected of him, rushing to Anne, telling her all, swearing his eternal devotion.

After James's fury over the incident with the scarf, not occasioned by husbandly jealousy but by the indignity of the lad opening preferring the queen to himself, Alexander had fled back to Ruthven.

Anne hugged her own secrets. She did not mention that the Earl of Bothwell wrote to her from exile. Or that she had received another letter from Alexander Ruthven informing of his return from Padua in Italy, where he had been studying with his tutor William Rynd. He and his elder brother John, Earl of Gowrie were about to take up residence in their town house in Perth.

Her thoughts returned to Tam Eildor. Perhaps she might be more fortunate with him as a devoted admirer or lover.

After all, she was queen of Scotland and for queens every fantasy could be made reality. That she knew so little about Tam made him even more appealing. That he was not of noble birth was an added titillation, since between the sheets stripped naked, men were merely men.

And this one would certainly outshine her kingly consort with his few grunts and his eagerness to get the necessary duty of procreation over with, his speedy return to his pretty young pages.

If only he could stay until the child was born, until she was free of this burden. Meanwhile she resolved that nothing – absolutely nothing – would make him available to James.

Unless he could be used for bargaining purposes. To restore her children to her, perhaps?

Chapter Ten

And so it was with many tensions within the Palace that the queen's Masque dawned. Blessed by the promise of a summer's day with not a breath of wind under a canopy of sunshine and cloudless skies, all was in readiness to transform the gardens of the royal Palace into a stage set for the benighted courtiers who had strayed into Arcady.

Such was the plot dreamed up by Queen Anne; and those who wished to endear themselves to her were lavish in their admiration.

Nymphs and satyrs, fauns and shepherdesses, local children dressed as fairies and even some well-washed sheep from the royal park. Their protesting ablutions heard from miles away aroused speculation among the townsfolk who, used to ignoring the strange sounds which regularly issued from the Palace, merely presumed that there was a slaughtering in progress.

No such ablutions were evident in the royal bedchamber where King James, still stinging from his wife's rebuff over Tam Eildor, was in the sulks at having to play second fiddle to Annie, who was much better at organising Masques than he was.

However, there was titillation in store. The theme was that some noble lords, who had gone hunting the wild deer, had fallen asleep in an enchanted forest – to be represented by a backdrop of highly artificial trees – and awakened to find themselves in the midst of a Bacchanalian orgy.

There at least the king found consolation. The garden fountains, with some considerable difficulty and a great deal of blasphemy, had been turned into fountains of wine, richly sampled by the labourers as they were put into effect.

There was one small difference in the theme. Titania, queen

of the fairies, was to be none other than Queen Anne herself. She was a somewhat obese and unlikely fairy, wearing an ill-fitting transparent robe which did nothing for an advanced state of pregnancy and a drooping and unappealing bosom. The least said about her extremities the better, but it was noted that large feet and heavy legs would present a serious handicap should she have wished to take to the air on suspended wires.

The lost huntsmen were ladies of her household wearing men's clothes, doublets and padded breeches, stamping about in boots that were several sizes too large for them, which must have been a terrible impediment to their hunting and no doubt the reason for the few rabbits slung on poles and a rather long-dead and odorous corpse of a deer which had apparently died of natural causes, old age being indicated.

The shepherdesses with whom the courtiers were to successfully make amorous advances – and there would be a lot of that sort of thing promised for later – were some of the king's younger pages wearing court dresses, some of whom became these costumes remarkably well. Bewigged and painted it would have taken a keen eye to know the difference. They at least were certain of having a right regal evening, since this notion was calculated to have special appeal for His Grace.

Spared any active role, King James would sit on his throne beside his fairy consort, in extreme discomfort on such a torrid evening by wearing his most elaborate state robes. The heavy crown would be replaced by his favourite ostrich-feathered tall hat, somewhat incongruously allied to coronation robes. But he would have his way and doubtless before the evening was out a lot of clothes would be discarded, especially if the heat of the day continued into darkness.

The satyrs and fauns were the youngest pages, very scantily clad despite the goats hair trews and rather inadequate codpieces, wearing woolly wigs with tiny gilded horns, their faces painted with seductively wide eyes. His Grace found them very appealing too. In fact, he wasn't quite sure if he would get around to distributing his favours to so many attractive creatures. There would be quite a queue later on.

Only Tam Eildor, the sheep and the doves, the latter to be picturesquely released, were themselves as God made them.

As dusk gathered the candles were lit on the huge tables with their tankards and goblets, the royal dais groaning with food that had been in preparation for several days and, alas, smelt less than fresh.

The royal chefs complained and looked heavenward and screamed abuse at each other. How could delicate meats and fish be kept fresh for more than a day in such weather, in such abominable heat?

A trumpet sounded, a hushed silence, and their majesties walked arm in arm like the best of friends down a central grove, a highly elaborate representation of tall trees, since the real-life ones were inadequately placed too far from the scene of the masque.

Tam had settled himself well out of the range of the lighted candles lining the processional route, some perched dangerously on lower branches of trees. Such was the stillness of that still hot evening that their flames did not even flutter.

In the clearing around a flower-girt fish pond – the creation of an earlier king – white pillars entwined with blooms indicated an Arcadian temple, the setting for the enchanted glade.

A royal trumpeter announced the arrival of children dressed as fauns and fairies, and looking every inch the part, which was more than could be said for the already sweating grown ups. The childish voices raised in a musical ode to Titania were accompanied, or not, depending on the state of one's ear for music, by the rattle of flute and fiddle not altogether in tune.

Obediently they trotted off, each leading a sheep or being dragged off in the wrong direction by creatures who had not read the queen's stage directions.

Tam craned his neck, looking for the five small girls he had encountered the previous morning, but could not distinguish them or even pick out their costumes, although he was pleased to see Jane proudly parading in court dress.

The children's departure was followed by the arrival of the courtiers with their bows and arrows, rushing about the stage set and falling exhausted into a deep sleep, to be awakened by a flight of shepherdesses, hotly pursued by satyrs.

Despite coy attempts at rescue the courtiers, refreshed by sleep, soon made their own intentions clear. Both hunted and hunters exchanged tender embraces which swiftly led to more robust lovemaking.

In no time at all, the evening had developed into a thorough-going orgy, over which His Grace's voice loudly proclaiming Latin quotations could be clearly heard.

After wild and undeserved applause, the unseemly lovers left the stage. No doubt, Tam decided, to sort themselves out of their borrowed costumes as speedily as possible.

While the wine and viands were tackled by those with robust appetites for other, less carnal, matters, His Grace was seen in deep flirtation and caressings with a couple of elegantly-dressed court ladies who, he would soon very pleasantly discover, were none other than John Ramsay and Aiden Proud, two of his favourite pages.

As an observer of this night's entertainment, Tam found this excuse for an outdoors orgy more than a little lacking in subtlety and entertainment.

Keeping well out of the king's range against one of the trees and shutting his ears to the noise he decided he would slip back to his lodging. About to leave, he turned round to find himself in the embrace of a handsome youth with a decidedly husky voice murmuring endearments.

This was too much, but Tam felt that he must humour the amorous creature, whilst fighting shy of those entangling arms.

'Release me, if you please, sir. I think you mistake me for

110

someone else.'

A chuckle vaguely familiar. 'Tam Eildor, is it not?' The voice faintly disguised.

Bowing he said, 'I have not the pleasure – if you will excuse me,' and started to walk away.

Laughter followed. 'That I certainly will not do.'

Hearing Tansy's voice he turned. And there she was, hands on the hips of those padded breeches. Grinning like an ape, she pulled off the bonnet.

'Tam, I have never seen any man so scared of a woman. I might have been the devil himself.'

'Or one of the king's pretty young men,' was the reply.

'Or the King himself. Was that what you thought?' laughed Tansy

Whatever Tam thought at that moment was lost as the still air was broken by an unmistakable sound.

Seizing Tansy he threw her to the ground as the arrow slammed into the tree where their heads had been a second earlier.

Tansy sat up, horrified and indignant. 'That was extremely careless. They could have killed one of us.'

'That, I think, was the general idea,' said Tam grimly, dragging the arrow out of the tree.

Tansy looked at it, frowning. 'I thought our lady courtiers were to carry toy bows and arrows. The queen shall hear about this –'

Tam shook his head. 'No lady could have wielded this one, not for play either. From a crossbow, the kind used by soldiers. A killing instrument – '

He had to restrain himself from the natural impulse of racing off in pursuit of the archer. But even if the assassin still lurked, most of the candles were out and the area from which the arrow had hurtled was in darkness that would make a search impossible and extremely hazardous.

'Tam – I don't understand. Why?' Tansy whispered.

'I wish I had the answer to that.'

'Do you think this has some – connection – with Mistress Agnew?'

'We both have enemies it seems,' Tam replied. He looked at Tansy in the dusk. She was shivering and he put an arm around her.

'Nothing like this ever happened before you came, Tam.' There was a hint of reproach in her voice.

Tam sighed. How could he tell her, warn her? He was certain that the midwife's death was a link, the prelude to some infinitely darker deed unsolved and the reason for his timequest.

'You say that the king wants rid of you, Tansy, and I have made one enemy – at least – among his courtiers. After his defeat at the royal tennis, I am fairly certain that John Ramsay would like to see my back, one way or another,' he added grimly.

The dusk was filled with distant shouts and laughter as couples made their way back to the Palace and in the area now deserted by the Masque servants were clearing up tables and removing furniture and chairs.

Overwhelmed by a feeling of utter depression, Tam said, 'It is cold. Let us go inside.'

Tansy nodded. 'I long to be rid of these silly clothes too. How men can wear them day after day – '

She stopped. 'A moment, Tam. My wine goblet. I left it on the table over yonder.'

Tam looked at her and smiled. 'Surely you have wine enough –'

Tansy shook her head. 'The wine goblet is special. I always use it at banquets. It has sentimental associations with my granddam – she always believed in carrying her own goblet.'

Leading the way, Tam followed her towards one of the tables.

A solitary candle guttered among the debris of food and goblets.

Tansy pointed. 'I left it right there.'

'Perhaps it has been taken away.'

'No, Tam. As you can see this table has not yet been cleared.'

'It could have fallen – been knocked down.'

Tansy was already searching. She did not have far to look. Under the long cloth that covered the table, an arm.

The arm revealed a hand and as Tam held the candle, Tansy said indignantly: 'One of the grooms. He's drunk – and that is my goblet!'

The servant made no attempt at resistance as Tam dragged him out.

Tansy attempted to remove the goblet clutched tightly in his hand. 'Waken him, Tam,' she said impatiently. 'Make him let go.'

'That I cannot do,' said Tam. With considerable difficulty he prised the goblet from the man's grasp. Sniffing it briefly, he held the candle closer, saw the contorted face.

He handed the goblet to Tansy. 'The death grasp.'

'What do you mean? He's dead drunk.'

'No, Tansy, Not drunk – dead!'

'Dead?'

'Poisoned.'

Tam drew the cloth over the groom's body and taking Tansy's arm said, 'There is nothing we can do for the poor fellow. We would be wise to make ourselves scarce and let someone else make the grim discovery.'

'Should we not – '

'No, Tansy, we definitely should not. I beg you, mention this incident to no one.'

'Not even Her Grace?'

'No one,' Tam repeated firmly.

Two attempts in one evening. And what better setting for success than the queen's Masque, in unprotected gardens surrounded by darkness and candlelight. How easy for an assassin to penetrate.

Tam was not surprised that the nervous king preferred to

113

hold such events within the safety of four walls where all doors could be guarded.

The groom's killing had certainly been an accident as the poisoned goblet, known to be Tansy's, was another deliberate attempt on her life. But by whom?

This was the second killing, or perhaps even the third, if Tam's suspicions were correct regarding the missing David Rose.

Chapter Eleven

Returning from the gardens, considerably shaken by their narrow escape from death, Tam and Tansy found that the Masque had extended its boundaries of carousing and romantic dalliance to their lodging.

Tam shook his head wearily, in no mood to take on the mantle of genial guest. Nor was Tansy, judging by her shocked face, capable of playing genial hostess.

Bidding each other goodnight, Tam whispered anxiously, 'Will you sleep?'

Tansy shivered. 'I have herbs for such matters. Goodnight, Tam.'

Some hours later, when the revellers had retired and the lodging was in silence, Tam lay sleepless, going over the night's events, his thoughts like a rat trapped in a cage.

The 'misfired arrow' and the poison attempt. The unfortunate groom had been no thief. That one sip of a half full goblet had cost him his life. And Tam wondered how that would be dealt with. How would it be dismissed?

"The poison was meant for someone else" would hardly be acceptable for those who grieved for him. Or were explanations always ready and conveniently at hand for such emergencies as the sudden decease of a mere royal groom?

At last the dawn came with cock-crow and the busy chirping of birds beyond the window to put an end to Tam's tortured thoughts.

Aware that any hope of sleep was impossible now, he decided to return to the garden with a forlorn hope that daylight might reveal some clues to the assassin's identity. For Tam was already certain that the man with the crossbow and the poisoner were one and the same.

Down the spiral stair and out into the gardens once more,

no longer regretting lost sleep, he revelled in breathing deeply the fresh pure air.

Already there was hint of warmth in the sunrise over dawn-wreathed hills revealing bruised grass, a few broken branches, the remains of a chair and some burnt foliage as evidence of the night's activities.

His footsteps leaving a delicate pattern on the dew-shrouded grass, Tam noted that the servants' task of clearing the debris of the Masque had been assisted by nature. Remnants of scattered food and bones from platters had vanished, the night creatures quick to avail themselves of this unexpected feast.

And with their industry, any possible clues, thought Tam wryly.

Deciding to have a closer look at the vicinity directly opposite the tree where he and Tansy had stood together, narrowly escaping the assassin's arrow, he touched the scarred trunk.

At almost exactly head-height, the archer had been very efficient, with a well-trained eye. Had it not been for Tam's exceptional hearing, the sound of a released arrow winging through still air, then the marksman would have found his target. Either he or Tansy would have been fatally wounded.

And Tam had no doubt of the ready excuse prepared for that particular tragedy. A misfired arrow by one of the actors.

Suddenly he realised he no longer had the gardens to himself.

Laughter, children's laughter. And he would have sworn the same children he had heard on the day before the Masque.

Looking over to the lawns, there they were, a glimpse of five little girls holding hands, playing in a circle together. Hardly had he blinked when they disappeared into the mist.

'Tam!' He almost leapt into the air at the unexpected voice behind him.

It was Tansy. 'What on earth – why are you about so early?'

he asked.

She smiled. 'I was about to ask the same thing.'

'Obvious, is it not? '

'Sleep was impossible. You did not hear me creep up on you,' said Tansy triumphantly. 'You were watching something very intently.'

Tam shrugged. 'Some little girls playing – over there. You must have heard them laughing.'

Tansy shook her head. 'I heard nothing.'

'I expect they are the gardeners' children.'

'At this hour of the morning? It is not yet five o'clock.'

'This is not the first time. I saw them the other day, at this hour. It was misty, like now. I presumed they were local children rehearsing for their parts in the Masque.

'They were already in costume.'

'In costume?'

'Yes. Days gone by. Five little girls – '

Tansy was regarding him strangely. 'Tell me about them – '

'Playing with a ball. The tallest one saw me first, smiled. They all curtseyed very prettily. I bowed. But when I looked up they were gone – swallowed by the mist.' Pausing for a moment, he added, 'There was something odd that morning. The air was – ' and, searching for the right word, 'I cannot describe it. Different somehow.'

He frowned, remembering. 'I decided they knew they should not be here.' And with a laugh, 'They had not expected to meet anyone and thought I would be angry with them.'

Tansy did not laugh. She shook her head. 'They had every right to be here, Tam, and they did want to be seen.'

'Ah,' said Tam with a sigh of relief. 'You know them?'

'Not personally. But I know who they are.'

'Gardeners' children? Was I right?'

'No, Tam. But I believe you know their identities, if you think about it.'

Tam shook his head, bewildered.

Tansy sighed, looked across at the deserted lawns and said,

'The five little girls are Queen Mary and her four Maries.'

'That cannot be!'

Tansy smiled sadly. 'Queen Mary loved Falkland, she often came as a child to play in the gardens and the woods nearby.'

'Are you telling me – what I have seen – are ghosts?' Tansy looked at him and said nothing as he went on, 'It cannot be. These children looked as real – as real as we are.'

Tansy gave him a tolerant sad smile, said gently, 'I do not think you, Tam Eildor, with your particular background, can offer a great deal on what is real and what is not. It would seem that there are others as well as yourself who are free to move across time's barriers.' She laughed. 'Although their presences are not quite as substantial as yours.'

That thought shocked Tam but before he could comment, Tansy went on, 'I have seen these particular shades too – ' Pausing, she sighed and added, 'Several times, and always before some momentous or tragic event.'

And, looking at him quickly, 'It is a warning, Tam. If you have any doubts, then let us walk to where you saw them.'

Tam followed her. 'Stop, Tansy. It was about here.'

Tansy looked at the ground. 'See – although the mist has lifted, the grass is still wet with dew.' And turning. 'There are our footprints – a clear track. Now look ahead, there is not a single human footmark, nothing more than a coney's paw or a bird's claw to mark the grass where the little girls were playing.'

Tam utterly bewildered, shook his head. 'I have never seen a ghost, Tansy. Never.' And regarding her solemn face. 'You see into the past?'

'Yes, Tam. And I sometimes walk there. I inherited this – sight – from my granddam, among other things.' Hesitating she looked at him, as if for a moment she yearned to discuss those other things. Then shaking her head, 'I do not care to tell any about it.' And glancing over her shoulder as if she might be overheard. 'Such matters are dangerous in this court. And I want to be like other people.'

Holding his arm as they walked back towards the lodging, she whispered, 'It is not safe to be different, Tam.'

'Does Will know of this?'

Tansy smiled. 'He does. He knows and understands, without having any such experience personally.'

As they went into the kitchens to break their fast, for it was not yet six o'clock and none of the servants were about, Tansy said:

'You must take this – visitation – very seriously, Tam. I beg of you, walk warily. You have been sent a message, heed it.'

Although his encounter with the supernatural revealed many things to Tam, it did not help him solve two murders, Mistress Agnew and the poisoned groom. And the murder attempt that failed – of himself or Tansy. To this he added the sinister disappearance of David Rose, where all evidence pointed to his presumed murder.

Most baffling of all, what was the motive for these murders? Was there some link connecting the victims?

He was to get part of his answer from Martin Hailes who arrived with Will later that day.

They were alone. Lady Gowrie was still unfit to travel and Beatrix had remained at Dirleton Castle to take care of her mother.

Tansy was delighted to see Will again but surprised to see Martin Hailes. Long aware of the old man's polite respect but faint disapproval of his cousin's choice of a life partner, she wondered if this unexpected visit signalled some change of heart that she had been accepted at last.

As she bade him warmly welcome, Tansy did not realise that the object of this change of heart was the desire to inspect the mysterious Tam Eildor.

Will, too, had been pleasantly surprised that his invitation so often rejected was now eagerly accepted. Martin had an additional reason. His brother-in-law, who lived near Perth, had constantly urged a visit from the lonely old widower since his dear sister's death.

'It is an excellent time to be absent from Edinburgh,' Martin told Tansy. 'The heat is so oppressive and I long for good clean air.'

Introductions over, Martin Hailes, with a glance at the two lovers holding hands and gazing fondly into one another's eyes, said tactfully, 'Would you walk with me a little, Master Eildor?'

'Gladly, sir.'

For a while they walked in silence and, as Martin took in the surroundings of the royal park and admired the architecture of the Palace, Tam assessed his companion.

The lawyer, although retired, still clung to the gown and velvet bonnet of his profession. He became it well and Tam realised that Martin Hailes had been an uncommonly handsome fellow in his youth and in old age retained fine bones, thick white hair, a luxurious beard and piercing grey eyes.

As conventional questions regarding Falkland Palace received conventional answers Tam was keenly aware, adjusting his steps to the old man's slower pace, that this walk was but a prelude to Master Hailes' reason for requesting his society and that he himself was under careful scrutiny.

A lawyer used to asking questions, Martin came to the point as quickly as the decent interlude of politeness allowed.

'I understand that you are from Peebles area, Master Eildor.'

Warily Tam nodded assent and Martin continued, 'I was very interested when Master Hepburn said that he had met someone bearing the same name as yourself at Morham Castle when he was living there as a small child with his granddam.'

Tam smiled. 'Indeed. So Master Hepburn informed me.'

There was a pause while Martin studied Tam intently, awaiting an explanation. When none was forthcoming, he went on, 'I realise that my young cousin must be mistaken. It cannot be the same Tam Eildor, since thirty-six years later, he would be a bearded old man – like myself.'

Again he waited. Tam shook his head. 'I have no explanation, sir, beyond those offered by William and Tansy – which I expect are known to you already.'

Martin gave him a wry smile. 'Indeed yes. The progeny of Border lairds and reivers outwith the bonds of wedlock.'

While accepting this as a likely possibility, the most natural and comfortable explanation, he had to also admit that there was something strange about this young man. And what he must take as coincidence – of a double a generation apart – was a matter that caused him considerable uneasiness.

Since this mysterious kinsman of Mistress Tansy Scott had appeared at Falkland Palace, there had been a murder of someone, William told him, who was a friend of hers.

Not that he wished to attach anything in the least sinister to the man walking by his side. Martin's profession had included taking risks regarding his clients' characters and over the years he had developed an almost unfailing instinct in such matters. Even on the acquaintance of one hour, he would have sworn to Tam Eildor's honesty. An open countenance with fine features. good-looking rather than outstandingly handsome but with remarkable wide-set eyes that had searching, almost luminous, depths to them.

Quite suddenly, Martin realised that there was a quality in Tam he could not lay a finger on and was unable to define. Except that it was not quite natural. It made him uneasy as he recognised that he had long been acquainted with it...

In the person of William's mistress!

Tansy Scott shared with Tam Eildor that extraordinary – something – that marked the two as completely different from the ordinary run of mere mortals Martin had encountered and had dealings with over so many years.

And it was and always had been, he had to reluctantly admit, this strangeness which accounted for his concern for his dear William's well-being in this stubborn and unflinching devotion.

'How long have you lived in Edinburgh, sir?' Tam asked.

'All my life. Born and bred there.'

A short pause and Tam said guardedly, 'This friend of Mistress Scott –'

'The one who was died recently?' Martin sounded calm enough but he was extremely agitated by William's story. Anyone connected with Mistress Scott, who might also involve his young cousin, however remotely, merited his deep concern. And he knew a great deal more about death by violence and how the widening circles of evidence engulfed both guilty and innocent alike.

'Did you know aught of Mistress Agnew?' Tam asked.

Martin, giving him a strange glance, shook his head.

Tam looked disappointed. 'We know that she was killed. We found her. And for Mistress Scott's sake, I want to find out who and why,' he added anxiously.

'So what is your question for me, Master Eildor?'

'Mistress Agnew was midwife to Queen Mary, the king's mother.' Tam paused before continuing, 'Was there any reason, sir, dating back to that time – any rumour concerning the late queen – that might account for Mistress Agnew's killing?'

Martin Hailes' eyebrows raised somewhat at this direct question. 'Edinburgh was buzzing with rumours which leaked out at the time.'

'Indeed!'

'It was said a document had been signed by two of the women who attended the queen.'

'And what were the contents of this document?'

Martin sighed. 'It was said that the queen had had a long and terrible labour. Never strong, she was at the point of death and in her agony would have only Margaret Agnew attend her. She sent her two ladies of the Bedchamber, Lady Reres and the Countess of Atholl, Marie Fleming's sister, out of the bedchamber and cried out for Janet Beaton –'

Tam observed the look of distaste on the lawyer's face at the mention of that name as he went on, 'The queen had implicit trust in Lady Beaton and, certain that both she and her child would die, believed only that the Wizard lady of Branxton – as Beaton was known and feared – had power to save them.'

Martin hesitated before proceeding cautiously, 'One can imagine the panic outside that bedchamber. The sight of Lady Reres and the Countess emerging in floods of tears convinced everyone that the queen was dead, the child stillborn. Grim looks were exchanged among the ministers. As orders were hurriedly sent for the mourning bell at St Giles to be prepared to tell the people of Edinburgh the dread news, suddenly the firmly closed door from which they were banned admission was thrown open.

'Lady Beaton appeared smiling. "Her Grace lives and has been delivered of a fine prince."

'Panic turned to rejoicing. Ministers rushed forward but Lady Beaton refused any admission. She held the door firmly against those whose right it was to view the newborn prince.

'"No one," she said to lords and statesmen, to all who waited in the outer chamber. "Her Grace is weak, she has suffered deeply. Now she sleeps. Let none attend her before her royal husband, King Henry. By her orders His Grace must be the first to see his son."

'There was no argument especially as Lady Beaton stood high in the queen's regard. And many feared her magic powers. If she had used these powers to restore the queen, then there would be sighs of relief and grateful thanks given to Almighty God.

'For the whole future of Scotland lay on a knife edge that day. Should the queen die, her realm was in direst peril from the might of Lord Darnley's family, the Lennoxes, who were biding their time for the appropriate moment to proclaim Henry king of Scotland.'

Martin paused. 'The queen was delivered at nine o' the clock in the morning. It was not until two in the afternoon that she presented Prince James to his father, saying "God has given us a son" and swearing before the assembled ministers that Henry Darnley and none other was his father.'

Martin stopped speaking and Tam looked at him. 'Was that truly as it happened, sir? As you have told me – is that your opinion?'

The lawyer shrugged. 'The only other possibility is that the queen was already dead when her two ladies-in-waiting left the bedchamber.'

'And the child?'

Martin nodded avoiding his eyes.

'If that was so then there must have been a substitute. Is that what you think?' Tam insisted.

'What I thought and continue to think, Master Eildor, is that five hours is a very long time to elapse between the birth and the infant's presentation to his father. Many things can be made to happen in five hours, hours vital, remember, for Queen Mary's kingdom.'

'But hardly enough time to produce a newborn child,' said Tam. 'And to get it into the queen's chamber unobserved.'

'Servants were admitted to the outer chamber, there were quantities of linen, basins carried in and out, watched over by Agnew and Beaton. As for the newborn child, it so happened, as fate would have it, that there was one, not very far away.'

At Tam's startled exclamation, Martin paused. 'Indeed. The Countess of Mar had come from Stirling to be in attendance at the queen's lying-in. She was not in evidence, however, since a few days earlier she was delivered of a son.'

A further exclamation of surprise from Tam. Martin gave a triumphant nod. 'And what we must observe particularly, Master Eildor, is that two days – two days, mark it well – after the birth of Prince James, the Countess was mourning her infant son's loss, for he had been born into the world incomplete, ahead of his due arrival.'

Tam looked at him. 'So you think that the Countess's newborn son was substituted for the queen's stillborn prince.'

And Tam thought how easy it would have been, this transporting of infant bodies, dead or alive. It would present no serious problems to midwives and servants scurrying back and forth with their baskets of soiled linen. Such domestic matters could be carried out under the averted eyes of the noble lords awaiting an audience in the outer chambers.

'But what became of the tiny corpse of that stillborn prince? The queen was very devout and the Roman Catholic Church are very particular about the immediate baptism of infants.'

Martin sighed. 'I try not to think about it, Master Eildor. But the rumour is perhaps more agreeable to swallow than the suggestion that James was the son of a baseborn servant, like Riccio.'

'You are not convinced.'

Martin shook his head and said wryly, 'I cannot imagine that lovely young woman who was so briefly our gracious queen taking an ugly little Italian as her lover. But regarding the other matter I have learned to respect rumour. There is always a thread of truth running through it somewhere. And in this case there is a shred of evidence.'

'Evidence?' said Tam

'Indeed. Whereas King James bears little resemblance to his mother or father, a strikingly handsome couple both over six feet tall –'

And Tam had a sudden vision of the small, slender, wizened young man who was the king, his dark scowling visage, heavy-lidded eyes, as Martin continued, 'However, the king bears a remarkable likeness to the Erskine family of Mar who brought him up at Stirling Castle. Whilst this could be accounted for by the fact that, as most of the Scottish nobility, they are remote cousins, it would also explain his devotion to his foster-mother and his insistence that she also fosters his own royal children.'

Tam smiled. 'Much to the chagrin of Queen Anne, so Mistress Scott informs me.'

'And the Countess's devotion to His Grace is possessive and demanding as any maternal love.'

'If these conjectures are true, sir, if the two women who were present when the late queen gave birth signed a document – lost, hidden or stolen, but in existence somewhere – then that is a very good reason why the king must recover and destroy it.'

'It is rumoured to be with the missing Casket Letters.'

'The letters that were used to condemn the king's mother?'

'Indeed. They were said to contain evidence of her plot to murder Lord Darnley.' Delicately he forbore to add that William's father, the Earl of Bothwell, was said to be her accomplice and added, 'The letters were forgeries mostly, but recovery of that ill-fated casket and its contents must haunt His Grace's dreams.'

Tam thought for a moment. 'Do you think the queen was innocent of deception? Do you think she knew and approved the substitution of the Mar child for her stillborn infant?'

'I think not. But even if she did, she is not to be condemned. She would have regarded it as a necessary action for the sake of the future of Scotland. She was never in any doubt of the dire consequences of Henry Darnley inheriting the throne.' Martin shook his head once more. 'I prefer to think in this too she was innocent of any deception. That weak and near death, she was not aware of what was going on around her.'

Pausing he looked at Tam. 'But the king knows. And the most revealing factor is his failure to protest, to fight for the stay of his mother's execution. From all accounts, he was indecently eager to get it over with so that when his godmother Queen Elizabeth dies, he will be king of Scotland and England. His one burning ambition, above all things and all people, for all of his life, and God help any who stood – or still stand – in his way.'

And Tam was considering how that burning ambition could be upset by such a document. Here indeed was the link between two women, Tansy Scott and Margaret Agnew, and their granddams, the two women intimately concerned with the substitution of an impostor prince.

Martin's solemn voice had echoes in a change in the weather. Above their heads was the distant rumble of thunder. He looked up at the sky.

'So ends our summer.'

'It was too good to be true, alas. Day after day, night after night.'

'And too hot for me.'

There were still questions Tam wished to ask, but at that moment Tansy and Will hurried down the path towards them.

'We have been searching for you,' said Tansy anxiously.

She glanced at Will who put an arm about her shoulders and said, 'Tansy has told me everything. We must leave Falkland immediately,' he added firmly. 'There is no time to lose. We are in the very midst of danger and death.'

And as if to stress their peril, the first raindrops, a shower of black coins, splashed down with unnatural violence on the path before them.

Chapter Twelve

Indoors again, watching the rain streaming down the windows, Martin, breathless from the speed at which they had rushed for shelter, sat down heavily. Overwhelmed suddenly by what he had imagined as a pleasant interlude at Falkland Palace to his family visit at Perth, he now found himself part of a tense drama of impending flight.

Sitting back in his chair and accepting the tankard of ale William thrust into his hand, he drank gratefully, his bewildered glance moving from one to the other.

Will turned to Tam and there was no mistaking the urgency in his voice. 'We wish you to accompany us, Master Eildor. From what Tansy has told me of the events of last night, we should go now. And quickly.'

Tansy said quietly, 'My thanks for including Tam, Will.'

Will bowed to Tam. 'That is my pleasure, sir.'

'I will ask leave of the queen,' said Tansy. 'She already knows that I am to go to Tullibardine for the Murray wedding, very soon, on the 5th of August.'

Tam and Martin did not miss William's grimace of revulsion, as she continued, 'Her Grace has given me permission to attend. However, since the Masque is over, my services as broiderer are no longer in urgent demand. And I have another reason. My foster brother Alexander, who is her good friend, is requesting that I might be allowed time to spend at Gowrie House.'

'Indeed, I thought you were to be at Kirktillo with me,' said Will sounding disappointed and looking a trifle cast down by this news.

'So I would wish, my dear. But John and William, who recently returned from Italy, are at present at Trochrie and intend to reopen their town house in Perth.' Smiling at

Martin, she said, 'It would perfectly fit your desire for good clean air, sir. It stands in the Inch, in a lovely situation commanding a splendid view of the river and the surrounding countryside. It is also better suited to my brothers; both are still unmarried, and in need of the society of other young people after their long absence.'

Will caught a whiff of matchmaking and suppressed a smile as Tansy went on, 'Gowrie House has long been sorely neglected and virtually unoccupied since their mother spends most of her time in East Lothian at Dirleton Castle. So Alexander decided that my skills with tapestries and draperies would be of great assistance in their refurbishing plans.'

'You believe that Her Grace will agree to your longer absence?' said Will.

Tansy shrugged. 'I do not think she will raise any objections – Alexander is a particular friend of hers – all will be well as long as I promise to return in good time for the christening robes for the babe due in November.'

She turned to Tam and said eagerly, 'I imagine there will be a place for you at Gowrie House. We will certainly be short of a steward.'

And spreading her hands in a triumphant gesture. 'Have I not done well? And if that does not please her, then I will think of some other plausible excuse.'

'You will need one,' said Tam drily. Distrusting the queen's ability to keep him in her household against the king's wishes, he added, 'Remember that I am commanded to take up residence as cupbearer in the royal apartments in a few days' time.'

Tansy groaned. 'I had forgotten – '

'I doubt whether His Grace has let it conveniently slip his mind,' said Tam.

Tansy bit her lip, stood up and said firmly. 'Then there is no time to lose. I will prepare the servants. Kirktillo first. It is not far, we will travel as light as possible.'

'Cousin Hailes will require a carriage especially for the remainder of his journey,' said Will and Martin gave him a grateful look. He did not fancy racing on horseback across the miles from Falkland to Methlour on the far side of Perth.

'I will arrange that. But first of all, I must seek an audience with Her Grace,' said Tansy.

The queen listened to her request to leave Falkland a week before the Tullibardine wedding.

'We fear it will not be an occasion to afford you much joy, Mistress Scott,' she said sympathetically. And fully aware that Tansy's long-time lover William Hepburn of Kirktillo was the bastard son of Queen Mary's notorious third husband, she added,

'We have not forgotten that it will be an ordeal for you to put in an appearance before your husband's family.'

Tansy gave her a weary smile. 'Your Grace is very understanding and I am grateful. The charade will be difficult, to appear to all the world that we are amiably disposed to one another.'

The queen leaned across and patted Tansy's hand. 'Then you, my dear, must appear lovelier than ever. You have our permission to take whatever gowns and jewellery from the royal wardrobe that will help you achieve this. We command you to be radiantly beautiful,' she added gently.

Tansy, though unstinting in her gratitude, decided that caution was needed in this matter. Overdressed at what was a mere country wedding would not do her cause any good. Walt would sneer and seek sympathy that his former wife looked like a royal whore. Even worse, and hardly bearable to think about, was that he might be so taken by her appearance that he wished to take full advantage of this false portrayal of connubial bliss. Overindulgence in food and wine in his mistress's absence and Walt might well assert his conjugal rights over Tansy.

Her reluctance was not lost on the queen who smiled sadly. 'Wives are subject to the worst of the marriage settlement, including the marital bed. It is difficult for us to always be ready to love, honour and obey.'

Her words were not lost and left Tansy to wonder if Her Grace's use of the royal "we" was significant or a mere politeness indicating the predicament of womankind in general.

Tansy then brought up the subject of Gowrie House.

'We are aware of this request from Alexander, his wish that you might be released from your duties with us to use your sewing skills.' As she spoke, the queen's tender smile told Tansy that Alexander ranked high in her affections and that she was pleased to grant him this favour he asked.

Anne did not tell anyone that she had been filled with such yearning to see the boy again she had kissed his letter and put it carefully in her locked jewel casket.

Asked when she intended to leave Falkland, Tansy said, 'Lady Gowrie has been ill with a fever at Dirleton. I imagine she will be returning to Gowrie House as soon as she is able to travel. I should like to see her again for a while before returning to Your Grace,' she added.

'You have my permission to do so. Perhaps while you are taking care of Lady Gowrie, Beatrix might return to our household. Tell her it is my wish that she does so. You are free to leave but you must promise to return to us in good time before – '

Pausing she touched her stomach delicately. 'In good time to attend to your duties concerning the robes for the christening. We trust that our lying-in will be here in Falkland for which we have a special regard. It was our morning gift from His Grace when we were wed,' she added sadly.

Her sentimental sigh caused Tansy to wonder if Queen Anne, as a fifteen-year-old bride, had once enjoyed great hopes of happiness and romantic love from an ardent lover only to be bitterly disillusioned when her bridegroom's true nature was revealed to her.

Kissing the royal hand and with a final promise to return in good time, Tansy curtseyed, feeling somewhat like a fairytale character who, failing to keep her word, might be transformed into a disagreeable toad at the stroke of midnight.

As she was leaving, Tansy found her way barred by the king and his retinue. On his royal way to the bear-baiting, he was breaking his journey at the queen's apartments. Not merely to pay her a pleasant afternoon but to discuss the urgent matter of an itemised account for the Masque.

A stickler for facts and figures, for pennies and silver in the royal purse, His Grace preferred to do his own additions and subtractions concerning small items of change, rather than trust such matters to the lofty discretion of the Keeper of the Royal Treasury.

Tansy curtseyed low and received a kingly scowl.

Closeted with his wife, James sniffed and said, 'Mistress Scott spends a deal of her time with you, Annie. What would she be wanting?' he demanded and, suspicious of anything concerning Tansy Scott, 'We doubt if it occurred to ye to seize the opportunity of an accounting for yer Masque's costumes.'

The queen shook her head. 'We had other more important matters in hand, sire.'

James gave her a furious look. 'Naething is of more import than siller, Annie. Naething.' And dragging at his beard, 'We would like her to tak a wee keek at yon gowns our godmother Elizabeth has sent us. That wee present, ye ken of.'

And pausing to shrug irritably, 'We dinna care to be regarded as a charity by our cousin of England and we would hazard a wee guess they are gey auld and full o' moths and lice.' With a vigorous nod, slobbering a little, he went on eagerly, 'But her gowns are well-kenned to be thick with precious gems, wi' pearls and rubies and sichlike. Aye, and worth a wee bit o'siller.'

Anne laughed. 'Not these, sire. We are sorry to disappoint you but you are mistaken. Your royal godmother holds a tight purse and her charity does not extend to precious gems.' She gave him a mocking glance. 'We thought you were aware that

132

Her Majesty of England shares your own interest in the acquisition of wealth.'

James scowled. 'We dinna get yer drift, Annie. What o' the jewelled gowns?'

Annie's glance mocked his anxiety. 'We observed that all the gems had been carefully – and indeed, some not so carefully – removed before they left your godmother's royal palace. Most will have to be repaired – '

'Worthless, eh?' James interrupted.

'Not at all. Some of the materials, the fur trimmings are quite exquisite.'

'You say so? Then get Mistress Scott straightway on to it then. See what she can save for our royal wardrobe.'

'We cannot do that, sire. We have given Mistress Scott leave to visit Perth forthwith.'

'Is that so? Aye, that is – ' James stopped confused. In the nick of time, cut short his grin, for he had been about to say, 'good news.'

Was he to be released at last from the sight of the hated Gowrie brat – and by peaceful means? Without scheme or blame, or his hands metaphorically stained with her blood? One less sin for the Almighty to forgive.

Anne watched him narrowly, cat-and-mouse awareness of his reactions to anything concerning Tansy Scott. She beamed upon him. With yet another blow to strike, she sat back prepared to enjoy to the full his discomfort at its impact.

'We have also given Mistress Scott our permission to go to the assistance of her foster-brother – ' A deliberate pause. 'Alexander Ruthven, whom you ken of,' she added coldly, 'in the restoration of tapestries at Gowrie House.'

James shuffled uncomfortably, wincing at the memory of the boy who had spurned him for his queen.

Anne was smiling. She was not finished yet. 'We have given our permission for Master Eildor to accompany her. It seems that Gowrie House is in urgent need of a steward – '

James had shot out of his chair and was staring down at

her. 'You – have – done – what!'

Anne repeated the sentence calmly and slowly, as if he were deaf, relishing the joy of the moment ignoring his anger, his frustration.

'Master Eildor will do very well. Do you not agree that it is a very suitable appointment for one of his station in life. They have asked for Master Eildor,' she added carelessly. The lie was delicious.

James was shaking with an almost uncontrollable fury. Anne did not at first recognise the danger she was in. That James wanted, more than anything else in the world, at that moment to raise his hand to his royal spouse Anne of Denmark. To strike her very hard across her gently mocking face, to remove forever that self-satisfied smile.

Tam Eildor to be removed from his presence. And, adding insult to injury to be under the roof and influence of his arch enemies, the hated Ruthvens and in particular, the boy who had mocked him.

Forgetting what he had come for, the urgency of those accounts, he turned on his heel and, since he did not trust himself to speak, he stormed out to join his courtiers who were patiently waiting to accompany him to the bear-baiting.

As he applauded and took wagers on the efforts of the brave but doomed series of dogs thrown into the pit to challenge the bear, roaring, chained and bleeding, scarred from its many wounds, James wished he could so readily dispose of Annie, the Earl of Gowrie and his brother.

How he would relish a savage and merciless delight in watching them torn apart and bleeding into oblivion.

Tam and Will had been waiting for Tansy on one of the stone seats in the garden. When she emerged and joined them, to discuss the result of her interview with the queen, the trio narrowly missed an encounter with King James. Fortunately he was not heading in their direction and as he possessed a very loud voice they were able to make their escape and take refuge by the dovecot. But here they were witnesses to a violent scene.

A middle-aged man was being forcibly ejected by the kitchen staircase.

Powerfully built, he was putting up a strong resistance to the palace guards, shouting and cursing those who struck him with the backs of their swords.

Looking round he saw Tansy, Tam and Will who were too far away to go to his assistance even if they had felt free and able to tackle his captors. He shouted in their direction:

'They will not let me see her. They tell me nothing. She is a prisoner in there,' and, indicating the kitchen, 'One of their whores.'

A guard kicked him, another struck him across the face. His mouth bleeding, they dragged him to his feet and, still protesting, marched him towards the gatehouse.

Tansy shuddered and whispered, 'I trust the bottle dungeon is not his destination. Men have been lost and forgotten there.'

It was another ugly scene of violence and although it did not appear to be any of their concern, Tam was glad indeed that he would be soon away from royal intrigues and enjoying the new experience of Gowrie House, which by all accounts sounded delightful.

What he would do there, what the future held after the Murray wedding, he had not the least idea. Perhaps this interlude was only what it sounded like, a short spell away from Falkland Palace before returning again with Tansy.

That he was bound to do eventually, anyway, as to return to his own time he must be in the exact place in the garden where Tansy had awakened him.

If only something would happen soon.

It would seem that so far his quest was a wild goose chase. Merely the unsuccessful investigation into the murder of a midwife who had been present at King James's birth.

However, Martin Hailes' sinister hints and information

had been suitably impressive and if it were possible he would have used all his powers to move back to Edinburgh thirty-four years ago, especially to meet the mysterious and powerful Janet Beaton.

Chapter Thirteen

An unexpected complication developed in their plans to leave Falkland, in the diminutive form of Jane Rose. Her deep attachment to Tam Eildor had now spread to Tansy and the prospects of being left behind, even under servant Martha's motherly care, terrified her.

'We will only be away for a short while,' said Tansy but Jane refused to be consoled.

'Please, Mistress Scott, dinna leave me here,' she cried, and to Tam standing by, 'Please take me with you, Master Eildor.'

Tam put an arm around her shoulders. 'Jane, if you come with us ... what if your uncle comes back? Surely he is the one you most want to be with.' He smiled. 'Staying here was only meant as a place where you could wait for him in safety.'

Biting her lip, Jane frowned. 'I ken that.'

For a moment it seemed that, overwhelmed by the grandeur of living in a royal palace, meeting new friends, she had forgotten the reason for her flight from Edinburgh in the first place.

Shaking her head stubbornly, she said with dogged insistence, 'But I like biding wi'you and Mistress Scott. That is what I want more than onything else.'

'Very well, Jane. We cannot promise but we will discuss it,' said Tansy.

Out of earshot, she said, 'I suppose there is no real reason why she should not accompany us. Another servant does no harm and besides she is very useful with her needle.'

They had not told little Jane of their suspicions regarding Davy Rose's mysterious disappearance. Since it was obvious he was unaware of her impulsive flight from Edinburgh and might be taken aback to find his little niece living in the palace, Tam decided that if she went with them to Perth, then word must be left with someone concerning her whereabouts. For the increasingly remote possibility that her uncle was still alive.

'The minister would be the most likely contact seeing that Davy used to work for him,' said Tam.

'Perhaps he will have some useful suggestion,' said Tansy with an uneasy feeling that she had been adopted by little Jane and that the child was looking to her to be responsible for deciding her future.

Tam wandered across to the church, empty but for the solitary figure of Rev Benton in deep meditation.

Tam's polite cough roused him and staring short-sightedly he presumed that Tam was one of his parishioners.

Before Tam could open his mouth, he said quickly, 'Ah yes, I remember. You lost a loved one very recently – it was, er –'

Frowning he looked hard towards the altar as though it might assert miraculous powers of supplying him with the deceased one's name. And ignoring, or more likely not seeing, Tam's shake of the head, he launched into an account of the many blessings awaiting the faithful in heaven.

Dismayed to find himself the recipient of what indicated all the symptoms of developing into a long sermon, Tam interrupted,

'Sir, you are mistaken.'

The minister's jaw dropped in shocked surprise. 'Mistaken, I am never mistaken,' he said sternly. 'We have the God's word on the subject – here.' As he opened his Bible to search for the relevant passage, Tam took the opportunity to say gently,

'Sir, the reason I came here at our first meeting was my search for David Rose. We met on a later occasion when I was taking his little niece to the Palace.'

The minister's face froze in disapproval, 'Quite so, quite so.'

An awkward silence followed. There were no more Biblical quotations forthcoming and Tam said, 'We ... I ... am about to leave the Palace and I hoped – '

Suddenly aware of the futility of leaving any message for Davy Rose and in the hope of a more permanent solution to the problem of Jane, he said weakly,

'I hoped that I might find someone to take care of her.'

Rev Benton's look of disapproval intensified. 'We have no charity for – for such – fallen creatures, I fear. Once on that wicked path they have chosen to travel, for these unfortunates there is no coming back. The Lord tells us – '

Once again Tam found himself trapped, a congregation of one, in a sermon on Biblical whores, fallen women and soiled doves, Jezebel being the one name he recognised.

He had no option but to listen politely, giving the minister his head and deciding that the unfortunate man was not only short-sighted but a little out of his wits, for Rev Benton had confused him with some other member of his parish. Aware of the popular duration of sermons lasting several hours and that time was of the essence, he chose a moment when the minister had stopped to draw breath.

'Sir,' he interrupted, 'I must leave. Matters await me. My apologies.' A quick bow. As he hastened down the aisle and out into the kirkyard, he was conscious of the minister's face glaring after him, shouting,

'Take heed, ye of little faith!'

Frustrated by the outcome of trying to leave a simple message for the perhaps permanently absent Davy Rose, Tam decided to visit his house once more and there leave a note concerning Jane in the hope of it being found.

The door was firmly closed. He let himself in cautiously but without any expectations of finding anyone at home.

One glance was enough to tell him that someone else had been here since his last visit two days earlier. The papers were no longer scattered on the floor and there was a general air of tidiness and occupation.

As he stepped cautiously inside, the door was closed violently and the man who had been hiding behind it anchored Tam in an iron grip around his neck.

Choking, he struggled to free himself as his captor cursed and shouted,

'At last! So you have come back. You villain – you will pay for this with your life.'

It was the voice he recognised. That of the man they had seen ejected from the kitchen of the queen's apartments. Suddenly his identity was obvious.

'Sir – ' Tam gasped with considerable difficulty. 'Master Rose – is it not?'

'Aye, that's me – ' he said, shaking Tam vigorously. 'And what have ye to say for yerself?'

'If you would release me, I will explain.'

'Ye have plenty o' that to do. Wretched creature – villain.' And so saying, with no intention of letting Tam go before he had dealt with him, he began a rain of strong and painful blows to his head and shoulders.

Davy Rose was bigger and stronger than himself. Tam, however, knew a great deal more about wrestling than was available to people living in the sixteenth century. In his own time there were no wars. Such conflicts had long been considered barbaric and obsolete. All nations were now united together, barriers down, in one world and it was left to individuals to rid themselves of aggressive feelings by studying the martial arts in the same manner as gladiators in the circus of Ancient Rome.

Memories of such expertise came back to him and twisting out of Davy Rose's grip, he threw him to the floor, from whence the man looked up at him stupefied and amazed. He was even more amazed when Tam held out his hand, dragged him to his feet and holding him firmly, in one swift movement sat him down at the table as if he weighed no more than a child.

Panting, he stared up at Tam, shook his head, wondering

what – or who – on earth was this creature who could lift a man almost twice his weight.

'Now, sir,' said Tam with a grin, 'might we call off our dispute and talk like civilised people?'

Rose nodded slowly, shaking his head again in a bewildered fashion. 'Who are ye?'

'Tam Eildor, not that it need concern you – you do not know me, we have never met. I saw you being thrown out of the royal kitchens by the guards the other day. How did you escape from the dungeons?'

'They only threw me out of the gatehouse, with a warning. But I will be back. I havena finished wi' them yet.' And with a furious look. 'I intend to find the foul beast who stole my little Jane – and kill him. Wherever he is – he will no' escape from me.'

Tam looked at him soberly and bowed. 'Your search is ended, Master Rose.'

The man's head jerked upwards. 'How so? Ye ken this – creature?'

'I do, sir. He is standing right before you now.'

That was too much. 'You are the vile bastard who sold her – as – as a whore.' And Rose sprang to his feet prepared to launch another attack.

With one hand, Tam thrust him back into the chair, held fast his flaying fists, ignoring his shouts and curses.

'Listen to me, Master Rose. I can assure you – and you can ask Jane yourself – I have never laid a hand on her, nor has anyone else. Any who did so would have me to answer to. She is my responsibility – she came to me seeking help – '

The man growled, 'Help, is that what ye call it – '

'Will you listen? I came in search of you one day and found her hiding under the bed yonder. She had walked all the way from Edinburgh to find you, she was cold and hungry.'

Pausing, Tam regarded Davy thoughtfully. 'Now explain, what makes you think she has been sold as a whore?'

The man scowled. 'That vile dress she was wearing. I saw

her in the pageant, I slipped over the railings. A bairn like her, dressed like a whore, her bosom – almost naked – '

'Stop!' Tam demanded. 'When she arrived at your door here, you were the only person she could turn too, she was in rags. We had to find some garment to cover her, and one of the queen's dwarfs' dresses was the nearest at hand. She liked wearing it ... she's just a child. Do you not understand, it was just like a pretty gown to her.'

Her uncle did not look convinced. 'Why had she left Edinburgh?'

Tam regarded him soberly. 'She was in flight from her foster-father.'

'How could that be? Was she being punished for wrong-doing?'

Tam shook his head. 'No, her foster-father, this Bart, was the wrong-doer.' And choosing his words carefully, 'He had attempted many times to – to come into her bed.'

Rose's eyes bulged. His face turned scarlet as he roared, 'That bastard – that villain – I will kill him for this.'

'What you do to him is your own affair. When I found Jane so distressed I could not leave her here so I took her over to Mistress Scott, who is the queen's broiderer. She has been looking after her.'

A thought struck Rose. 'What were you doing in my house in the first place, Master Eildor?'

'I came looking for you to – inform you – about Margaret Agnew,' he said leaving it at that as he wondered how much Rose knew already.

Davy Rose put his hands over his face and sobbed. 'My poor Margaret. I didna ken about her accident. I knew naething until the minister told me and I saw her grave.'

Tam put a hand on his shoulder. 'I am sorry for your loss. Mistress Scott too, for they were friends.'

With considerable effort, wiping away the tears. Rose looked up at him and whispered, 'What happened? What caused it? – she was such a careful lass.'

Tam took safe refuge in the official version of the accident with the shears, rather than reveal that Mistress Agnew had been murdered, which would certainly have driven such an inflammatory person as Davy Rose into instant and fatal action.

He ended his account by asking, 'Where have you been this past week?'

Rose bit his lip, studied Tam for a moment and whispered, 'Can I trust ye? Ye have the look of an honest man. I had been called away – my cousin was sick and dying in Perth. I stayed twa days and when I came back – I realise now that must have been the very day Margaret died – I surprised robbers in the room here.' Pausing, he looked around recalling the scene. 'They were riffling the press over yonder – searching through papers. Instead of running away, they seized me, dragged me out of the house with them.'

'Why should they do that?' asked Tam, knowing perfectly well what the answer would be.

'They said they had questions to put to me.' And with a shudder, 'They said if I didna oblige then there were – other means. I kenned well they were hinting at the boot –'

Tam decided this was confirmation of his own thoughts. No ordinary robbers but men with an official task, with instructions about what and who they were looking for.

'They didna get very far,' said Rose. 'I managed to over-power them in the darkness, gave them the slip. One was a weaselly-looking craiter,' he added contemptuously. 'But I decided to be cautious and stay away for a while, so I went back to Perth – in time for my cousin's funeral,' he ended sadly.

There was a slight pause before Tam asked, 'Did these robbers find what they were looking for?'

Rose smiled craftily. 'I think not.'

'Did you know what it was they had in mind?'

An evasive glance, a shake of the head.

Tam studied him carefully. 'May I ask – had it something to

do with Mistress Agnew?'

That question was obviously unexpected, for Rose looked at him sharply, demanded, 'Why do you ask that? What do you –'

He bit his lip, stopped and Tam finished the sentence for him. 'What do I know? The answer is nothing.' Hesitating, he added, 'May I ask you what was your relationship to Mistress Agnew?'

Rose shrugged. 'Man to man, I can tell you. She was my wife in Scots law – by habit and repute. I would happily have made her my legal wife, since I have been a widower for the past twenty years. But she would have none of it, she said marriage was forbidden in royal service without the queen's permission.'

'Had she any dependants of her own, family of any kind?'

'Bairns, ye mean. None – or kin that she ever mentioned. She had been orphaned early, brought up by her granddam. She was like myself widowed early, but she never talked about her man.'

He looked at Tam. 'Why are ye so interested in Margaret Agnew? The robbery had naught to do with her, I assure you.'

'I just wondered, seeing that she was midwife to the queen, perhaps she was in possession of confidences.'

'What kind of confidences would that be?' was the cautious response.

Tam shrugged, said casually, 'Documents, perhaps.'

Rose shook his head, looked vague but considerably ill at ease. And Tam knew in that instant that Davy Rose was perfectly aware of what he was talking about.

It was all falling neatly into place. The missing document Martin Hailes had told him about signed by the two midwives present at the king's birth.

And now all too late, on the eve of his departure from Falkland, Tam believed he had the answer to why Mistress Agnew was murdered.

Aware that he would get no more information from Davy

Rose, he said, 'With regard to Jane, Mistress Scott happily employed her as a seamstress.'

Rose looked surprised. 'That wee bairn?'

Tam smiled. 'She is thirteen. How long is it since you saw your niece?'

Rose sighed. 'Not for several years. I thought her to be younger than that.'

'She is very happy with Mistress Scott and has settled down well. Unfortunately Mistress Scott has leave to go to her family at Gowrie House for a while.'

'Gowrie Palace, they used to call the Ruthven's town house. I ken it well. One of my cousins was steward there,' he added proudly.

'I am to accompany Mistress Scott as Jane has no idea that you have returned home. I take it she did not know of Mistress Agnew's part in your life.'

Rose shook his head. 'They never met.'

Tam continued, 'Jane is very unhappy at the prospect of being left behind when we depart, frightened and bewildered. She would like to come with us.'

'There is no need for that. Her home is with me. I dare not show my face near the Palace again, so bring her across, if you please. I believe it is time we both moved on. And I have a safer haven in mind,' he added wryly.

And so Jane and her uncle were speedily reunited to their mutual delight. Jane, with promises that she could rejoin Mistress Scott in the sewing-room once she returned from Perth, set about her temporary farewells to the other servants. Most especially to her exciting new friend, the Captain, in whose company Jane had become an almost daily visitor to the kitchen.

Once in royal service in the Netherlands, he claimed to be newly returned from official duties on the Queen's behalf, with her brother, King Christian of Denmark. The Captain had many tales to tell of intrigues and exciting adventures especially for the wide-eyed simple lass from an Edinburgh close who hung upon his every word, intoxicated by the vicarious pleasure of living in Falkland Palace and rubbing shoulders with a servant of the Duke of Lennox, the king's cousin.

A smiling kindly man, with two bairns of his own he told her, the Captain brought her small gifts, urging her to talk about her uncle Davy and what had brought her to Falkland.

Praising her bravery in facing that long horrid journey, he was disappointed to hear that she had met her caring uncle but once at her mother's funeral. Afterwards he had stayed long enough to see the orphaned Jane settled in St Mary's Close with his daughter's friend and her man, the notorious Bart.

Coming down to the kitchen and finding Jane's new companion laughing and enjoying a tankard of ale with Martha, who dearly loved a gossip, Tansy would have been surprised to know that the visitor had a less genial side.

He was in fact Sandy Kay, one-time servant to her husband Walter Murray, and was being paid to spy on her, while enjoying a similar role with the Duke of Lennox, who was anxious to investigate and bring down Tam Eildor.

She would not have been so welcoming had she known that this ex-soldier was the wielder of the crossbow that had almost cost her or Tam their lives. And, that the same hand had slipped the poison into her goblet at the Masque.

Bowing her out of the kitchen, Kay decided that he had not finished with either Tam or Tansy yet. Their leaving Falkland meant that his lucrative mission was at an end. However, as Master Murray would pay exceeding well for the privilege of appearing in the role of grieving widower at the Tullibardine wedding, should a convenient accident befall his estranged wife, Sandy Kay soon had the matter in hand.

Kirktillo was only a few hours ride from Falkland and it was there she would be staying with her paramour, Will Hepburn, until the wedding.

Jubilantly he decided that Fate was playing into his hands

with an opportunity not to be missed, which would offer grateful and lucrative rewards from both Walt Murray and the Duke of Lennox.

Chapter Fourteen

Agreeably disposed towards the Ruthvens, in particular to young Alexander, Queen Anne was pleased to offer assistance to Tansy in the matter of refurbishing Gowrie House by placing at her disposal a carriage and coachman from the royal stables for the journey.

Tansy was suitably grateful. In addition to herself, in charge of the many items from her sewing-room, Martin Hailes would also welcome being a passenger, having received a message from his brother-in-law Simon who intended to meet him at Kirktillo.

And so, in the misty dawn of the first day in August, the carriage rattled through the gatehouse of Falkland Palace with William and Tam as outriders.

Tam did not care for horse-riding, but he had learned to adjust to it as a frequent necessity of his quest-life which often offered no other means of transport. He had also discovered that, having a natural affinity with animals, even horses appeared to understand and make allowances for his clumsy lack of skill.

The long dry spell had hardened the earth and made roads considerably more accessible than they were in winter or in wet weather when they disappeared into muddy tracks and became not only uncomfortable but extremely hazardous for travellers both outside and inside carriages.

So it was with a certain lightness of heart that the four left Falkland behind and journeyed through the still-sleeping landscape, along avenues of great trees, whose drowsy heads drooped under their heavy burdens of summer leaves. Birds and small animals darted across their path and as the moon faded high in the sky, the morning yawned its way into another day.

They travelled through small villages and hamlets until at last they emerged from a glen above the twisting river Tay. Far below, a cluster of houses and a church steeple indicated the fair city of Perth.

Will halted the carriage to give the coachman directions to Kirktillo and to allow the passengers to stretch their legs.

Looking down on the scene before him, he said, 'Folks who are better travelled than I am consider it similar to Rome, both built on the banks of rivers, Rome having the Campus Martius and Perth, two majestic parklands called the North and South Inches.'

'And our destination, Gowrie House, is on the west bank of the river yonder,' said Tansy, adding with a happy sigh, 'For me, this is always homecoming. In truth Perth means much more than any royal palace.

'Once it was the capital of Scotland until some 50 years ago when the court moved and Edinburgh became the seat of government,' said Tansy for Tam's benefit. 'But some of the old customs remain. In the order of procedure our Lord Provost – ' 'John Ruthven, who happens to be my foster-brother, takes precedence over Edinburgh's Lord Provost,' she added proudly.

'I am often confused when people refer to it as St Johnstoun,' said Will.

'What brought about the change of name?' Tam asked.

'A derivation of Aber-tha – the mouth of the river Tay,' Will exlained. 'Which became the Roman fort of Bertha, an important trading post on the river and a defence against the wild northern tribes.'

Pausing he pointed in the direction of the church tower. 'After the Romans left, Christianity came. The church over yonder was built in the twelfth century and dedicated to John the Baptist. The settlement grew and became known as "St John's Town at Perth."'

Looking at Tam, Tansy smiled. 'When I can be released from my activities in Gowrie we will have time to walk by the river. You will of course be expected to attend church on Sundays. The minister Mr Galloway is renowned for his sermons. On occasion he gets quite carried away by his own oratory.'

Tam groaned inwardly at the prospect. As they crossed the bridge heading towards the Inch the townsfolk were already wide awake with a bustling market of noisy livestock in full spate.

'We go first to Gowrie House,' said Tansy, 'and make the carriage lighter by depositing most of the heavy luggage to await my return.'

Tam was very impressed by the approach; far exceeding his expectations of the Ruthven's town house, the building had the monumental dimensions of a castle. The additions of a turret at each corner to the simple tower house purchased by the present Ruthvens' grandfather, Patrick, had earned it the local description of "Gowrie's Palace".

And such it appeared to Tam. The main gate was locked, so the carriage with Martin had to remain outside while he followed Tansy and Will, who unlatched a side gate and crossed the small courtyard and up steps to the main entrance.

That door too was locked. Neither bell nor stout blows yielded any result. There were no caretakers visible and as the three walked around the building, occasionally stopping to shout up at the windows, it became obvious that the occupants were either very soundly asleep or still absent.

As Tansy continued to look up at the windows, staring like vacant eyes upon them, Tam was overcome suddenly by the sense of desolation that empty houses gave him. As if they had souls of their own, dreams – and nightmares – to be hidden from the world.

And at that moment he decided that Gowrie House repelled him. It emanated something that chilled his heart. A long-dead house, biding its time, dark and secret, waiting for something to happen.

Tansy came to his side and, as ever, had that strange ability to interpret his thoughts. She smiled sadly. 'So long neglected, I dare not think of the tasks that await me inside. It needs laughter to bring it back to life.'

She laughed. 'Alexander and John will soon do that. I am certain of that. There will be merry times ahead.'

And seeing Tam staring gloomily at gunloops and keyhole windows, she said, 'Do not be put off by those sinister tokens of an age gone by. It really is a lovely house.'

Watching Tam's sombre expression as they walked back towards the gate, wanting his approval, she said almost apologetically, 'So many different histories in its making. Originally built for defence, but those days of bloodshed are long past. Perth is a peaceful law-abiding city now.'

Will, who was walking alongside looked back and said, 'I fail to understand why people who own one castle want to have a town house of this size.'

To which Martin awaiting them by the gate added, 'Nor I, William. I much prefer Edinburgh's town houses. Even the highest in the land, earls and lords, were quite satisfied with them, conveniently situated close to Holyrood Palace or the Castle.'

'But consider the fresh air of Perth – the abominable smells of Edinburgh's High Street,' said Tansy.

A small argument about the relative merits of Gowrie House was terminated by their return to the carriage.

Half an hour later and a few steep slopes brought them within sight of Kirktillo. Perched on a hill with sweeping lawns down to the river, it aroused a very different set of feelings in Tam. Little more than a modest tower with none of the architectural grandeur of the house they had left in Perth, the morning sun on its walls seemed to emanate warmth as if it beckoned a welcome to the arrivals.

Will noted Tam's approving glance and smiled proudly. 'Once it was moated and approached by a drawbridge. That was long since replaced by an ordinary wooden bridge over the steep rock-sided burn. Good for fishing, Tam,' he added with a laugh.

As they escorted the carriage slowly down the slope, Will said, 'We will need to take care. The bridge is quite narrow and we rarely see anything as large or grand as this carriage.'

All was well until they were in sight of the bridge when two of the Kirktillo servants rushed forward, waving their arms frantically.

Will recognised his steward Thomas. Before he could ask what was amiss the man said, 'Sir, it is dangerous to proceed any further. The bridge has been damaged. You must leave the carriage on this side and lead your horses across in single file –'

Dismounting Will asked, 'When did this happen? Has there been a storm?'

The steward shook his head, looking bewildered. 'An accident, sir. A gentleman was almost killed just hours ago.'

'Who on earth –'

'A gentleman – he came to escort Master Hailes.'

And Martin stepped out of the carriage with a cry of alarm. 'Simon Fuller – is he injured? Where is he?'

Thomas turned to him. 'Sir, he is uninjured apart from a few bruises. He had a very lucky escape. He was driving his carriage across the bridge when the left-hand parapet collapsed and fell into the burn. The carriage was overthrown and the gentleman would have been hurled down into the burn. He escaped injury by clinging to one of the spars. Fortunately the gardeners who were at work heard his cries for help and ran to the rescue. We had arisen before dawn to have everything prepared for the Master,' he paused and bowed towards Will, 'so we were able to make the gentleman comfortable whilst he awaited your arrival.'

'How is he in his spirits?' asked Martin anxiously.

'A little shaken, sir, as might be expected from such an ordeal. But there were no bones broken, only a few bruises, which he assured us were quite trivial.' Thomas shook his head. 'A fortunate escape, thanks be to God.'

Peering over, they saw that the parapet on one side had fallen and disappeared into a pile of matchwood in the burn. The whole structure of the bridge was now precarious and completely unstable. They walked very carefully with the servants leading their horses and warning them to keep well to the undamaged area.

Gazing over the edge to the rock-sided burn Tam realised that it was steep drop of some twelve feet, enough for a carriage to be crushed and its occupants severely, if not fatally, injured in the fall.

A groom led their horses away to the stable and with servants carrying what Tansy had removed from the carriage as their essential luggage, the four walked up to the sloping lawns to the house with Martin leaning on Will's arm.

Reunited with Martin and introduced to the newcomers, Simon immediately launched into the story of his misadventure, of how, as the carriage set onto the bridge, the structure began to vibrate and shake.

'There was an enormous sound of breaking wood, I looked out, saw the parapet leaving the bridge and I jumped clear. Not clear enough, I thought I was going down into the rocks too, but I grabbed hold of one of the hanging spars and yelled for help.'

As he spoke, Tam observed that Simon Fuller was considerably younger and fitter than his brother-in-law. His quick wits doubtless accounted for his surviving a particularly nasty accident, where an older less agile man might not have been so fortunate.

'Master Fuller's carriage will need repair, sir,' said the steward.

'The carriage was provided at my good lady's suggestion for Martin's convenience and comfort, Thomas,' said Simon.

'We will attend to its repair,' said Will. 'You shall both continue your journey in the carriage we have on loan from the royal stables – at present reposing on the other side of the burn.'

'That is very handsome of you,' said Simon. 'Thankfully my faithful horse escaped injury – a splendid animal. He is in your stable with a good feed of oats.'

Will declined sitting down with his guests as they took the food and ale set before them to break their fast. Motioning to Thomas to follow him, Tansy thought that he looked very worried indeed as they retreated towards the study. As for Tam, he was delighted to observe that Tansy was regarded by the servants as mistress of Kirktillo.

While Simon regaled Martin with news of this late wife's family, Tam remarked on the comfort of their surroundings, the elegant furniture much superior to Tansy's lodging at Falkland Palace.

Tansy looked pleased. 'In many homes of the wealthy tables such as this have replaced the board on a trestle.'

'As in the gardens at the Masque?'

Tansy nodded. 'Indeed. Before Will's time here, in his granddam's day, they sat down twelve to fourteen on forms before a long board against the wall. Now most houses of quality have individual chairs, like you are sitting on now.'

As the servants hovered awaiting Tansy's requests. Tam saw that the dishes were of pewter and many bore Lady Morham's coat of arms. They had come from Will's childhood home, as had the silver laver and jug to pour water over the diners' hands into a handsome silver basin held by one of the servants, with linen over his arm in readiness to dry them.

On one side of the small room with its two windows overlooking the garden, a tall dresser with a display of silver, cups, goblets, bowls and spoons both table and dessert, since the latter were for fruit and sweets often taken in an ante room away from the dining-hall.

It seemed all very civilised to Tam and he noted the huge stone fireplace with logs already crackling, a welcoming sight lit in readiness for guests in the chilly early hours of a summer morning. He was wondering how this room, so snug and comfortable and easy, could cope with any more than half a dozen guests when Tansy provided the answer.

'Will uses the parlour for informal dining, with a few friends or when we are alone together. The walls used to be tapestried but Will changed over to panelling which is much warmer. There is a large dining hall, much grander but, I fear, far less comfortable. Come and I will show you the house,' she whispered and glancing at the two men in deep conversation on the other side of the table, 'They will never miss us and Martin knows it well.'

Following her down to the kitchens, Tansy's popularity with the servants was immediate. Serving-men bowed, maids curtseyed. All clustered around her smiling, delighted to have her home again. They talked of not only practical domestic matters, but homely topics concerning their families, who had been born and who had died. At last released, laughing and happy, she led the the way up the wheelstair. Turning, she asked eagerly, 'So what do you think of Will's home?'

'I am very impressed. It is remarkably comfortable.'

Again she laughed. 'But you are just at the beginning, there is much more to see and admire.'

Pausing as stairs suddenly changed direction and led to the smaller tower wherein were set the guest chambers, they reached the second storey where, she told him, the handsome windows overlooking the garden had been a recent renovation.

'Fifty years ago they were little more than arrow slits but Will changed all that. He wanted fresh air and light.' And opening the doors into what had once been the Great Hall with its two massive fireplaces one at either end, Tam noticed that, as well as handsome chairs upholstered in velvet and brocade set back against the walls, there were mirrors and on the floor, carpets and rugs.

Tansy touched one with her foot. 'A great improvement. Once upon a time such a house as this would have had only bent grass as a covering. Frequently changed but not very healthy and smelling like a hayloft.'

Tam had walked across to a corner containing musical instruments; fiddles, fifes, a harpsichord and virginals.

'Do you play and sing?' he asked eagerly.

'A little, sometimes – only to entertain Will,' she said modestly. 'I do not rate it as one of my best achievements.'

Tam looked at her fondly. 'Perhaps you will sing for me sometime?' he whispered hopefully.

'Perhaps, Tam. Perhaps.' And as always she moved quickly away from him, as though afraid or embarrassed by their closeness.

His expectations no more than a gentle kiss, feeling spurned and a little hurt, Tam followed her through the house which was considerably larger than it appeared from the outside.

At one time the house provided accommodation for many guests and their servants, for glimpsed through opened doors were dark panelled walls, polished floors, rooms dominated by postered beds with exquisite bed-hangings.

When he remarked upon such luxury, she smiled wryly. 'If you look closely you will see that these particular ones were once a bishop's vestments. Most of the tapestries in the house have a similar clerical origin, as you will see.'

So speaking, she hesitated briefly before a room with a handsome carved oak door. A moment later, opening it somewhat reluctantly she said, 'This is the grandest room in the house.'

Tam walked across to the turret annexe whose three windows overlooked the garden and a sweeping vista of the Perthshire hills.

'This is Will's room, the master bedroom.'

Tam looked at the massive bed Tansy shared with Will, the room spread out with their personal possessions of clothes and books. Suddenly her reluctance became embarrassment as she waited for him at the door.

Descending the stone spiral to the distant murmur of voices below, she said, 'Will intends to have all these walls plastered in due course. He believes it will add to the warmth of the house. One more place to see then I will release you.'

Opening a door, she said, 'This is the Tapestry Gallery. It spans the area over the Great Hall. Many of these hangings are very ancient and very valuable. After the Reformation, like the bishops' vestments, these were looted from despoiled churches and found their way into private homes.'

She paused, trying to read Tam's expression as he looked at them. 'Will has been very generous. He has promised that I may take as many as I wish to Gowrie House, where I am sure they are sorely needed.'

Gazing upward critically, she said, 'What do you think, Tam? Do you feel they are right for two young men who might not share a taste for such sombre offerings in their bedchambers?'

Tam was in full agreement with Tansy. He would certainly have no wish to be surrounded by scenes of bloody battles from Ancient Greece and of Biblical themes, mostly of a worthy but highly depressing nature like a wild-eyed Abraham, knife raised, preparing to sacrifice his beloved son.

Tansy was inspecting the handwork. 'They are beautifully embroidered, in petit point and must have taken years in the making.'

'And many pairs of hands,' Tam said. 'I feel that a second opinion is advisable here, that you should consult your foster-brothers before removing them.'

'I agree,' said Tansy. 'Nothing is more embarrassing than a very valuable but completely loathsome gift.'

Returning to join the three men in the parlour, Tansy suggested that they might like to see the herb garden.

They were observed by Will from his study window, where, closeted with his steward Thomas, he had just heard related a sinister and terrifying account of the events behind the accident to Simon Fuller's carriage.

Chapter Fifteen

Had not Simon Fuller been a habitual early riser and keen to arrive at Kirktillo in readiness to welcome his elderly brother-in-law, the carriage from Falkland Palace bearing Tansy and Martin would have been the first arrival. With its passengers, coachman and two horses plus heavy luggage, crossing the bridge would have had fatal consequences.

Such were the horrifying facts imparted to Will by his steward.

'There is no doubt, sir,' said Thomas with a solemn shake of his head. 'The whole structure would have collapsed under the carriage's weight.'

Will also heard a very different story regarding the cause of the morning's near tragedy.

'It should never have happened, sir. If only your message had reached us earlier.'

'What message? You were informed of our arrival several days ago.'

Thomas shook his head. 'I am not referring to that, sir, but to the more recent one.'

Will stared at him. 'A moment, Thomas, if you please. I sent you no other message.'

It was Thomas's turn to regard his master incredulously. 'But, sir, the two men you sent yesterday – they brought your order to reinforce the bridge against your arrival – '

Will held up his hand. 'Wait – what – men?'

Thomas sighed and repeated patiently. 'They arrived at dusk last night with instructions that Master Hepburn had observed on his last visit that the bridge was becoming unsafe. Realising that it might not bear the heavy weight of a carriage and horses, you had given orders that they were to reinforce the parapets and strengthen the understructure immediately – '

'Thomas! This is nonsense. I have never made such an observation to anyone,' said Will indignantly. 'I was not aware until this morning that the bridge was in disrepair. It has always seemed perfectly safe to me.'

Pausing, he regarded Thomas sternly. 'Did these men present you with written instructions, as would have been the usual procedure?'

'No, sir. I asked to see their orders, but they insisted that there had not been time for such to be issued by you. That you had apologised but stressed that the matter was too urgent.' He hesitated and added, 'They assured me that you had insisted that I would understand.'

Then, feeling guiltily that he had been at fault, Thomas shuffled uncomfortably and said in his own defence, 'It appears, sir, that they were right, the bridge was unsafe, but it would appear they did not get the repairs completed in time.'

'But someone gave that order, Thomas, and it certainly was not I. Did you perhaps recognise these two men?'

'No, sir, they were not from these parts.'

'How would you describe them?'

Thomas thought for a moment. 'Not labouring men, sir. They seemed like men with authority, used to folks obeying them. Stern – like soldiers.'

Tansy, Tam, Martin and Simon emerged from the herb garden and Will said, 'I need to look further into this matter.' At Thomas's gloomy expression he added, 'I assure you that I do not consider you are to be blamed for any of these unfortunate events.'

'Thank you, sir.' Bowing, Thomas managed a relieved smile.

Dismissing him, Will added, 'Would you please ask Master Eildor to attend me here.'

Watching Tam walking with Tansy across the lawns, Will marvelled at how lightly he moved, his steps swift, graceful.

Certainly Tam Eildor stood out from normal men of his acquaintance, and it defied all logical explanation that he could be the same young man whom he had first met at Morham thirty-six years ago.

Tam was considering an excuse to leave Tansy and have a look at the bridge alone when the steward approached and said that the Master wished to see him.

Tansy looked surprised, perhaps that she was not included, and caught up with Martin and Simon to continue their walk around the gardens.

In the laird's study, a grave-faced Will asked Tam to sit down.

As he repeated what the steward had told him. Tam listened without comment. Apart from the story of the two false labourers and their instructions regarding the renovation of the bridge, Master Fuller had already repeated several times in full detail his harrowing experience, stressing particularly the marvel of his escape unscathed, more or less, from the wrecked carriage.

How fortunate it was, he told them, that he was driving his own modest carriage alone that morning with his very biddable horse who obeyed his every command. His listeners shuddered obligingly as he added that had his dear wife and small children been passengers, the outcome might have been such that he dare not even think about.

At the end of Thomas's version of the morning's events, Will looked at Tam and said, 'I was aghast! I have never so much as hinted at the bridge being dangerous! Do you not agree that there is something very alarming about this story?'

Tam nodded. 'I would hazard a guess that the bridge was deliberately made unsafe.'

Will was silent a moment for Tam had confirmed the full impact of his own suspicions. Shaking his head he said, 'This conversation between us is in strictest confidence, Tam. I do not wish the others to know the full story. And for reasons

160

that are no doubt obvious to you, I want it kept from Tansy at all costs.'

And leaning forward, Will regarded him anxiously. 'I had to tell someone. For in the light of recent events at Falkland I am fearful for her safety. Since you hold her in such high esteem and you will be with her at Gowrie House, I am relying on you to take very good care of her.'

Stretching out his hand he smiled and took Tam's arm in a friendly grasp. 'I know I can trust you, Tam Eildor.'

'I am flattered by your trust in me,' said Tam, 'but let me ask, how trustworthy are your servants?'

Will smiled. 'I would trust Thomas with my life. He has been at Kirktillo with me for twenty years and in all that time I have never had reason to doubt his honesty. I have been happy to leave the running of the estate in his hands and I have never had any reason for doubt or complaint. Everything runs smoothly and he has shown a natural shrewdness about choosing reliable servants.'

Pausing he shook his head. 'I can assure you none of them would or even could have made up such an elaborate and fantastic story about the bridge.' And spreading his hands wide. 'Let us consider, what would any of them have to gain by such a fabrication. Especially as the servants are all devoted to Tansy.'

Tam had seen evidence of this as Tansy walked him round the house.

Biting his lip, Will continued, 'You see, I have a very unhappy feeling that neither myself nor Martin were the objects of this wicked deed. Or yourself. Why should any wish to harm you?'

Tam could have given him two plausible answers to that question. Namely the Duke of Lennox and John Ramsay, King James's favourite, but he preferred to remain silent on that particular issue.

'Have you enemies among your neighbours, Will?'

'None that I am aware of. I believe I share a very harmonious relationship with others in the area. My cousin Hailes is an infrequent visitor, so the attack could hardly have been directed at him. And as I rarely use my carriage, I always ride, the trap was certainly not for me.'

Pausing, he added solemnly, 'One thing is perfectly clear. Somehow the plotters knew in advance about a carriage on its way to Kirktillo. Very precise information, even down to the day and – almost – the very hour.'

Tam had already reached that conclusion as Will continued, 'So, who had these villains in mind? Who did they want to kill – for killing was certainly their plan? There is only one person left,' he added grimly. 'And that is Tansy.'

Perhaps he hoped for some reassuring denial from Tam but, aware of the murderous attempts at the queen's Masque, the crossbow arrow that could have been intended for Tam, the poisoned goblet left no room for any doubt about who the assassin had in mind.

A gentle tap on the door announced Tansy. Her pretext of discussing with Will somewhat urgently whether he would prefer mutton or beef to be served at his guests' next meal seemed somewhat flimsy.

Tam suspected that she had been listening outside and, excusing himself, he decided to continue his inspection of the bridge.

Minutes later as he crossed the lawns, he was hailed by Will hurrying to catch up with him.

'I presume we have the same destination in mind.'

Silently they approached the area of the old moat and Tam slid carefully down the rocks where the broken parapet lay scattered like matchwood across the stream.

After him, scrambling on hands and knees, Will watched Tam leap sure-footed across rocks and tangled shrubbery, as if such hazards were no more than stepping stones. It was quite extraordinary, thought Will. Where had he learned to move so fast, with such agility. And to walk so softly?

From a point underneath the bridge, Tam called to him. 'It

is as I suspected. The posts below road level had been cut through.'

'Damned villains,' said Will.

'And very recently,' said Tam grimly. Clinging to the vegetation along the swift moving burn, evidence of sawdust and shavings.

He let them run through his fingers. This was the final confirmation that a deliberate attempt had been made, a death trap set for the carriage from Falkland.

At his side Will repeated, 'Damned villains. A horseman, one person, would have been unscathed or only slightly unnerved by the instability of his crossing. But the weight of a fairly large carriage with passenger or passengers would guarantee disaster.'

Both had the same thought in mind. That a fourth determined attempt had been made to kill Tansy. And that the order could only have issued from her lodging at the queen's apartments or from the stables at Falkland Palace where their plans were known.

As they walked back towards the house, Simon Fuller, in the stables, was making another sinister discovery concerning his narrow escape.

Making sure that his horse was being well-cared for, he was having a friendly word with the coachman from Falkland.

As they were talking, one of the young grooms, Jock, came in.

Simon instantly recognised his rescuer who, first on the scene, had raised the alarm.

'Ah, there you are. I hoped we would meet again.' And so saying Simon handed him a fistful of silver coins.

'That is for saving me from a very nasty fall.'

Jock stared amazed, open-mouthed. Bowing, murmuring thanks, for he had never had so much money in his life.

Simon smiled at the coachman.

'There I was clinging like a monkey to a spar when along comes this lad like a guardian angel.'

The lad looked from one to the other. 'It was just luck that I was on the spot – '

The coachman Mat winked at Simon. 'At that hour. Not just luck – I would say he was up to no good.'

Shamefacedly the lad avoided their eyes. 'It is a good place to snare a coney in the early morning and I have some snares under the bridge.'

Mat laughed and indicated Jock's fist tight-closed on the coins. 'And you reaped a better harvest than a few coneys!' Pausing he added, 'Does Master Fuller know what you overheard?'

Jock looked diffident and stood twisting his bonnet in his hand, shaking his head.

'And what would that be?' Simon asked.

'Tell him, lad, it might be important,' urged the coachman.

'I dunno. It might have been just a jest,' was the reluctant reply.

'Some jest, lad. This kind gentleman might have been killed.' And looking at Simon he said earnestly, 'I think you should hear this, sir.'

Jock shuffled uncomfortably, staring at the ground as Simon smiled reassuringly. 'Tell me, lad. You have my word that whatever it is, I promise not to get you into trouble with the Master.'

Jock looked at him and then it all came out in a rush. 'I was looking for my snares, keeping quiet because I sometimes catch the young ones with my hands if I am fast enough. I was right under the bridge, keeping well out of sight when I heard the noise of the carriage. The next thing, the terrible noise above my head. I thought my end had come when you fell right in front of me, hanging on to that spar.' And, pausing to draw breath, 'Just as I was coming to get you, I heard them – '

'Them?'

'Aye, sir, these two men on the bridge. One looked down and said, "We got the wrong one. It was a woman we were meant –" The other man cursed and told him to keep his mouth shut. Then he said, "Shall we just finish him off?" I heard the gardeners running towards us and knew you were safe. I yelled and they both bolted.'

Simon was shattered at this information. Could it be true?

'What were these men like? Would you know them again?'

'They looked like ... soldiers,' said the lad, shaking his head.

'Why did you not tell Master Hepburn all this?' Simon demanded sternly.

The lad shook his head. 'I was scared. About the snares, I mean. I take the coneys to my mother and sisters across yonder. I could get into trouble for doing that.'

Heading back towards the house, Simon wondered what he had got himself into. Confused and deeply worried, he realised he must tell Will. Even aware that the penalties for poaching were very severe. On some lordly estates tenants were hanged for such offences. But he could not imagine a laird as kindly as Will Hepburn ever putting more into effect than a good scolding.

'"Meant for a woman." That's what the lad said he heard them say. What does it all mean?' he asked a grave-faced Will.

And before he could reply. 'I came only to collect my brother-in-law, pay my respects and linger for an hour or two. Instead I am almost killed – by mistake – and find myself in some sort of political intrigue. For that is what it sounds like.' Pausing he said, 'Are you to tell me what this is all about, Will?'

Will shook his head. 'I cannot do that, Simon. But I can assure you, you are in no further danger. The carriage will see you safe home before returning to Falkland. One thing, before you leave, I must beg you.'

'And that is?'

'Tell no one. Keep your suspicions to yourself. God knows

they are only that. We have no proof. But do not, on any account, discuss this with cousin Martin. It will only distress and worry him.'

Simon put a hand on his arm. 'Have no fear, William. I realise the depth of his feelings – for you are like a son to him,' he added gently. 'You may rely on my discretion.'

And looking out of the window at Tam walking with Tansy towards the stables, 'I believe you can rely on that young man to take very good care of your lady.'

Smiling he added, 'They are alike, are they not? Surely very close kin.'

Chapter Sixteen

Tam was acutely aware of the air of tension as the two guests prepared to leave Kirktillo. Everyone put a good face on it, but the sooner there was some distance between Simon and Martin and the sinister events of the collapsed bridge, the happier everyone would be. Will, especially, looked particularly grave, hoping that Simon's discretion could be relied upon as they watched the carriage depart on the short journey to Methlour, with Martin inside and Simon as outrider.

Having arranged for repairs to the damaged carriage, Martin again apologised most profusely for the unfortunate accident, while Simon did not seem in the least perturbed.

He repeated that the carriage was only used on occasions involving the whole family. Like Will, he prefered to ride his own horse. Treating the incident in a light-hearted, almost merry manner, he hinted that such an escape would be a worthwhile adventure to entertain his dear wife.

'A fine fellow,' Will said to Tansy waving them farewell.

Tansy interpreted his anxious look. 'Indeed, but he does talk rather a lot. Some of his conversations are quite exhausting. Martin was in severe danger of dozing off – one needed a good deal of concentration to keep track of it all.' To Tam she said, 'Even you looked a little glazed on occasions. And you were very silent.'

Tam laughed but the warning glance he exchanged with Will indicated the real source of his silence. Both shared the fear that Simon might reveal to Martin what the stable lad had overheard.

That Tansy was the target of the villainous plan.

As they returned across the lawns to the house, each of them nursed their own secret anxieties.

Tansy was increasingly apprehensive as the day of the

Tullibardine wedding approached. Although she tried to make light of it to Will, she told Tam privately that there was no escaping the fact that it would be a considerable ordeal for her.

She sighed. 'Alas, dissembling has never come easily to me. And I fear that my feelings – my loathing for a husband I have not met face to face for three years – will be transparent for all the world to see.'

'It is just for a short while,' said Tam consolingly.

Tansy shook her head. 'Family weddings last days, Tam. The Murrays have kin from many parts of Scotland. And I shall have to put on an amicable portrayal of a happy marriage, of a docile obedient wife, for the benefit of Walt's family, since his inheritance might be in serious jeopardy should his staunch Presbyterian father suspect his son's double life.'

'Do they not know about his mistress?'

Tansy shook her head. 'I think not. Or at least they pretend not to.'

Tam laughed. 'Then that is the weapon you hold over him. Threaten to tell all.'

'Oh Tam,' she wailed. 'You do not understand a husband's power. He is a violent man and I am terrified of him.' She looked at Tam imploringly. 'You must suspect, as I do, that many of the things that night at the Masque had his hand behind them. He wants my death. I know it!'

Tam could not deny that. Aware that it may be true. Aware in addition what they were at pains to conceal from Tansy. That the deliberately damaged bridge had been intended for their carriage from Falkland.

Instead he said reassuringly, 'One day, perhaps two or three at most to endure, then it will all be over and you will be back here with Will.'

'One day,' she repeated and with a look of panic, 'The wedding might last for several days. And nights. And I will be expected to share his bed.'

'Surely not. Some excuse – '

'Surely yes! What reasonable excuse could a wife give for such a denial?'

Before Tam could think of any answer to that, one of the servants appeared. Mistress Scott was required in the kitchen.

Will had disappeared indoors. With the talkative Simon no longer his concern, he too was concerned and anxious about the Murray wedding. He had long since guessed, from Tansy's description of her earlier life, the kind of ruthless, violent man she had married. A man who had brutally cast her aside because she was unable to bear children.

Will had no doubts however that as Tansy grew lovelier with the passing years and with their own love fulfilled, Walt might also be aware of this change and see her through new and lustful eyes.

Aware that she had found happiness and love, he was capable of delivering the final degradation. By making her share his bed and forcing himself upon her. How that would delight his depraved spirit.

Will clenched his fists and groaned at the sight he was trying not to imagine. The hours, God forbid that it should be days, when she was at Tullibardine would be a nightmare for him and he tried instead to concentrate on her return.

A few days here together then he would see her safely installed at Gowrie House. Near neighbours, he had known the four Ruthven boys all their lives and the two eldest, John, the Earl of Gowrie, and Alexander, the Master of Ruthven, had been constant visitors.

They knew of the circumstances of their foster-sister's unhappy marriage and that she had found a new life with Will Hepburn and he was sure that they would gladly and often make him welcome at their town house.

Tam had his own misgivings, none of which had any connection with the Murray wedding. He was deeply concerned about the future, realising that this was a smooth plateau and only part of the picture had been revealed to him. There were threads in plenty but he had no idea where they fitted into the main event of his chosen time-quest which still lay ahead, some unsolved episode in Scotland's history.

He had been taken by surprise. Imagining that they would be safe after their flight from Falkland, he saw that he had been unprepared for the pattern which begun with Mistress Agnew's murder, and culminating in the attempted murder of Tansy – and himself – at the Masque.

Helpless to speed up the pace of time he must keep patient vigil with Tansy and Will, who he had once wistfully regarded as a rival for her affections.

But Tansy had made perfectly clear that she was Will's and his alone. And even if Tam could have had her love, it could only, he knew, have been an interlude. Now he enjoyed a growing friendship and respect for them both, recognizing that they had much in common with himself, despite belonging to centuries which were six hundred years apart.

Will had a great love of poetry and an excellent library although most of the books were of an intellectual depth and language beyond Tam. But the paintings were more easily understood. Portraits and landscapes are not so affected by the passage of time.

Most striking of all was their common delight in nature, in the outdoors, for Will was the perfect laird. Eager to accommodate his guest while Tansy took over the reins of mistress of Kirktillo and spent many hours in earnest conversation with servants, setting this and that to rights, talking patterns for bed-curtains and windows, Will and Tam spent many hours in companionable silence fishing in the burn, which in a more turbulent existence had qualified as a moat.

An inadequate catch at the end of most days did not bother either of them. If fish were small then Will threw them back and said, 'Swim in peace, grow in splendour.'

Perhaps it was Will's exceptional general knowledge of the animal world that Tam found most appealing as well as their mutual love of Tansy. On occasions she joined them and they picked cherries and berries in the orchard to reappear later that day in the appetising form and smell of baked pies.

Tam decided this was a good life and he was grateful. One day all too soon, it would end. Tansy would return from the dreaded wedding and together they would leave for the re-adornment of Gowrie House.

Meanwhile, he would enjoy the peaceful interlude of Kirktillo's tranquil gardens. He grew increasingly fond of his delightful room up the crooked stair over the gatehouse, with panelled walls that still retained the smell of fresh wood and a windowseat overlooking the garden.

Had he been born into this century, he decided, this would have been his ideal household.

Here he was offered every comfort, servants at his command, with warm water for his ablutions each morning and night, to wash and shave. Changes of linen were also laid out for him.

In the fireplace, logs were set ready for lighting against chilly evenings. But the summer weather continued and in his south-facing room he loved the night air – although it was commonly regarded as highly dangerous – and found it pleasant and refreshing to unlatch the window.

From his deep, soft, many-pillowed bed, its sheets perfumed with lavender and rosemary, he watched the sky. Night brought a blaze of stars, so close that he could almost reach out a hand and touch them, marvelling that these same stars and moon also shone on that other world, still far away in time, that he had temporarily abandoned. Although he was denied all memory of it, it existed somewhere out there in space.

Sleeping dreamlessly, he awoke to the sounds of the early morning with birdsong and bees already busy amid the honeysuckle growing close to the window.

How good it was. He had an ominous feeling that the sprawling Gowrie House in the centre of Perth would be far less accommodating. He hoped he was wrong and that the chilling exterior, so unwelcoming on their flight from

Falkland, was due to its long emptiness and neglect.

He had not confided these feelings to Tansy or Will, of his particular sensitivity to houses.

He yawned and opened his eyes, hearing the house below stretch itself into day. Servants voices, some girl who sang with a sweet voice, laughter too, dogs barking. Horses in the stables, neighing a greeting to the grooms.

The sound of a galloping horse.

A rider – urgent – with a message.

And such a message. Coming sleepily downstairs, Will and Tansy had awakened to a small miracle.

They were hearing that all their present anxieties were at an end. No happy ending but a happy beginning.

In an instant the whole story of their lives had changed.

Walter Murray was dead.

The messenger who brought the news to Tansy had been redirected to Kirktillo from Falkland Palace. He was offering condolences, bowing. Sad and respectful.

Tansy asked him to repeat it. Fearful that her white face meant she was about to faint, he looked at Will helplessly.

'Your husband, madam, Walter Murray, is dead.'

Tansy sat down. 'What happened?'

'Two days ago when he was hunting, his horse refused a fence and threw him. He was carried home.' Pausing, the messenger shook his head. 'But he was already dead, his neck broken in the fall.'

Tansy stared at him, conscious of Will's hand upon her shoulder. 'I beg your pardon. We will get you some refreshment.'

And in a desperate attempt at normality, 'Your name, sir?'

'John Jeffers. I am – was – your late husband's lawyer. The funeral has been arranged by Mistress Embleton. It will take place on Monday afternoon in the village church. Master Murray will be laid to rest in the family vault.' He looked down at Tansy and said sternly, 'Mistress Embleton does not expect you to attend either the service or to appear at the kirkyard.'

'Mistress Embleton?' said Tansy dazedly.

Then at the man's confusion she remembered Judith Embleton was the name of Walt's mistress. She nodded and smiled weakly.

Straightening his shoulders Master Jeffers plunged on. 'Mistress Embleton, as you might imagine, is distraught with grief and she hopes you will abide by her wishes in this respect.'

'That I will do gladly. Please offer my condolences.'

Tansy was tempted to add her gratitude to that request. More than that she had a sudden vision of the unimposing white-bearded grey-faced lawyer in the unlikely role of her guardian angel.

Master Jeffers had brought her the best possible news that she need no longer hate or be haunted by fears of Walt Murray. She was free.

With a certain diffidence, the lawyer was mentioning the legalities which had occasioned his personal visit to the estranged wife.

Tansy listened, her heart suddenly racing with joy. Walt had long ago changed his will to leave all to Judith Embleton and the son she had borne him.

'Inform Mistress Embleton that it is not my intention to contest my late husband's will, and I gladly relinquish any rights that I might have had under the law to moneys and property from his estate.'

Master Jeffers bowed politely, although he must have been well aware for several years of his client's matrimonial situation. Declining Will's offer of bread and ale, on the excuse that he had matters to attend in Perth, the lawyer eagerly took his departure and rode away from Kirktillo, greatly relieved at the outcome of what had promised to be an extremely difficult visit.

A patient listener for some years to horrendous accounts of

the iniquities of Master Murray's legal wife and their disastrous marriage, he had been prepared for a sharp-toothed vixen of somewhat the same category as Mistress Embleton.

Instead he had been greeted by the gentle and quite lovely Mistress Tansy Scott, who was obviously deeply shocked by her late husband's sudden death.

Deeply shocked indeed, but not quite as the good lawyer imagined.

Closing the door on him, Tansy turned and flung herself into Will's waiting arms. Bewildered still, as he held her she whispered, 'I am free, Will. Free at last – after all these years. I cannot believe it.

'Nor can I, my dearest.'

'I do not know whether to laugh or cry. I fear that I might wake up and find that it was just another dream and that Walt is still alive and waiting outside the door to brutally ill-use me.'

There was panic in her voice as she clung to him. 'Tell me that will not happen, Will. Tell me this is no dream.'

Tenderly Will kissed her, cradled her like a child in his arms. 'No more bad dreams, my dearest love. Not ever again. Now you are mine forever.'

'I only ever wanted to be free of him. Not his death,' she whispered. 'And although he treated me so badly, I am sorry for the child who has lost a father and for his grieving mistress. Like myself she has been an unofficial wife for many years.'

'I should not waste too much sympathy in that direction. Think instead of how many times the two of them must have wished you dead,' said Will sternly. 'Aye, and done more than that. Remember the incidents at the queen's Masque. Think how he would have rejoiced had news of your death been carried to him. To have heard that you had been the victim of a misplaced arrow or a goblet of poisoned wine,' he added grimly.

'We must tell Tam,' said Tansy.

Tam was greatly relieved at the news. Like Will, he suspected that Walt's hand could have directed the attempts on Tansy's life. Now he too could also breathe freely at last, with one less item on his growing list of concerns.

'Now we can be wed,' said Will. And to Tansy, 'We need not wait any longer. Not one day. Tomorrow will be our wedding day.'

'How can that be?' asked Tansy softly, gazing at him adoringly.

'We have long been man and wife in the sight of God, now only the legalities remain. I shall ask Reverend Wilton to perform the ceremony. Here in our own home.'

To Tam he explained, 'Reverend Wilton is our parish minister and has always shown a great deal of understanding for our living together as man and wife which was not of our choosing, but forced upon us after Tansy sought refuge at Kirktillo long ago – '

'A moment, Will dear,' Tansy interrupted. 'Make it the day after tomorrow,' she begged.

'You say that – after waiting so long. My patience, dearest love, is at a very low ebb. I want to claim before the whole world that Tansy Scott is now Mistress Hepburn, until death do us part.'

And so saying, he whirled Tansy around in his arms, while she laughed, kissing him and calling upon him to desist, that the whole world was whirling about her ears.

At last on terra firma again, Tansy said excitedly, 'We must invite John and Alexander from Trochrie. They shall be our witnesses.'

'We need a man to give the bride away,' said Will. And smiling at Tam, 'A father's duty, but as Tansy's true friend, one you will perform very well indeed.'

Tam bowed and as Tansy hugged him and kissed his cheek, he decided wryly that she could be very bold at displaying her affection. Especially since he could not take her in his arms, as he longed to, in front of Will.

Chapter Seventeen

Into this happy scene rode a newcomer.

Alexander Ruthven, on his way to Gowrie House from Trochrie, had decided to call in at Kirktillo and pay his respects to his foster-sister and his dear friend and neighbour Will Hepburn.

An onlooker, Tam found himself in the midst of family jubilation at the announcement of their unexpected wedding.

Embracing Tansy and Will, Alexander shook Tam warmly by the hand and said that this was the best possible news. He had never met Walter Murray but anyone who was unkind to his dearest Tansy was his enemy for life.

Tam, observing the bond of affection between the pair, realised that Tansy had been more fortunate in her foster-family than many orphans are with their own kin. In too many homes, the unfortunate child thrust upon them to rear as a matter of grudging duty becomes the jealous target of foster-siblings and, bullied and ill-treated all round, is regarded as little more than the lowest unpaid menial.

Tam's thoughts on the matter were confirmed when Alexander, with his arm about Tansy's shoulders, kissed her cheek and said to him, 'There is no blood kin between us and had dear Tansy not this very day promised to be Will's wife, then I would have married her tomorrow.'

'You would not,' laughed Tansy. 'I am far too old for you.'

'A mere fourteen years,' sniffed Alexander indignantly. 'A mere nothing if our roles were reversed. Old men take wives young enough to be their grandchildren,' he added earnestly.

Will produced a bottle of fine claret and a toast was drunk to the wedding. Amid talk of Lady Gowrie's health and whether she was making a good recovery at Dirleton with their sister Beatrix, as well as other matters relating to the family in which Tam had no part, he had a chance to observe the Master of Ruthven.

Alexander had a fiery nature to match his fiery red hair. A nineteen-year-old whose life was already full of passionate loves and passionate hates.

Listening to tales of Padua from whence he had recently returned, and his revolt against the appalling conditions among the poor and the imprisoned, Tam decided they must have been dire indeed to make such an impression, considering the lives of such poor wretches in his own native land.

It was not difficult to make an assessment of Alexander Ruthven. Intensely chivalrous, he was ready to spring into action to right wrongs, fight imaginary dragons and rescue damsels whether or not they were in distress and whether or not they even wished to be rescued.

Tam had an unhappy awareness that Alexander Ruthven was one of time's misplacements born at least two hundred years too late. He belonged to the medieval age of knightly deeds and tournaments, and would have served well in the Crusades.

The wedding of Will and Tansy was planned with remarkable speed to take place immediately and Alexander went back to Trochrie to fetch his brother.

To Tansy's anxious question whether Martin should be invited, Will shook his head. 'Summoning cousin Hailes will delay us by at least another day and politeness would mean including Simon, his wife and family. And who knows how the word might spread and the crowds gather?'

He shook his head. 'No, my dearest. Neither of us would want that. To all who know us, for all intents and purposes except the legal ones, we have been long married. Martin will understand. You have been my wife in his eyes for a long time now. He can but add his blessing when next we meet and I have a fancy to take you to Edinburgh.'

'And Edinburgh is not too far from Dirleton and my dear foster-mother. She will be so happy.'

Tansy was secretly relieved at his decision for she felt this small miracle, this bubble of happiness, was fragile as thistledown on a summer's day and any delays might cause it to blow away and vanish for ever.

So Will summoned the minister from the parish church to prepare with all possible haste and in the late afternoon, accompanied by the two Ruthvens, the wedding party set off on foot to walk the quarter-mile across fields to the parish church.

There Tam led a radiant Tansy down the aisle. She looked at him and smiled, a little self-conscious, pleased but feeling somewhat overdressed for a simple country wedding. The wreath of wild flowers on her red-gold hair was not quite appropriate for the elaborate satin dress that the queen had given to her for the other wedding which would be taking place a few miles away.

As Tam handed her to Will, she blinked away tears. For the day that she had dreaded having to live through, so fraught with menace, with misery and fear had, by God's grace, turned out to be the fulfilment of her heart's desire, her own wedding day.

As Tansy and Will stood before the altar they made before God and those witnesses present the vows to love, honour and obey, until death did them part – the same vows that made them man and wife which they had sworn to each other privately so many years ago.

While Will slipped the ring back once again on Tansy's finger, the sun beamed through the windows, touching their heads in benediction. And outside, the minister's words were in keen competition with a blackbird singing most obligingly on a tree nearby.

Over the empty echoing pews, two butterflies, radiantly blue, fluttered and danced, while a bee droned, busily sipping nectar from the posy of wild flowers that Tansy had set aside.

As they left the church she smiled, kissed her foster-brothers and Tam. 'If only this day could last forever,' she whispered and added wistfully, 'There will never be another day – not in my whole life, I know – as happy as this one.'

And despite the warm sunshine, Tam shivered. For an instant the little group were frozen in time. The faces of bride and groom, the two handsome foster-brothers sharing in their wonder and delight.

'It can never come again.'

Tam felt Tansy's wistful words hung on the air, and he wanted to push back the moment of prophecy, the darkness still to come which might blight all memories of that golden day.

A simple wedding feast awaited them in Kirktillo. Wine and a joint of lamb with vegetables from the garden and a splendid apple pie.

With his first chance to get acquainted more closely with the two brothers, Tam, expecting another edition of Alexander, decided that it was fortunate for the Ruthvens that John, his senior by three years, had inherited the title.

Now Earl of Gowrie, he had been appointed Lord Provost of Perth when only fifteen years old. It took only half an hour in their company for the difference in their temperaments to become obvious. John was a much more cautious and responsible young man who regarded his fiery sibling with the apprehension of a man holding in check a team of wild horses.

Alexander had a special place in Tansy's heart and, walking ahead of the others in the gardens, he was eager to hear about Tam Eildor.

In common with everyone else who first met him, Tam had made a deep impression on the boy.

'Distant cousin, on my granddam Beaton's side,' was Tansy's prompt response in reply to Alexander's first, expected question.

'I guessed that,' he grinned. 'Two people so alike must be

related. Brother John deeply regrets that he never met Lady Beaton. Was she really a witch?' he asked.

Tansy laughed. 'Dear Alexander, you have asked me that question so many times and the answer is still the same.'

'Indeed?' he said eagerly.

'Indeed. To me she was simply my granddam, loving and kind. And wise with herbs and simples. I never saw her in any other light.'

'John would be disappointed. Despite that sober and scholarly manner, my brother became particularly interested in alchemy and necromancy when we were in Padua. He often said he would have liked to discuss it with her, that she might have been uncommon knowledgeable about it. He insists there is much to learn about that other world. What do you think, Tansy?'

'I have no opinions on the subject,' was the careful reply.

Alexander frowned. 'But even as a child, you saw things – things that other people were not aware of.'

'Did I? An impressionable child. That was a long time ago,' she said and, ignoring his look of disappointment, she hurried him in the direction of the other three, their heads bent in conversation.

A dangerous topic for discussion, but she did not doubt that Tam could have shed a great deal of light on John's curiosity about that other world beyond time that so intrigued him.

The fact that Tam was devoted to Tansy was enough recommendation for Alexander to decide without knowing anything more about him that here was an excellent friend, a boon companion in the making.

And had he needed further information, the knowledge that he was in retreat from Falkland Palace having spurned the amorous advances of King James was an unbreakable bond.

He already felt he had found a brother in distress and once again he rode his favourite hobby horse, the degradation and iniquities he had suffered for that mercifully brief time before he had quit royal service as Gentleman of the Bedchamber.

Banging his fists together, his eyes blazed that his friend Tam Eildor should have also suffered at the hands of the lustful king.

'That murderous wicked man – who killed our father – expected me – his son – to be his catamite. If only I could make him suffer, for Master Eildor and for myself.'

And quite suddenly, Alexander had an inspiration, a plan that would avenge them both.

Visiting his mother in Dirleton he had met Robert Logan, an old conspirator whose stronghold was Fast Castle, on the wild Berwickshire coast. Lady Gowrie was well aware of her young son's vulnerability regarding stories of hidden treasure. She considered Logan a black-hearted schemer, a man not to be trusted and to be treated with extreme caution.

But in common with many schemers, Logan also possessed plausibility and charm, attributes which he was ready and willing to shed on any who he thought might be useful to him. It took him less than an hour to impress the boy, who was incapable of seeing beneath the surface exterior of anyone who was kind and heavy on flattery.

Logan was no friend of King James. Listening to Alexander's tale of woe, of his grandfather and father both executed plus his own indignities at Falkland Palace at the hands of the king, Logan was quick to see opportunity lurking within his grasp.

Telling Alexander just enough to encourage his interest, he hinted at a vague plan in the making to kidnap James, take him by boat from Leith to Fast Castle and keep him prisoner until he agreed to their terms, unspecified to Alexander.

The only words which he listened to were, 'To keep him prisoner as once your father kept him in Ruthven Castle.'

Logan did not add that he had paid for it with his head.

Alexander was bound to secrecy. On no account was he to tell anyone. He could be discreet when necessity demanded, however, he could not resist gleefully telling brother John of his meeting with Logan and the plan to abduct the king.

John was horrified, appalled at such an idea. Proud to be the peace loving, respected young Earl of Gowrie, Lord Provost and God-fearing Presbyterian and keen upholder of the Protestant faith, he was eager to keep it that way and at that moment was conscientiously working on a sermon to be delivered at St John's Kirk on Tuesday, 5th August.

'Let it go,' he warned his brother. 'It is folly and far too dangerous. There can be no good outcome to such a scheme. Remember what happened last time – to our father, I entreat you.'

'Do you not see, this is my very reason – and it should be yours too, brother.'

'Alexander, we are living in peace now. The old wounds are forgotten. Or should be, for it is time to do so, if we wish to have any future.'

And at his brother's stubborn look, he added, 'I absolutely forbid you to go ahead with this mad scheme. I warn you of its dangers and I want no part.'

Alexander, disappointed, feeling let down and betrayed, thereupon decided that Tam Eildor, a brother in spirit, bold and fearless, would be the perfect accomplice.

He had it all worked out. Together they would make the king smart, put the fear of God in him.

And so Tam listened to his vague hints and tried to dissuade the impetuous Alexander with his wild ideas emanating from Logan, about whom he knew nothing, but could guess quite a lot of what was in his mind, when Alexander spread a plan of Fast Castle on the table before him.

'Take a look, Tam, see what possibilities it has for us,' said Alexander excitedly. 'It stands on the very edge of a perpendicular cliff, its only access by a natural staircase cut in the living rock.'

Pausing, he looked eagerly at Tam. 'Already it is known as the meeting-place of smugglers and Papist spies with gold in their purses, chosen because it is an impregnable fortress, with the wild North Sea on one side and landward a waste of bent and dune from which it is severed by a narrow rib of rock over a deep gorge spanned by a drawbridge.'

Tam tried in vain to reason with him. How could he hope to accomplish all this, kidnap the king with a handful of loyal servants – there were about six only at Trochrie who would be going with the Ruthvens to open up Gowrie House.

'There is a saying that twenty men could hold Fast Castle against all Scotland,' said Alexander triumphantly.

'That may be so. But first you would need a whole army to get him there, from Falkland to Leith and down the treacherous Berwickshire coast.'

Alexander pondered for a moment. 'We could take a ship from Perth down the River Tay – '

At that Tam stopped listening. He decided that the boy with his fantasies was not really dangerous. He was just a little mad. A madness, he hoped, that age and wisdom would cure.

Back at Falkland Palace, the arch conspirator Sandy Kay was also mad.

Mad with rage. News of Walter Murray's sudden death had deprived him of a reasonable income, based on plans to rid his one-time master of Tansy Scott, his legal wife who was now his widow.

Since the attempts on her life had failed miserably he could not expect to be reimbursed for the fracas of the mistimed accident with the bridge at Kirktillo. It had cost him the services of two out-of-work mercenaries hired at a local inn.

As they were now out for his blood – quite literally – he decided to quit Falkland Palace quite sharply since he had also failed the Duke of Lennox in that other important mission.

To discredit Tam Eildor. A task no longer necessary, since Master Eildor had been removed from under His Grace's amorous eye to Gowrie House.

Ludovick Stewart had no quarrel with the young Earl and his brother. His first wife Sophia, who died some eight years ago, had been their elder sister, a relationship he was not inclined to brag about, aware of James's violent antipathy to any mention of the hated Ruthvens.

Chapter Eighteen

The early morning of August 3rd saw Kirktillo in a flurry of activity.

The newlyweds were leaving for Edinburgh, and thence to Lady Gowrie at Dirleton Castle. But first they would call upon Simon Fuller and bring the glad tidings of their marriage to Martin Hailes, with the certain hope that he would offer to accommodate them at his Lawnmarket house.

The bridge repaired, Will took out his seldom-used carriage with a groom delighted at the chance of a rare jaunt to Edinburgh.

Tansy embraced Tam in farewell and said, 'This is just a short parting, you will see me at Gowrie House very soon. As soon as my dear husband here will release me,' she added with a mock curtsey in Will's direction.

As Tam glanced quickly at Will who smiled, Tansy said defiantly, 'I gave my word. They need my assistance. Two young lads, helpless as babes where refurbishing a house is concerned.'

Will laughed and kissed her hand. 'I think I can spare her for a short while. I cannot be greedy – what are a few days when she has the rest of her life to spend with me?'

They radiated happiness, the certainty of a future which stretched ahead exactly as they had always imagined. The dream they had believed in for so long had at last come true. And watching the carriage depart, wishing them God-speed, Tam closed his eyes, willing it to be so.

Willing it to be so, he thought again as, ready to leave for Gowrie House with his saddlebags, he headed for the stables. Why should he suddenly prickle with terror of the unknown? If only he knew its nature and could warn them.

'Tam!'

The horseman racing across the bridge was Alexander. 'I met Tansy and Will on the road.' He laughed. 'My timing could not have been better. Now you are to come to Gowrie, John is already on his way there, but I told him I would collect you. John has a great deal on hand at the moment. He is to deliver a sermon at St John's Kirk in two days time. He send his apologies.'

Walking alongside, Tam bowed in acknowledgement, thinking this was a great deal of trouble for the Earl and his brother to personally escort a servant from one house to another, only a few miles distant.

A groom appeared leading Tam's horse and as he mounted, Alexander said, 'A moment, where, pray, is your luggage?'

'Here, sir.' Tam patted the saddlebags. 'A servant, even a steward, needs little luggage, sir. Merely a few necessities.'

Alexander shook his head and said sternly. 'No servant, Tam Eildor and no steward, for we have one already from Trochrie. And no "sir" either. You come to Gowrie as our dear friend and honoured guest.'

As they rode out, Tam marvelled at such a generous invitation on a mere three days' acquaintance. Alexander called across to him, 'You shall hunt with us if you have a mind to it and perhaps advise on certain other matters before you return to Peebles.'

That was the story Tansy had told Alexander allowing Tam an open door and the freedom to leave when he must. As for those 'certain other matters', Tam hoped that young Ruthven had accepted his final word on the madcap scheme of the king's kidnapping.

Riding swiftly down through twisting lanes from Kirktillo on to the tree-lined roads that led to Perth, the countryside had the mellow look of a hot summer that had burned itself out, its day almost over.

The distance was short and Tam was thankful.

He was able to handle a horse competently enough. Even

the wild stallion whose life he had saved from King James's wrath had settled down very happily to domestic life with Queen Anne's mares.

At last the roofs of houses and the tall spire of St John's Kirk appeared above the distant treetops and a few minutes later they were riding towards Shoe Gait, or South Street, the city's chief thoroughfare, crossed at right angles with Spey Gate on the right and Water Gate on the left.

There, behind high walls with locked gates, glimpses of handsome turreted houses half-hidden by trees, were the homes of Perth's richest citizens and merchants and the town houses of county lairds.

The gateway of Gowrie House was directly opposite the end of Shoe Gait, with a wall extending the length of the Spey Gate and concealing vast gardens stretching down to the River Tay.

Recalling their earlier unsuccessful visit en route for Kirktillo and the uneasy atmosphere exuded by the empty house, Tam hoped that a sunny day would bring about a great improvement.

There was none; the house, a pile of buildings of assorted dimensions like an inverted 'L' faced east and west. Only late afternoon would obliterate the dark shadows of its north-facing courtyard and warm west-facing apartments with the gleam of a sunset sky.

Grooms took their horses and Alexander led the way into the house by-passing a door which lay open revealing a narrow spiral staircase, which Tam presumed to be the main entrance.

Alexander shook his head. 'That is another way. Quicker access to the upper apartments of the house, but so dark and dismal it has always been known as the Black Turnpike. Follow me.'

The main doorway led up a great wheel-staircase to emerge into the Great Hall dominated by a handsome stone fireplace and bare stone walls. Beneath lay rolled tapestries and carpets while items of furniture, dust-sheeted chairs and tables, stood everywhere, awaiting distribution.

'This will appear a great deal more comfortable once Tansy gets to work on deciding how and where the tapestries should be hung,' said Alexander, almost apologetically, as if, Tam thought, he was indeed some honoured and distinguished guest.

As Alexander opened a door on the left Tam had a glimpse of a panelled room whose central table and chairs proclaimed it as a dining-room before following across the hall through a door with an external stair which he said led into the garden.

Back on to the main staircase, Alexander pointed to a door into the family apartments and said, 'We shall find you a place there, Tam.' Another door and they were in the Great Gallery hung with paintings which Alexander pointed out had been gathered from all over Europe by his father.

Facing south it was the warmest and most welcoming area of the house. Windows gazed down on sunny tree-lined gardens. Beyond them like a twisting silver ribbon, the River Tay.

'This is magnificent,' Tam said.

Alexander sighed. 'It is indeed. It was the inspiration of our late father, the Earl, who had it built and supervised its decoration,' indicating the painted ceiling with its ornate cornices and carved wooden panels depicting scenes from Greek mythology. And leading the way across the floor, 'The gallery extends above the dining-room and the hall we have just left and over there,' he pointed to the right to a door in the wall. 'That is the Gallery Chamber. Its windows face on to the Shoe Gait.'

Tam followed him into the room. It was so cold after the warmth of the Gallery with its sunny windows, that it gave him a sense of shock, as if ice had been thrown over him. At the extremity of one wall a door led into a turret, a small circular-shaped study where one window looked down to the gateway, the other to the street.

Alexander was opening a small door to the right. At first

glance, Tam thought this to be a cupboard, since it was completely dark.

'Down there is the Black Turnpike. Now you will observe how easy it is to reach the upper floor by anyone entering the quadrangle and avoiding the main door.'

The Gallery Chamber was empty, one wall draped loosely by a curtain. Even on this warm August day the room had a brooding atmosphere which chilled Tam to the bone.

He wondered if Alexander felt it too as he went across and dragged the curtain aside, to reveal the full-length portrait of a man in fine robes. A falcon on his wrist, deerhounds staring up into his face, he stood proud but faintly smiling against the distant backdrop of what was presumably Ruthven Castle.

'That is my father, Tam. The man the king so cruelly put to death,' said Alexander, his voice bitter and angry. 'I hardly knew him. I was only three years old, but I loved him. Indeed, I do still love him and it is my whole life's intention to avenge his death.'

Tam said nothing. This was the same statement Alexander had made at Kirktillo, the same sentiments which he guessed were expressed over and over again to all who would give him hearing.

Treasonable sentiments which could be extremely dangerous if they ever reached King James's ears.

Alexander was regarding him eagerly as if he expected some response.

The appearance of a servant at the other end of the gallery saved Tam the necessity of emphasising once again that such schemes were doomed to disaster and would inevitably end with the hangman's rope and the drawing and quartering reserved for traitors.

The servant announced that the Earl wished to speak with his brother.

Alexander took Tam by the arm. 'How selfish I am being, keeping you to myself like this. John must also be waiting impatiently to welcome you to Gowrie House.'

Tam followed him downstairs to the dining-room, now occupied by the Earl with a spread of papers on the table so that his first impression was not of welcome but of intrusion.

As Alexander pushed him forward, introducing him with great affection, John looked askance and with an impatient frown set down his pen. Embarrassed by Alexander's fulsome manner, John's reaction suggested that his request for his brother's company was for some matter to be discussed privately. He had not expected to see him accompanied by Tam Eildor.

Although John greeted him civilly enough, could Tam have read his thoughts, they would have revealed some surprise and confusion that this newcomer, who he had understood from Tansy was to be employed by them as steward, had been suddenly elevated to his brother's dearest friend and their honoured guest.

John hoped that his misgivings were not evident for this was a path he had walked wearily many times before. His impetuous younger brother, the Master of Ruthven, lacked all discernment in choosing companions. This man Eildor was typical of the kind of friend he would often choose from a lower strata of society.

A better choice, he had to admit, than Robert Logan who John dismissed as a dangerous plotter and cautioned his brother against as a reckless schemer.

Certainly this man Eildor was unusual enough to stand out in any crowd. Not a flamboyant character like Logan, rather the opposite. Scholarly and reserved but neither sly-seeming or secretive.

Taller than average, well-built, his looks were strange. There was something about his face that John had never encountered before in a man and yet it was familiar and he suddenly realised what had been lurking at the back of his mind.

Eildor bore a strange resemblance to their foster-sister

Tansy. Had he hit upon the very reason why he appealed so strongly to Alexander, John thought triumphantly?

Poor Alexander, periodically in hopeless infatuation for some fine lady or other who was older, married and either inaccessible or unresponsive to him, had always been a little in love with his foster-sister.

Regarding Eildor, however, John was certain his feelings towards this man were not unnatural, since he was tired of having to listen to the tale of Alexander's attempted seduction by King James and how he had fled to understanding Queen Anne. He had also been in love with her and hinted that she returned his affection.

'Do not encourage her for that is a dangerous pursuit for a queen,' John had remarked. 'Heads have fallen for less.'

John sighed. The sooner his brother found a wife, the better, and there was an interesting possibility of matchmaking in the immediate future. After his sermon at St John's Kirk on Tuesday, he was proposing to break his journey to Dirleton to see his mother by calling on Lady Margaret Douglas at Seaton Palace.

John had met Lady Margaret several times and found her company quite delightful. Teased by Alexander, he had slyly mentioned her younger sister who he had to reluctantly admit was clever as well as being the acknowledged beauty of the family.

John soon realised his error. He should have known better. Experience should have taught him that anything he suggested or hinted at prompted immediate opposition. This was no exception. His gentle proposal regarding a visit to Seaton Palace received the inevitable reaction.

'I cannot bear clever young maidens. They never learn how to laugh and they take life far too seriously. But the sister sounds a good choice for you, brother, for you must take a wife, and soon.'

When John did not comment or appear to take this message to heart, Alexander continued solemnly, 'You must provide an heir for our dynasty. If you do not marry then my son will be the Earl of Gowrie some day.'

John laughed. 'You are racing ahead of yourself, Alexander. First get your wife, then your son – and then come back to me with your warning.'

Thinking it over though, John decided that Alexander was right, for once. The title inherited early carried with it undoubted responsibilities. Many lairds and noble lords of his acquaintance had already produced heirs by the dynastic necessity of arranged marriages at the age of twenty-two.

Thus far he had never met the one woman who so out-shone all others that he yearned to spent the rest of his life with her alone. Had he been so inclined, the alternative of taking a mistress was forbidden by strict adherence to his Presbyterian principles.

He decided that he could afford to be leisurely about the future. Time was on his side. Time without the encumbrance of a wife, to indulge in his scholarly activities and the fasci-nating subjects opened up to him in Padua, especially necro-mancy and alchemy.

Tam's first impression that the two Ruthvens were poles apart was confirmed over the meal that evening. While they did not actively quarrel over any particular topic under dis-cussion, their personalities were constantly at war with each other and unrelated even by colouring, John was taller, tougher looking with thick fair hair, a beard and the high cheekboned face of the Lowland Scot while Alexander, red-haired, slight and mercurial leaned towards Celtic origins.

Living under the same roof with the brothers promised to be a trial. Without serving any useful purpose at Gowrie House, except to play friend and honoured guest for Alexander's benefit until Tansy returned, Tam realised he had found himself in the middle of a somewhat trying domestic situation.

With John vaguely disapproving of his presence and ready to throw cold water on Alexander's wild schemes that smelt

of treason and danger, the future seemed to stretch endlessly
ahead.

Chapter Nineteen

In what remained of that first evening, Tam sighed with relief when the conversation switched to the less inflammatory topic of the young Earl's travels in Europe. In Geneva he had met the famous reformer Beza who, he alleged, was devoted to him. After Switzerland came Paris where he met, among others, the exiled Francis Stewart, fifth Earl of Bothwell, and bastard nephew of Will's father, James Hepburn.

Together they had laughed over Francis' attempts to terrify King James and become a perpetual thorn in his flesh. A more productive meeting had been with the English ambassador, Sir Robert Cecil who, in common with Bothwell, had little cause to love King James.

Accepting Cecil's invitation to the English court, John soon discovered that Elizabeth had found no good reason to change her opinion of James as "that false Scotch urchin".

'What thought you of the Queen of England?' asked Tam curiously.

John smiled. 'A formidable lady indeed. No one could doubt she was her father King Harry's daughter. Not one you would wish to make an enemy of.'

'How can you say that, brother?' demanded Alexander. And to Tam, 'He is being modest as usual.'

'I was very well received.'

'And although she is never lavish with her gifts, you were given a cabinet of plate,' said Alexander sharply.

'No doubt they thought I might be useful to them,' said John.

'Perhaps you allowed them to believe that you had more influence with King James than was completely truthful,' said Alexander somewhat bitterly. 'Why do you not tell Tam about how jealous he was of your reception by the queen, his many jests and petty taunts?'

And to Tam he added, 'We have it on good authority that when crowds came out to welcome John's return to Edinburgh, the king said that there were more with his father when he went to the scaffold. Do I not speak truth, brother?'

John shook his head. 'As we did not hear it with our own ears, we can only dismiss it as rumour.'

'You are so – reasonable,' said Alexander fiercely. 'Even about a man as treacherous and murderous as the king. Have you no stomach for revenge after all he has inflicted on this family?'

And they were back again on Alexander's favourite hobby-horse. A merciful interruption by the steward Henderson had Alexander leaping to his feet and leaving John and Tam alone at the table.

John swilled the wine in his goblet, regarded it thoughtfully and asked, 'Tell me about yourself, Master Eildor.'

'There is not a lot to tell, sir. Not a great deal of note happens in Peebles,' and quickly changing what might become a dangerous and awkward subject to lie about, he said, 'I was pleased to visit my cousin Tansy at Falkland. Life at the Palace was an interesting new experience.'

'And Gowrie House is yet another.' Raising his goblet, John added with a laugh, 'I wish you joy of it, for once Tansy returns I do not doubt she will keep us all in order,' Bowing, he excused himself. 'I have matters to attend to. I wish you goodnight.'

It was growing dusk outside, the long gloaming of a Scottish summer, and Tam decided on a walk through the gardens and down to the river. The fish would be leaping for insects flying above the water. Such peace would make an agreeable end to the day.

Descending the stairs, he heard whispered voices and came upon Alexander in earnest conversation with Henderson, who was looking ill-at-ease.

Not wishing to interrupt what appeared to be some domestic crisis, Tam turned on his heel.

Alexander saw him and looking guilty said, 'I apologise for abandoning you to John's hospitality.'

As Alexander dismissed Henderson, who was showing a tendency to linger, Tam said hurriedly, 'My apologies. Please do not let me interrupt you.'

With little desire for Alexander's company on his quiet evening stroll he abandoned the project and said, 'I was considering retiring if you would be so good as to show me to my room.'

'A pleasure, dear Tam.'

Climbing the stair, Alexander led the way to the family apartments alongside the gallery and opened the door into a small but comfortable bedchamber overlooking the courtyard and stables. Thanking him, Tam's relief at being able to retire was short-lived.

Taking his arm firmly Alexander said, 'But you are not for bed yet, Tam, for I have one more place, a very special one, that I have decided to show you.'

He led the way along the Great Gallery. In the curious twilight glow with the rags of a sunset, paintings took on a spectral life. Trees in sombre landscapes seemed to move and castle windows gleamed anew, high above rivers whose waters sparkled and endlessly flowed.

They had almost reached the door leading to the Gallery Chamber when Alexander turned and said, 'I am about to let you into a great secret. But first I must have your promise that you will tell no one.'

Wondering what it was all about, Tam was too curious to refuse. 'You have my word.'

Alexander nodded approval. 'In particular you must promise not to tell my brother,' he added urgently, pulling aside a tapestry that hid part of the wall.

'Here is magic for you, Tam. Behold!' and touching a carved wooden leaf, the panel slid open to reveal a tiny staircase leading upwards. 'Follow me.'

Tam could scarcely stand upright in the room, which was no more than six feet high and seven feet square. There was no window to the outside but faint light was provided by an oblong at eye level.

'What do you think of my secret place?' whispered Alexander and without waiting for a reply, 'This is a priest's hole. Built by my grandfather, for those were troubled times and he favoured the Catholic cause.'

Angling Tam towards the faint light, he said excitedly, 'Look down there – what do you see?'

Below him, Tam saw the whole of the Gallery Chamber with its corner turret. Like a stage set, every part was clearly visible, barring the entrance door directly under where he stood.

'Is it not wonderful?' asked Alexander.

Tam laughed softly. 'It is quite incredible. I do not recall this – ' he pointed to the oblong frame.

'That was because it just appeared as part of the ceiling above the door. What you are looking through is very fine glass thinly painted to resemble wood from inside the chamber. And therefore invisible. It came from Italy, is it not a marvellous invention?'

Tam agreed but before he could question the use of such an elaborate device, Alexander said, 'My grandfather considered it useful if he had a priest hidden away, but at other times it served as a laird's lug – and eye. He would invite those he distrusted to meet in the turret chamber below and listen to their conversations. And I believe it has also been the bridal chamber on occasion, so that the activities of the bedding might be enjoyed in secret by the guests.'

He laughed. 'Now, is it not a marvel?'

Tam could only agree. Whatever his thoughts concerning the revelations of the Earl's ingenuity in spying on his guests, he had to remember Gowrie House had been built in troubled and dangerous times.

Alexander was in no hurry to leave. Clearly, he wished

Tam to enjoy and relish the prospect offered by the laird's eye.

It was remarkable. One window looked out on the front court gate and main entrance to the house, the other window opened on to the main street. This was the most publicly situated room in the house, a great vantage point for an earl who was also a voyeur.

Although the light was fading, Tam could see the church spire, the wooded hills and he could both see and hear the citizens of Perth walking or riding homewards down the main Shoe Gait beyond the house walls.

So the laird's eye served another more useful purpose, he decided, as an eeyrie from which a careful scrutiny could be kept on what was happening by conspirators within, and approaching enemies without.

Returning towards Tam's bedchamber, Alexander said, 'Sleep well, dear friend. And sleep late,' he added mysteriously, 'for you will not see me. I am for Falkland.'

Tam smiled. 'I am an early riser from habit. Why Falkland?'

'I go hunting with His Grace the king,' was the mocking reply. 'My brother also had an invitation to join the hunt, but he will be sermonising at the kirk. So I am to go alone.'

This was indeed a change of heart thought Tam. 'This is indeed good news. So you are to be on friendly terms with the king once more.'

'Only for an hour or two,' said Alexander firmly. 'I am to bring him here to Gowrie.' Pausing, he gave Tam an intense look. 'It is all part of my plan. My great plan.' Tam's heart sank. What mad scheme had he in mind? Surely he was not still planning to kidnap the king. And what was more important, thought Tam, how could such a disaster in the making be prevented?

'What plan is this?' he asked, knowing full well.

'A new one, Tam. The king cannot resist a treasure. And we have one such in our possession, under our very roof here at Gowrie.'

Pausing to give Tam a look of triumph, he said, 'This is a

treasure that has eluded him for years and years. He has searched high and low in vain. What do you think about that, Tam?'

'It must be very important indeed.'

'It is, it is! His very life depends on it. His very future as king of England and Scotland when Queen Elizabeth dies, depends on his finding it.'

'Treasure, Alexander? Surely money could not buy him such a future.'

Alexander wagged a finger at him. 'That is where you are wrong, Tam. This treasure chest does not contain money. It is a casket of letters. Letters that my grandfather had from his mother, Queen Mary. Letters that her deadly rival, her cousin Elizabeth of England, tried in vain to purchase from him.'

'And what makes these letters so important to the king?' asked Tam, again knowing full well from conversations he had had with Tansy.

'Among those letters allegedly written to Lord Bothwell from the queen, and mostly forgeries, indicating her guilt concerning her husband Lord Darnley's murder, there is another item. A document.'

The fatal document, thought Tam grimly.

'You see, if this casket is opened, it will also reveal the truth that the king has murdered and tortured so many to hide. And if Elizabeth ever reads it all his hopes of inheriting her throne will be gone forever. And I will have avenged my grandfather and my dear father's deaths.'

Tam wanted to know more, knew such information was vital, but before he could frame any questions, Alexander said, 'I must leave you now, for I have people to see and I am to be up and about at dawn to join the king. He leaves Falkland at seven in the morning.'

Tam went back to his room and closed the door. He no longer felt like sleeping. Was the missing document in the Ruthven's possession all this time the cause of Margaret Agnew's murder and sundry foiled attempts on Tansy and himself at Falkland?

And was the next murder attempt to be that of King James? Was this the reason for his time-quest?

He went over to the window. Alexander had not gone straight to bed. He was walking across the courtyard to the stables.

A moment later he was joined by the steward Henderson and they were again in deep and earnest conversation, perhaps a continuation of what he had interrupted earlier. Whatever the context, Henderson was not happy about it. He shook his head as if in ignorance or protest whereupon Alexander gripped his arm and adopted an almost threatening attitude. At last some compromise seemed to have been reached and the two returned indoors.

Tam slept badly and awoke early, in time to hear horses in the courtyard and see Alexander ride out with Henderson at his side. Going downstairs, he met John who sighed and repeated what Alexander had told him. He had been invited to hunt with the king but, alas, would be giving his sermon this morning.

Showing no desire to linger, and mentioning as an excuse that he still had final notes to prepare, he left Tam to break his fast alone in the dining-room, served by two silent but attentive maids.

Thanking them, Tam went outside wondering how he was going to fill in the day. Irked once again by having so little to do, he walked down to the river and decided that he might take refuge in his favourite pastime, as the fishing promised to be excellent on such a day.

As he sat for a while by the riverbank before returning to the house, he wondered whether Alexander would manage to persuade the king about the treasure awaiting him. If Alexander's scheme was successful and King James arrived at Gowrie House, then Tam decided to make himself invisible. He had no wish for any further encounters with the lustful king or for a royal command which would enrol him as a victim of the Royal Bedchamber.

Hopefully he told himself that the king was most probably fickle where young men's affections were concerned and by now had forgotten the existence of Tam Eildor.

That alas, was not so. At the royal hunt not only was treasure in the form of a casket of letters being whispered in the king's ear but also the mention of one Tam Eildor.

Now conveniently downgraded by the Master of Ruthven from "dear friend and honoured guest" to "our honest steward", Tam was to provide the final lure for the amorous king.

Chapter Twenty

The royal hunt was in progress and the prize, a fine buck, was leading the huntsmen and Alexander Ruthven a merry dance. In vain Ruthven was urging King James to proceed with all possible speed to Gowrie House where the man he had found with the treasure that His Grace longed to possess was being kept chained in a secret room, awaiting His Grace's interrogation.

The hunt had lasted four hours, from seven until eleven, far longer than Alexander had expected and when at last the buck, sensing its doom, returned to its own territory they were back almost at the royal stables.

Again stressing the urgency of returning to Gowrie, Alexander found the king reluctant to leave before his personal ceremonial butchery of the buck. The moment which ended with James being up to his elbows in its blood was his particular and most anticipated delight of a successful hunt.

'The treasure, Sire. I entreat you.' Alexander's whispered reminder at his side.

James frowned, looked at the waiting huntsman. There would be other fine bucks, perhaps not as splendid as this, but the chance of capturing the treasure awaiting him at Gowrie House was urgent and might not come again.

So, grudgingly, he made his choice. He would leave immediately without even changing his horse, exhausted as were the other beasts by the long morning's hunt.

'We will accompany you,' he told Alexander, gesturing towards Lennox and the Earl of Mar.

Alexander panicked. 'Sire, it is meet that Your Grace come alone.'

James sharply demanded why, to which Alexander conceded that he might make an exception for His Grace's royal cousin, Sir John Erskine, keeper of Stirling Castle and guardian of Prince Henry in the royal nursery, plus one or two servants.

At the king's doubtful expression, Alexander bowed and whispered that too many noble lords who were present with him at the hunt might mar the whole purpose of the visit.

When James somewhat reluctantly agreed Alexander, with a sigh of relief, bowed again.

A short distance away, just out of earshot, Lennox and Mar, who had been observing young Ruthven's frantic behaviour during the hunt and at this short interview with the king, marvelled at James's obvious excitement.

Lennox shook his head. Whatever the two were discussing it had to be strong indeed for James to relinquish the climax of morning's exhausting hunt and the garroching of the buck, the quarry that had eluded them for several hours.

Riding alongside, James leaned over and whispered confidentially, 'Ye canna guess, Vicky man, what errand we are riding for. We are to get a treasure in Perth.'

He then told Lennox the story that had been carefully prepared for those not in the plot. Last night in the fields around Perth, Alexander had come upon a rough base-like fellow. This stranger had had his cloak drawn up to his mouth and faltered in answering young Ruthven's questions.

He behaved so suspiciously that Ruthven began to look at him more closely and saw there was something hidden under his cloak. Dragging it aside he saw a great wide pot under the man's arm, full of coined gold in great pieces and, taking the man back secretly to Gowrie House, he chained and locked him in a safe and private room.

Then aware that the coins might be treasure trove he set out to Falkland at four in the morning to inform the king.

'What d'ye think o' that?' James demanded

A pack of lies from beginning to end, was what Lennox would have liked to say. And James, normally so astute, must be out of his wits to believe it. But he had a suspicion there was more, much more in this little tale than he was being told.

So in reply to James's question, he did what he always did best. When in doubt, bow, his smile and slight inclination of the head to be taken as agreement.

James put a finger to his lips. 'Ye're to tell no one, Vicky,' he warned. 'Aboot this treasure, no' even the breath o' it. D'ye understand?'

Again Lennox inclined his head, but he wanted to know more.

'Foreign gold, is it, sire?' he asked, his curiosity tinged with caution for he prided himself on being was somewhat less vulnerable than his royal cousin, whose soul leaped at the first whiff of gold.

James laughed. 'No' gold exactly, no' in so many words, ye ken. But a treasure, aye, Vicky. The greatest treasure in the world to us,' he added solemnly. 'If we get this one which we have long sought then all our troubles, over the succession and sichlike, will be resolved. Now, what think ye o' that, Vicky?'

Considering young Ruthven's odd behaviour during the hunt, his wild dashing hither and thither and scowling at everyone, Lennox now was forced to the conclusion that Ruthven was not the only one out of his wits that morning.

Trying to sound casual, he asked lightly, 'What greater treasure is there, sire, if not gold?'

'Ye're no' listening to what we are telling ye, once again, Vicky,' said James shortly and frowning he asked anxiously, 'Ruthven wishes the matter to be kept a close secret.' Pausing, he added, 'Think ye that the lad is discreet?'

James was a worried man. Lennox detected the note of caution and judging by the odd and erratic behaviour he had witnessed that morning alone, he would not have personally placed a substantial wager on discretion as one of Alexander Ruthven's overwhelming virtues.

As for the treasure story, it was preposterous. But if James wished to believe it then who was he to incur his royal cousin's wrath by putting up a convincing argument against it. So choosing his words carefully, he said, 'I believe Ruthven to be a discreet and honest gentleman.'

'Ye do, eh, Vicky? But can he keep a secret?' Without waiting for the reply which Lennox would have found extremely difficult James, removing his hat to scratch his head, added, 'Did you hear aught strange about him?' And pausing for a moment to look closely into his face, 'Ye ken, in yon time you were wed to his sister?'

'Sire, that was eight years ago,' Lennox protested. 'Alexander was but ten years old.'

Lennox's marriage to Sophia Ruthven had been brief indeed. She had died the following year and now happily remarried he preferred to forget, as far as James was concerned, that he had ever associated with one of the hated Ruthvens.

Leaving the remainder of the hunt behind they progressed swiftly towards Gowrie House with Alexander still riding back and forth in the same demented fashion. At last, when the spires of Perth were in sight, he came alongside the king, drew rein, bowed and said,

'Sire, have I your permission to ride ahead and announce to the Earl my brother that Your Grace is at hand?'

Tam heard the huntsmen's' horns.

There was no mistaking the sound that interrupted John enjoying a leisurely meal of mutton broth and fish. Having just returned an hour ago from St John's Kirk, he was now in jubilant mood, associated with relief that the ordeal of the sermon, which had been very well received, was over.

As for Tam, he realised that this was the first intimation of the king's imminent arrival and that no messenger had been sent ahead as would have seemed advisable.

Tam also decided that it was also clear from John's agitated behaviour that he was taken completely by surprise and that Gowrie House was ill prepared for a visit from King

James. He further concluded that Alexander had also failed to advise his brother of the plan he had in mind which he had put to Tam the night before.

Summoning servants, John gave hasty instructions while listening impatiently to panic-stricken accounts of the contents of the larders. How long it would take to prepare a meal and including their reproaches that having just arrived a few days ago from Trochrie, there had been no opportunity to stock up on lavish provisions that would be expected by a royal visitor.

As Tam listened he realised he had no excuse to leap away and hide before the king arrived. His assistance was also needed in the scene of frantic activity, moving furniture and setting a table where, as was his usual custom, the king would dine alone separated from his retainers at the far end of the hall.

By the time King James entered, there was a semblance of normality. Apart from John, who still looked flustered and angry, his grim manner suggesting that once alone with his brother he would use harsh words for springing this particular surprise on him without even the courtesy of a messenger in advance.

John was particularly aggrieved at his brother's thoughtlessness, especially on his sermon morning, since Alexander knew full well that it was something of an ordeal however well prepared and that John had looked forward to enjoying the rest of the day in pleasant and tranquil pursuits.

There was no escape for Tam. Having been warned by Alexander to expect his presence at Gowrie House, King James beamed at him across the room.

Dismissing the customary welcome from the Earl with a vague nod, he shambled over to where Tam was standing among the serving-men.

Tam bowed low and James put a hand on his shoulder, stroked his arm and touched his cheek fondly, much to the astonishment of the other servants. Then, turning, he regarded critically the still unfurnished hall, its unpacked trunks stacked hastily against the walls.

Frowning, he pointed to the table set aside for him. 'Here, Master Eildor. Sit ye down, here by us. Tell your king what news.' And pointing to the chair opposite, waiting until Tam was seated, his raised hand a royal command that they were to be served forthwith.

Leaning forward, he gazed intently into Tam's face and patted his hand. 'We await most eagerly your return to our service, Master Eildor. 'Twill be Edinburgh this time though, not Falkland since we remove there directly.'

Tam was thankful for that small mercy at least, trying to pretend to be unaware of hostility hovering a short distance away in the disapproving face of the Duke of Lennox who had entered at the king's side. Normally James dined alone and the fact that he had been excluded from the royal table in favour of Tam Eildor was a personal affront.

Lurking nearby, Lennox was aware of John Ramsay. Assured of being happily reinstated once more as James's favourite after Eildor's departure from Falkland, Ramsay wore a similar expression of anger for although the two had never been friends they were both united in the hope that they had seen the last of the upstart fisherman from Peebles.

Taking the wine offered him, James dismissed the Earl with his apologies for the delay in having meat ready to put before his royal guest. Leaning forward, he dragged his chair closer to Tam and asked confidentially:

'D'ye ken aught o'this man with the pot o' gold that the Master apprehended in yon fields outside the town last night? He tells us that he brought him here secretly, bound him and locked him away in a private room, his gold with him. Aye, gold – this treasure for us to examine.'

And listening to the story, Tam realised this was a pack of lies invented for general distribution. Alexander had never met any such man, having retired early to leave for Falkland, as he had informed Tam, at four in the morning.

'We have told young Ruthven that we canna interfere in such matters. No man's treasure that is a free and lawful subject, can appertain to the King, except hid under the earth,' he quoted and added virtuously. 'But the lad maintained that this wild fellow was about to do that very thing.'

And with a shake of the royal head, 'A tricky situation, Master Eildor, aye, verra tricky, was it no'? Ye ken, this might be foreign gold brought in for the Papist cause. We may have to go to law to sort it all out.'

Tam wondered why he was being treated to all these confidences. With his knowledge of Alexander's declared intention to himself, was he being set in place as alibi – or witness? Utterly confused, he wondered should he warn the king of a possible kidnap plot?

But caution dictated the terrible results of setting such a revelation in progress. Not only for himself but, remembering James's taste for vengeance, for the Ruthvens – and that included Tansy.

And he comforted his conscience with the thought that Alexander dealt in fantasies that he could never hope to put in effect when it came down to practicality.

A platter of cold meats was set before James. A not very inviting repast, thought Tam, noting James's expression and also the fact that no repast of any kind was set before himself.

The implication was obvious: his favoured position had gained disapproval all round. Averting his eyes from the king stuffing cold mutton into his mouth with both fists and then wiping them on his breeches, Tam took note that although James attempted to converse with John lingering nearby, he received few direct answers.

Indeed, John seemed very much out of sorts and whether this was the natural unease at being a rather poor host to his royal visitor or whether it had some deeper meaning was beyond Tam.

There were other guests. Despite Alexander's warning and instructions, James had brought fifteen retainers with him in all. Including Lennox and Mar they were seated at a board at the other end of the gallery.

As far as Tam could see no food was coming their way either and Lennox, grown hungry and impatient, took the situation in hand.

He came forward, bowed and whispered in his cousin's ear.

James turned and regarded the disconsolate group staring reproachfully in his direction.

Motioning to John he said, 'You are neglecting your guests, sir. Is it not time that some repast was put their way? Aye, and wine too, for hunting is thirsty work and naught has passed their lips since the early hours of this morning.'

John bowed and looking more agitated than ever went hurriedly towards the kitchens.

Tam looked round curiously for Alexander. He had disappeared a while ago. His continued absence worried Tam. Where was he and what was more important, what was he planning?

Unable to leave the royal table without the king's permission, opportunity arose when James sprang to his feet, quaffed down the rest of the wine and ambled over to the garderobe to relieve himself.

John had returned and as he was engrossed in directing two of the servants, Tam seized the chance and went in search of Alexander.

He found him in the Great Gallery. In earnest whispered conversation with a man in armour. A man who carried a sword and wore a dagger.

Tam's unexpected arrival took both men by surprise. They sprang apart guiltily then Alexander laughed.

'Do you not recognise our steward Henderson, Tam? He is to be our knight in armour, watching over the king's treasure,' he added slyly.

Tam decided that he had never seen a less happy knight ready to guard anything. Henderson was shaking, the sword trembling in his hand.

'Has the king now dined?' asked Alexander.

Tam said yes and Alexander gave a nod of satisfaction. 'Then all is in readiness. Come with us, Tam.'

Tam stood his ground firmly and shook his head. 'First, tell me what all this is about.'

Alexander sighed. 'Tam, you know full well what it is about. We talked about it last evening,' he added wearily. 'We are to spring a surprise on the king. He is expecting a man with a treasure, a casket containing certain items he has long yearned to possess. Instead he is to find a man in armour with a sword.'

And pausing dramatically, he laughed. 'Imagine!'

Aware of the king's horror of naked swords, how they were forbidden the court, Tam had no difficulty with that.

'Imagine, Tam,' Alexander repeated. 'His gibbering terror. Then I will tell him that it was all a jape. We will witness his humiliation. Come.'

Tam was watching Henderson, shaking and fearful, his anguished expression showing that he had no liking for Alexander's plan either.

But was that all the fiery unstable young Master of Ruthven had in mind, thought Tam, remembering those earnest conversations he had witnessed from his window last night?

And Tam realised he was faced with a dilemma. The nightmare that he was to be unwillingly part of this plan and that all Alexander's overtures of friendship had been leading up to this fatal moment.

Was it too late to try to dissuade him against this folly, this stupid dangerous game – if game was all – of making King James the Sixth of Scotland (who considered himself divine as God's Anointed) a laughing-stock.

It did not take much imagination to foresee that such a plan could have terrible consequences for any and all involved.

'Alexander, you must think again, I beg of you,' Tam said.

'I for one, will not be party to this mad scheme.'

But Alexander shook his head and set off, marching the reluctant Henderson ahead of him towards the Gallery Chamber. Helplessly Tam followed them, protests and pleadings falling on deaf ears.

Turning, Alexander smiled and took hold of his arm. Keeping his grip strong he wrenched aside the curtain hiding the door to the priest's hole.

'You are to hide in there, Tam. And watch carefully. You are to be our witness of the king's humiliation. Go, Tam, as I bid you. I promise no harm shall come to you. It is but a game.'

Tam decided to humour him. If he made a fuss others might arrive on the scene and poor Henderson, armed with a sword, might well be the first to bear the brunt of the king's personal interrogation under torture of the boot.

He had a plan and hoped it would work as he climbed the stair into the tiny space and looked down through the oblong of the laird's eye into the Gallery Chamber.

It was empty. As he had expected there was no bound man with a pot of gold or a treasure casket waiting for King James.

Henderson, who had been thrust in by Alexander, was looking very agitated while being directed to the exact place where he was to stand at the ready, menacing the king, sword in hand.

'Try to look the part of a dangerous man,' said Alexander impatiently. 'And for pity's sake, hold the sword steady. You will not have long to wait. I will return directly with the king.'

Tam saw Alexander leave, heard the key turned in the lock on the unhappy Henderson. He could not release him as he had hoped. Sadly that part of his plan had failed. However, he would intercept Alexander and James with an urgent message, some excuse to prevent them entering the Gallery Chamber.

But would that be sufficient to avert Alexander's mad scheme, this catastrophe in the making?

In the room below, Alexander stood behind the king's chair

and whispered that it was time to go to "that quiet room" but that he wished this to be kept secret from his brother, at present doing his duty by belatedly playing host to the neglected courtiers.

'We would have Lennox and Mar accompany us,' said the king. 'Inform them, if you please.'

Alexander bowed. 'Sir, it is of great import that Your Grace's treasure be kept secret between us and neither the Earl my brother nor anyone else must know of the prisoner who awaits Your Grace's interrogation.'

James arose and looked reluctantly towards Lennox, just out of earshot with John Ramsay, both of whom had been watching and were trying to appear casual, intrigued by the king's conspiratorial whispering to Ruthven.

'If it please Your Grace, command that none follow,' Alexander pleaded.

James nodded and leaning on Alexander beckoned to Lennox and said, 'We are to be private together – to discuss urgent matters of state.'

Lennox bowed while Ramsay gave Alexander a glance of jealous hatred. Visualising all his regained prestige and advantages slipping away, the nature of being private together left him in no doubt whatever of the king's intentions. Ruthven, had left the court in disgrace, rumour had it, for spurning the king's advances? Had he now regretted that impulse and was in a more agreeable state of mind?

Tam heard their approaching footsteps, Alexander's voice and the king's ringing tones which echoed the length of the Gallery.

'The treasure, lad. You shall receive our best love and trust for this day's work.'

With his invented excuse, an urgent message for the king to return to Falkland, Tam ran down the tiny staircase and pushed the panel door.

It did not open. The voices drew nearer.

Again he tried. Again it remained firmly closed.
He was trapped.

Chapter Twenty-one

Tam thought quickly. What was he to do?

His struggle with the jammed panel had gone unheard, lost in the king's excited voice and Alexander's replies as he unlocked the door of the Gallery Chamber.

Tam considered shouting, calling for help but rejected that. By making a lot of noise he might bring about the very situation he dreaded. Danger for the innocent Henderson, dragged unwillingly into his master's wild scheme. Even danger for the king himself.

As for Alexander, he would have to find his own way out of this once the king knew that he had been tricked. For Tam, it was now too late to intervene and he went back to the laird's eye with its view of the Gallery Chamber and the door leading down the Black Turnpike stair, which he guessed had been locked by Alexander to prevent Henderson escaping.

Below him, Henderson was also in full view, quaking with fear as the king entered. As Alexander turned the key behind them, James stared at the armed man, dismayed the at sight of naked steel and the absence of the casket he had expected to see.

Turning to Alexander, he whispered urgently, 'The treasure you promised us, lad. Where is it?'

At that, Alexander went to the portrait and wrenched off the curtain and, snatching the dagger from Henderson, he turned to the king with a threatening countenance and demanded,

'Whose face is that? Who murdered my father?'

Pointing with his other hand to the face in the portrait he advanced towards the king, pointing the dagger to his breast.

'Is not thy conscience burdened by his innocent blood? And the blood of my grandfather? King you might be but you are the basest black-hearted villain at heart.'

Unable to avert what was no mere jape to humiliate the king, no kidnapping attempt and as the full extent of what lay ahead became apparent, Tam realised that he was to be witness to a royal murder.

He saw James armed with only with his hunting horn standing between two traitors. One, a stranger to him, Ruthven's servant, trembling inside his armour. But the king's astonishment was for Alexander's changed attitude, his betrayal.

Staring unbelievingly at the dagger pointed at his breast, he said in a voice remarkably calm considering the dangerous situation,

'Alexander, we were but a minor, when your grandfather the Earl of Gowrie was executed. We were guided by a faction who overruled us and the rest of our realm. What was done was done by the ordinary course of law.'

Alexander laughed mockingly at this as the king continued,

'If you take our life, you shall not be King of Scotland for we have sons and daughters – '

'It is neither your life nor your blood I want,' Alexander interrupted.

'What is it then ye want, man, if ye do not want our life?'

Alexander shook his head and glanced towards Henderson, as if he did not wish to discuss this in front of him. 'Only a promise,' he muttered.

'Aye – what promise would that be?' As Alexander hesitated again looking at Henderson, James said, 'Then go and fetch your brother.'

Alexander seemed reluctant to leave and Tam listened to James trying to appeal to his captor's conscience by reminding him that he had restored the Ruthven lands and dignities after the executions of their father and grandfather. How two or three of his sisters were in attendance on his "dearest bedfellow, the queen".

When James saw that this was making little impression, he reminded Alexander of his religion, of his education under Robert Rollock, Principal of Edinburgh University, from whom he had never learned such cruelty.

Alexander's stubborn scowl turned him momentarily into a mutinous schoolboy as James said reproachfully, 'We have loved thee like one of our own family.' Pausing to let that take effect, he added as the final plea; 'If ye spare our life and let us go, we will never reveal to any living flesh what has passed between us nor allow you to receive punishment for what was betwixt us at that time.'

This statement seemed to satisfy Alexander. 'Sire, if you keep silent then nothing will ail you. I will fetch my brother and by making this same promise to him all will be well.'

At the door he said, 'Sire, I will promise you your life, if you hold your tongue. Do not make any noise or open the window until I come back with my brother and him only.'

'Ye have my word,' said James.

Alexander nodded and turning to Henderson said, 'I make you the King's keeper and you keep him safe upon your own peril.'

As he went out and was locking the door behind him, Tam ran down the tiny staircase, rapped on the panel and called,

'Alexander, I am locked in. The door has jammed. For God's sake, let me out.'

Alexander either did not hear him or did not want to, for all he heard were his footsteps retreating across the gallery.

Tam looked round frantically. He considered trying to burst open the panel but decided that was too dangerous. The noise might startle the nervous Henderson into violent action. The king, thinking help was at hand, might even attempt to disarm him with disastrous results.

Voices from below had him rushing up the tiny staircase again.

James was asking Henderson if he meant to murder him.

Tam heard Henderson's quavering reply, 'Sire, I was forced

into this room and locked in only a short while before Your Majesty arrived. As the Lord shall judge me I was never told of any purpose behind this and knew nothing of any conspiracy against Your Grace.'

Tam listened, his sense of inescapable nightmare growing. Small wonder Henderson was so distressed. He had obviously realised too late his terrible predicament and peril, an unwilling accomplice in a plot against the king's life arranged by his masters in which he was to be the scapegoat.

'Sire, I would shield you with my life,' he pleaded.

'Is it the Earl and the Master's intention then to murder ourself?' asked James, and Henderson's heart sank to new depths. The king's expression as he said the words indicated that he thought their servant was in the plot too.

'Sire, if that is so, then I have never been privy to it,' Henderson argued feebly. 'And I shall die first,' he added hoping to convey fierce and gallant loyalty.

James pointed to the turret. 'Then open the window,' he commanded.

Henderson went at once to the one facing the garden.

James said, 'The other window, facing the street.'

As Henderson obeyed, Tam heard footsteps below and Alexander's key in the lock. He entered the room alone.

Seeing the turret window open, he shouted to James, 'By God, Sire, there is no remedy. You must die,' and producing a cord attempted to catch both the king's hands and tie them.

James struggled and tried to reach the open window shouting, 'I was born a free King and shall die a free King.'

Tam waited no longer. Running down the staircase he hurled his full weight against the panel door. It did not move. He ran a few steps up the stairs to give some impetus and launched himself bodily, using his shoulder as a battering ram, against the panel.

There was a crack, and the agonising pain that stunned and sickened him was enough for Tam to know that his shoulder had also fractured in the onslaught.

But he was free and struggling out of the panel. He ran the few steps to the door of Gallery chamber. To be thwarted once again, for Alexander had locked it behind him.

Tam thumped the door with uninjured arm, shouting, 'Let me in, Alexander. For God's sake, let me in.'

No one listened or even heard him above the noise of raised voices – Alexander's and the king's – inside the room. Other sinister sounds, scufflings and the rasping of steel on steel.

'Bind his hands – '

'Help! Treason!' from the king.

And again from Alexander, 'Are you not going to help, Henderson? You will get us all killed.'

There were more yells, sounds of swords clashing...

With no hope of getting into the room, Tam remembered the other entrance on the outside of the house by the Black Turnpike.

Praying that he could summon help on the way, he fled across the gallery and down the main staircase. But there was no one in evidence.

Looking through one of the windows, it appeared that the guests had all removed into the garden and were enjoying the sunshine of a perfect summer afternoon, completely unaware of the drama that was taking place a few yards away in the turret facing on to the street.

Tam blinked in disbelief. Could this nightmare be really happening? There were swans on the river beyond the garden. An idyllic scene with a glimpse of courtiers eating cherries.

Was it possible that in such a world, on such a day so tranquil and serene with birdsong and laughter drifting up to him, he had imagined the scene he had just left?

Rushing out of the main entrance he ran to the hedge and yelled at the courtiers to follow him, for unarmed he could do nothing. They turned startled faces in his direction, regarding him reproachfully and exchanging bemused glances with one another.

Had this servant gone stark raving mad? Some shook their heads and went back to picking cherries.

'The king is in danger. Come, for God's sake!' Tam yelled, running up the turnpike stair.

The door was locked. From inside the Gallery Chamber. Hammering against it, he could hear sounds of fighting, scuffling, cries and groans as if the two were locked in mortal combat, Alexander's voice screaming that James would die if he attempted to cry out of the open window.

'Help! Help!' the king's strangled yell. 'Treason! I am murdered. Help!'

And the men who had been eating cherries so peacefully a few moments earlier and had seen Tam disappear up the turnpike stair now caught a glimpse of the king. His face in great distress pushed through the window, while a hand was seen grasping his throat trying to pull him back.

Tam, shouting to Alexander to open the door, heard a key fall, and the fumble of it retrieved and turned.

A voice called to him to wait a moment. Not Alexander but presumably Henderson, still inside and trying to escape, to run for help.

As the door opened, there were footsteps on the stair behind him.

Heartened to think there was help on the way, he was pushed roughly aside as Ramsay, the king's falcon on his wrist, rushed inside.

As Tam made to follow him, Henderson in his heavy armour emerged like a bat out of hell, cannoned into Tam and sent him spinning down the stairs. As he stumbled and fell, his injured shoulder striking hard against the stone wall, Henderson stepped over him, and disappeared down the stair.

Stunned and faint, with the agonising pain intensified, Tam stumbled through the open door.

To his surprise James had the situation well in hand.

220

Alexander was on the ground, his head tucked firmly under the king's arm.

James was shouting, 'Kill him, Johnnie. Strike him low.'

Even as Tam entered, Ramsay struck at Alexander with his hunting knife. Disfigurement was more to the favourite's taste and smiling, ignoring the king's instructions, he dealt two vicious slashing blows across face and neck.

Watching the blood spurt Tam ran to Alexander as he fell. As Ramsay called for help from the open window of the turret, Tam tried to raise the fainting Alexander, taking his weight on his good arm.

Appalled by the brutality he had just witnessed, Tam realised that he must somehow get him down the turnpike and quickly find means to staunch the blood flowing from the terrible wounds on his face.

Before Tam had dragged the by now unconscious boy more than a few steps across the floor, they were beset by those who had heard the king's cries and were rushing to the scene.

The Earl of Mar thrust Tam roughly and painfully aside, shouting; 'He has murdered our king,' and before Tam could do more than cry, 'No!' the Earl thrust a rapier into Alexander's heart.

In his last breath Alexander turned to Tam and grasping his hand said, 'I had no knowledge of this. I never intended to kill the king.'

His eyes glazed over. The gallant knight would never slay another dragon.

At that same moment, out of earshot, John had been conducting some of his guests through the garden and down to the river. Suddenly aware of a hubbub and people shouting, he realised there was some terrible conflict going on in his house.

'The king has been murdered.'

Hearing the terrible words, he paused only to pick up two swords from the armoury on the ground floor before rushing up to the Gallery Chamber to find himself in the midst of fighting men.

He shouted, 'Where is the king? I am come to defend him.'

Suddenly he noticed a man's body lying in one corner covered by the king's green hunting coat, with Tam Eildor crouched against the nearby wall, covered in blood – Alexander's blood – and looking near to death.

'Has the king been killed in my house? My God, what can this mean?'

As Tam began to gasp out an explanation that it was Alexander lying beneath the coat, Ramsay rushed at the Earl and, raising his hunting knife, pierced him through the heart.

Although John died at once, falling alongside his brother's body, Tam remained on the floor, kneeling alongside the murdered brothers, wanting somehow to restore life to them, to wake up and find this was nothing but a nightmare.

Completely unable to believe what he saw before him, that he was part of this scene of dreadful carnage, he saw James kneel on the bloody floor, heard him praying and thanking God for his deliverance. He had not a scratch on him and had stood silent through all the killings with one foot firmly on the falcon's leash.

Fighting for breath, in fearful agony, trying to rise, Tam would also have died in that moment, for Ramsay raised his sword and said,

'This for me, Master Fisherman.'

Tam though injured, was still instinctively capable of lightning movement. He rolled aside, and the knife that was to have been his deathblow struck him in the arm.

A deep gash, just above the wrist bearing a small dark triangle that the king had once commented upon.

The area that contained a microchip. The guarantee of his return to his own time.

Ramsay loomed over him again, knife upraised. He heard the king's voice saying, 'Fie, leave him, Johnnie. He had no part in this.'

The room faded and was lost.

Chapter Twenty-two

Late that same afternoon, Tansy and Will arrived by coach in Perth. Made so warmly welcome at Simon Fuller's home in Methlour, they had needed little persuasion to stay an extra day and night, relieved by Martin Hailes' reception to the news of their marriage.

Despite all his earlier misgivings concerning the rightness of Tansy as wife for his dear cousin, Martin was genuinely delighted by the surge of well-being and happiness that radiated from the newlyweds.

He insisted, as they had hoped he would, that his house in the Lawnmarket would be at their disposal for as long as they liked, in order that they might enjoy the pleasures that the great city had to offer.

So at last they were continuing their journey to Edinburgh, where they would spend a few days before returning to Kirktillo to resume their domestic life. Before doing so Tansy would fulfil her promise to her foster-brothers and help them with her expertise on tapestries and like matters of furnishing for their planned reopening of Gowrie House.

On an impulse, Tansy had decided that they should look in and see the young men.

'They are not expecting us,' said Will. 'Perhaps they will not be at home.'

Tansy shook her head. 'I know, Will, but I wish to see Tam. To see how he is faring with Alexander.'

Will looked at her and smiled. 'I am sure Tam will be well able to keep young Alexander in check. As long as we do not stay too long. I should like to be settled in Edinburgh before nightfall.'

Tansy nodded in agreement.

But Will was uneasy. Her mood had changed suddenly. She

was no longer jubilant and carefree, with the light-heartedness that had characterised the few days since their marriage. Since setting out from Methlour, she was more silent than usual with a tendency to stare out of the window at every passing milestone and the distant prospect of Perth.

Tansy could not tell him that last night she had had a dream.

She had dreamt that Tam was dead.

Much to their surprise since this was not a market day, Will and Tansy found their way to Gowrie House barred by a crowd of citizens. People who looked anxious and frightened.

Will leaned out of the window, asked what had happened.

A scared old man looked up at him. 'The Earl – our Lord Provost – has been killed.'

'And his brother, the young Master,' said a woman at his side.

'Both dead. Both brutally slain. In that turret up yonder,' the man pointed upwards.

Tansy turned white. Her hand flew to her mouth as she choked out, 'Dear God, no! Not John and Alexander.'

'Aye, lady. Both of them. And the king had a hand in it,' he added darkly.

'Aye,' whispered another man. 'We can be sure o' that.'

As if in confirmation, the gates swung open and four of the royal huntsmen pushed the crowd aside ushering ahead of them a group of terrified servants, their hands bound.

'They are for the Sheriff court,' said the man bitterly, 'to be tried and hanged, nae doubt, for trying to protect our Lord Provost.'

'Aye, treason, they'll call it. An attempt to kill the king.'

'It'll no stop there,' his companion predicted. 'The king will kill them all, all our noble Ruthvens, that's for certain.'

Another man agreed. 'Aye, he will want his revenge and he will get it. Who can oppose him, tell me that?'

Tansy leaned back in the coach, clutched Will's arm. 'Dear

God – William and Patrick. They are at Dirleton with their mother.'

'They are just youths,' said Will.

'Youths or no,' said Tansy grimly, 'they are the next in line. We must reach them, warn them,' she added frantically.

'Tansy, we cannot get to Dirleton before tomorrow.' Will had no desire to add that by that time, they would probably be too late. A swift horse and a messenger from James might already be on the way.

'All we can hope for is that one of John's servants was not among those we've just seen,' he said. 'That he had sense to ride off and warn them.'

A guard rode alongside, stared in at them. 'Move this coach. The street is to be cleared, by royal command.'

The Kirktillo servant who was driving awaited Will's instructions.

'Perhaps you would be so good as to clear a passage for us,' Will told the guard.

Leaning over he looked into the coach, demanded suspiciously, 'Your name and business?'

'William Hepburn. My wife and I are travelling to Edinburgh,' said Will, aware of Tansy trembling at his side.

'Clear the way, clear the way there.'

Moments later, they were heading past the gardens of Gowrie House towards the Speygate and the city walls.

There Tansy commanded the driver to stop. 'We cannot leave like this, Will,' she sobbed. 'Where are we going?'

'We are going home to Kirktillo. We can do nothing for John and Alexander, my dearest. I know how hard this is for you to bear, but my main concern now is for your safety.'

'What about Tam? We cannot abandon him. And I am in no danger.'

Will put his arm around her. 'Dearest, that is where you are wrong. You are in the very greatest danger from James at this moment. Anyone who bears the name of Ruthven or who has connections with them will be hunted down and executed. You saw the servants, innocent men and women. You know as well as I do what will happen. You know what his vengeance is like.'

Pausing a moment, he added quietly. 'And you have said yourself that he hates you.' Letting that take effect, he went on, 'I have no wish to abandon Tam, my dearest, but you and your safety must be my first concern.'

Obstinately Tansy shook her head. 'I cannot leave without knowing whether Tam is still alive or –' Her voice broke. 'What are we to do?' she cried.

'We must abandon any thoughts of Edinburgh and return home. That I think would be the wisest move. Rest assured that if all is well with Tam he will find us there,' said Will, aware that his words sounded considerably calmer than his thoughts at that moment.

Had the queen told James that Tansy planned to be at Gowrie House with her foster-brothers? Would the king in his search to hunt down the Ruthvens remember that Mistress Scott also had a connection with Kirktillo?

As for Tansy, she sank back weeping helplessly, like one living in a nightmare from which there was no awakening. John and Alexander dead and that other inescapable vision of Tam, fighting to protect them, lying dead in his blood beside them in Gowrie House.

She was quite certain that he was gone, that she would never see him alive again. And as they rode back towards the road leading to Kirktillo, Tansy knew that she had never been so shocked or grief-stricken in her whole life.

After these terrible events she could not imagine ever being happy again. This day would remain with her forever, its remembrance a dark cloud over her future life.

And it seemed so unfair, this cruel blow of fate when she and Will had at last achieved content in that long dreamed-of marriage.

'Oh, Will, we were so happy,' she wailed.

The coach had stopped to negotiate a narrow bridge near the city boundary. Fearful of pursuit now, Tansy leaned out of the window, looked back along the road they had travelled.

It was empty and down below at the river, a girl who had been filling pans with water was hurrying back up the slope.

She looked up at the coach, shaded her eyes and then yelled,

'Mistress Scott. Mistress Scott! Please wait!'

It was little Jane Rose.

Inside Gowrie House, King James, wearing his tall hat with its ostrich feather, sat slumped in a chair. A very angry monarch, smouldering with rage and frustration. He had been tricked, he who was born divine, God's Anointed, had been deceived and someone, aye, countless someones, must pay for it.

'What are your orders, sire, for the bodies?' asked Mar. They were still lying upstairs in the turret room where they had been struck down.

'Sire, shall you give the order of their removal for burial?' In the normal way this unpleasant task would have fallen to the next-of-kin. But James hoped that there were no such Ruthvens alive or ever would be again, if his orders to seek out the two younger brothers at Dirleton had been carried out.

As for the Earl, but most particularly Alexander, he would have liked to leave them up there, to rot away. But he had a better plan.

Remove them for burial? Nay, he wanted them kept intact – more or less – but without their vital organs. Their corpses kept unburied awaiting his pleasure. Even dead they should not escape his wrath.

He gave the orders. To be carried to Edinburgh, put on trial and tried for treason. The sentence to be hung, drawn and quartered, the end reserved for traitors. And in the Ruthvens' case, their name extinguished, their estates and all worldly goods to revert to the Crown.

But the main cause of James's anger was the vital casket

once in the first Earl of Gowrie's care. The casket that Alexander had promised him, had hinted was still in Gowrie House. It must be somewhere. It must be found.

And he thought of the document it contained, that evil genius signed by the midwives at his birth, a document which could sound the death knell of his hopes for the Crown of England.

Now sitting alone at a table in the murder's house, he listened to furniture being moved, tapestries and pictures pulled from walls, sounds indicating that the search he had commanded, with results he hoped for and was impatiently awaiting, was being conscientiously carried out.

It had begun with the corpses of the two brothers lying on the floor of the turret room. Ordering a search of their pockets for alleged conspiracy papers, naught had been found on Alexander.

On John, the royal invitation to that morning's hunt, that had retreated into the past like some episode from a bloody history of Ancient Greece. The invitation John had declined on account of his Tuesday sermon. But there was something else, a packet containing tiny dolls, magical characters, brought doubtless from Padua, symbols of his interest in necromancy.

Perhaps the Earl carried them believing they would bring him good fortune. At such a thought, James suppressed a cynical laugh, his first of the afternoon.

As the searchers returned one by one, each with a negative result, he banged his fist on the table before him. Soon every room would have been scoured as minutely as possible. It should not have been difficult when there was so little furniture for the casket to remain concealed. But in so vast a house, it was almost impossible to detect a concealed document.

He sat isolated, the brooding heavy eyes, the melancholy expression set as if in stone and those who approached him shivered, fearing his wrath, ready to descend with unforeseeable consequences on any who displeased in thought, word or deed.

As the two bodies were taken out of the house, so too the summer day removed itself from the royal presence. The warm cloudless skies that had seemed such an anathema to a day of terror and bloodshed suddenly gave way to a storm of great magnitude.

Thunder rattled through empty rooms as rain-laden clouds burst over the roofs of Gowrie House. Hailstones and rivers of water streamed down the window, tapestries shook under thunderclaps and eerie winds came from everywhere and nowhere.

As darkness engulfed the city it would have struck terror into the heart of a less sensitive man, suggesting that the earth itself cried out and mourned the slaughtered Ruthvens.

The lords who had been his huntsmen that day were cold and weary. Since the Ruthven servants had been carried off to jail, there was no one left to prepare food for them, had any of them been hungry enough to eat anything after the events of that afternoon.

Shivering and apprehensive, even the boldest longed to be quit of this place, to be back in Falkland and the comfort of their own apartments.

Lennox, watching his royal cousin, marvelled at his calm, his cold and precise orders, for he was one with the noble lords in longing to be in his own rooms and to shut out the horrific scenes he had been party to that day.

He felt sympathy for the huntsmen, forced to stand in the king's presence unless invited to sit. And he remembered how the fisherman Eildor had sat with James as he ate earlier that day.

Lennox presumed that Eildor was also dead, remembering the hatred on Ramsay's face as he watched the fisherman favoured by the king. Remembering that Ramsay had killed the Earl, seeing Eildor fall under his onslaught.

He had last seen him bleeding on the floor beside the two

dead brothers. He kept visualising Ramsay with his hunting knife stabbing Eildor and now he wondered why he had hated that young man so much, for he had never really been a danger to his position in court. Not in the same sense as John Ramsay.

Lennox had never liked Ramsay and decided philosophically that Eildor was one less favourite to worry about. There was no doubt in his mind that Ramsay had saved James's life, had not James told him so and that he would be suitably rewarded with honours. But for Lennox there was something desperately evil about a youth with the face of an angel and a devil's heart.

He turned his attention to Mar who was standing near James. Was his conscience bothering him at having delivered the death stroke to young Ruthven? Sir John Erskine was a man known to keep his own counsel. James's closest friend, four years his elder, he was son to the Countess of Mar and the two boys had been raised together in the royal nursery at Stirling Castle.

Lennox was aware again of the striking resemblance between the two, so strong that they might have been brothers.

The last of the searchers, Hew Moncrieff, approached James who came suddenly alive again, looked up eagerly.

Moncrieff bowed. 'Alas, sire. Nothing. We cannot find any trace of the casket Your Grace describes.'

James impatiently rustled the pile of documents on the table beside him. Each of the searchers had been instructed to bring before him any that was found, but not one related to that damning piece of evidence James had sought so tirelessly and for so many years.

Lennox came over. 'Sire, the weather is worsening. Is it your wish that we remain here until morning?'

James sprang to his feet. 'Nay, Vicky. We are for Falkland. We have urgent matters to attend before the morn. We can do no more here. We have despatched Sir John Sandilands to

Dirleton with orders to arrest William and Patrick Ruthven. We will have them brought before us for trial with their two brothers by and by. They will all be sentenced together.'

And Lennox had a nightmare vision, quickly quenched, of two long dead corpses side by side with two lads of fourteen and sixteen. He shuddered in disgust.

'What of their sisters, sire?'

'We shall persuade Annie to give them up to us. She canna have any excuse to keep traitors in her household. And that goes for any who are known to have associated with the Ruthvens,' he added grimly.

Such as Mistress Tansy Scott, thought Lennox, who had never known how tirelessly her late husband had angled for her death through Sandy Kay. She still had one enemy left more resourceful than Walter Murray had ever been.

There were sighs of relief quickly suppressed and changed into loyal and respectful bows as the king gave the order to leave Gowrie House.

And so they rode out hastily like desperate men through pelting rain and darkness on the long treacherous ride back to Falkland Palace.

Chapter Twenty-three

'Mistress Scott!'

Tansy could hardly believe she was seeing Jane, the sewing maid she connected with her lodging in Falkland Palace.

'Uncle Davy and I live here now.'

And Tansy remembered Tam telling her Davy Rose had decided to take Jane away, alarmed that the search of his house and his subsequent rough-handling might have a sinister connection with the killing of Margaret Askew.

'It is good to see you again,' said Tansy and burst into tears.

Will put his am around her. 'Her foster-brothers, Jane, the Earl and his brother – at Gowrie House – ' he began.

Jane shivered. 'We know. Will you come with us, sir? We live just along there.' Pointing to a narrow street, 'You can leave your coach at the inn by the bridge here. It will be quite safe.'

Giving instructions to the coachman, they followed her down a narrow street where gabled houses leaned toward each other across the cobbles.

With Will gallantly insisting on carrying one of her water bags, she led the way up a forestair, knocked twice on the door, hesitated and then twice again.

'This is just a precaution,' she whispered. 'So that Uncle knows it is me. He is mortal afraid that we might have been followed from Falkland,' she added as a key was turned in the lock.

The door opened to be filled by the massive frame of Davy Rose.

His puzzlement and pleasure at these unexpected visitors was quickly quenched by a glimpse of Tansy's white tear-stained face.

Gently he led her to a chair, produced a goblet of madeira

for her to sip and as she waveringly introduced Will as her new husband, Jane clapped her hands but looked mildly astonished, having heard something of Tansy's sad first marriage.

Tansy smiled shyly and reached for Will's hand. 'We have known each other for many years. We were on our way to Edinburgh and stopped to – to look in at Gowrie –'

Suddenly she burst into tears again and Davy said, 'A terrible business. Both young men – ' He stopped, too shocked to continue.

'And Tam too,' Looking at Jane, she clutched her hand and whispered, 'Master Eildor, Jane.'

Davy and Jane exchanged glances. 'You had better tell them, Uncle.'

Davy nodded. 'We heard the town bell and went to see what it was all about...'

In the turret room of Gowrie House, that same bell ringing the alarm to rally the citizens of Perth stirred Tam. He had lain as one dead on the floor beside the lifeless bodies of the Earl and the Master of Ruthven.

Weeping, he looked for the last time on those two young faces, Alexander so disfigured by Ramsay's knife as to be unrecognisable and John's face untouched, pale and serene in death.

The effort of getting to his feet was agonising. Somehow he staggered down the turnpike stair and saw a discarded cloak. Tearing off his shirt, he wrapped it round his arm which was bleeding heavily. Wearing the cloak tight around himself, praying that he would not be stopped and challenged, he kept to the shadows and slipped across the garden where a side gate led on to the main thoroughfare.

Hoping to lose himself among the ordinary citizens of Perth who were milling about the area, aware only that he had to put some distance between himself and Gowrie House, he crossed the road into a narrow entry.

That last effort, the agony in his shoulder and the loss of blood was too much. Too weak to continue, he sank down on the ground and huddled in his borrowed cloak, shivering uncontrollably.

He would wait for the king's guards to find him, make him prisoner. But they were already too late.

For this was death...

'And that was where we found Master Eildor,' said Davy. 'We had taken the quick way to the Shoe Gait and we saw this body lying there. I hardly recognised him again. But I was sure he was dead –'

Hearing Tansy's cry, Jane put in quickly, 'He is alive. Tell her, he is here, safe with us.'

At Tansy's bewildered face, she added, 'You will find him through there,' she whispered, pointing to a door. And with a proud glance at Davy, 'Uncle carried him home.'

Tansy looked at him gratefully. For a moment all else of the day's horrors put aside in this one miracle.

Her dream had been wrong. Tam was still alive.

'He is bad hurt,' warned Davy. 'We are doing what we can but he has lost a lot of blood.'

Tansy followed Jane quickly into the other room.

Tam was lying on a pallet. He was very still, corpse-like, his face as white as her own.

Kneeling beside him, she took his hands, chafed them in her own. 'Oh, Tam – I thought I would never see you again. You are alive. Thank God!'

He opened his eyes, as if that action took considerable effort. Seeing her he smiled weakly. 'Only just, I fancy. And thank Davy Rose, for I was near death when he found me.'

Leaning over, Tansy kissed his forehead and noted with some alarm that it was fever-damp. 'You are safe now and we will soon have you well again.'

And at that, the practical Tansy took over. 'Now let us see this arm,' she said. Blood was seeping through Jane's rough bandaging. 'We must stem the flow,' Tansy said to her.

Jane nodded. 'I have water heated, and clean linen ready.'

Carefully Tansy bathed his arm, observing how narrowly the dagger thrust had missed the dark triangle on his wrist. That was a miracle too, she thought. And opening the small leather purse she wore around her waist, she took out needle and calmly threaded it.

Tam watched her idly, as if all this was happening to someone else.

'Have you usquebaugh – some strong spirit?' she asked Davy. He said yes and produced a goblet, thinking it was for Tam to drink.

Tansy smiled. 'A small receptacle, a saucer would be enough. This is to make sure the wound is clean.'

And to the man lying there, 'This is going to hurt, Tam.' Holding the two gaping edges of the dagger thrust together, she dabbed on the liquid and took up needle and thread. 'This must be done. Otherwise you will bleed to death.'

'They told me your stitches were delicate. So let us see some of them,' he said bravely.

He had winced when she dabbed on the liquid but the sewing was much worse.

And pain was not at an end. Once his right arm was bandaged there was even worse to come. He fainted clean away when Will held him while Davy thrust his shoulder back into its socket.

When Davy grinned and said it had been wrenched out and not broken, he should have been relieved and grateful, but the agony was just as great.

Eventually it was over and he was able to tell them what he had witnessed in the Gallery Chamber of Gowrie House, being cautious and sparing with details, observing Tansy's white-faced anguish and saying only that both brothers had been stabbed and died immediately.

He ended quickly, touching lightly upon how he had also been daggered by John Ramsay and of his escape through the gardens with the angry crowd gazing up at the house.

'I saw them leading the servants away, but there was nothing I could do.'

'And we were just a few yards away from you,' said Tansy.

Tam shook his head. 'I had no idea where I was heading. I had some vague idea about getting back to Falkland once darkness fell. But I had no money – nothing. All my possessions were in Gowrie. When I collapsed in that alley I had no hope of survival.'

Pausing, he looked across at Davy and Jane. 'And then you came on the scene.'

Davy grinned. 'We almost fell over you.'

Lighting candles against the growing darkness, Jane said, 'It was like a miracle.

Some twelve miles away at Falkland Palace, King James was preparing his own miracle for consumption by a gullible public.

Pursued by the relentless storm, he and his courtiers had arrived back at the royal apartments. James rode in, wet and angry, expecting to be met by a queen distraught at the dangers that had beset her "dearest bedfellow" and giving thanks for the miracle of his survival.

Instead, unconcerned for his discomfort, his Annie reviled him. For she had heard about the murder of her dearest Alexander and his brother John.

Screaming at him for daring to suggest that she should dismiss Beatrix and Barbara Ruthven from her service, she shuddered at his approach, at his very presence in her bedchamber.

There was the blood of the Gowries on his hands, and the hands of all his huntsmen. The sun that had so innocently arisen that morning, like so many others in that warm summer, had died in blood.

The king left her presence closing the door on her cries and fury. There was no dealing with Annie in such a mood, for she seemed almost out of her wits with grief for the slaughter of the Ruthvens. The first to dare question him and to assault him with angry reproaches.

'There was no treason, James. This was plain murder, the motive I do not doubt was gold.'

So now he, King of Scotland, God's Anointed, had to justify his actions to the whole world. Sleep was impossible. He wished to make his case and so he sat down and wrote eight thousand words, "A Discourse of the Vile Unnatural Conspiracy" that the Ruthvens had wrought against him.

In it the missing casket with its damning document that he had sought so wildly had undergone a transformation. It was now once more a pot of gold in a field outside Perth, hidden under a man's cloak.

James included his speech with Alexander Ruthven, his pious reference with some inevitable Latin tags on the difference between such gold and treasure trove.

The news reached the Edinburgh preachers by nine o'clock on the following morning, August 6. By ten o'clock the Privy Council received a letter from the king, the preachers were called first "before the council of the town" and the King's epistle read to them.

'It bore that his Majesty was delivered out of a peril, and therefore that we should be commanded to go to our Kirks, convene our people, ring bells, and give God praise and thanks for His Majesty's miraculous from that vile treason.'

After due deliberation they decided that "they could not be certain of the treason" but would speak of delivery "from a great danger". Or they would wait and when quite sure of the reason, would blaze it abroad.

James was furious at not receiving the preachers' full support and his arguments and threats fell on deaf ears. Later he was to say, in justification to the one minister, Robert Bruce, who stood out refusing to accept the validity of his report on the conspiracy: 'If I had wanted their lives, I had causes enough. I needed not to hazard myself so.'

To Bruce and many others, this was tantamount to saying that he regarded the two Ruthvens as dangerous traitors and the day he rode to their house in Perth, he had deliberately played hostage and put his life in danger despite this knowledge. Not for the sake of an illusory pot of gold the traitors had used as bait to trap him, but in hope that the real object of his search about which they were in total ignorance would be revealed.

James had learned through the years to be cautious, that even with sufficient causes for a man's death, it did not always pay to hustle him to the block by judicial process. He had rushed the young Ruthven's grandfather, the first Earl, to the scaffold but it had not secured him possession of the casket letters. That secret had died with him.

Others through the years who were suspected of damning knowledge, an ever growing-list, had been turned over to the executioners but also died without revealing anything concerning his secret.

And so for James it had become a case of waiting and watching with the young and vulnerable Alexander Ruthven and taking a chance, hazarding his own life when it seemed that success in his long-drawn out enterprise was in his grasp at last. The certainty that the secret he dreaded was firmly confined in some press or hiding place in Gowrie House conjured up the final desperate degradation that James could inflict, so that the corpses of the two dead brothers not only had their pockets turned out but also had their home ransacked.

In an effort to win the popular support, he issued a proclamation guaranteed to please all his loyal subjects. August the fifth was to be observed in perpetuity as a public holiday, a day of thanksgiving and rejoicing with prayers said in all churches for His Majesty the King's miraculous deliverance.

In the days that followed while the preachers, sceptical and unimpressed by this bounteous gesture, awaited further developments, Tam Eildor lay not far distant from the ill-fated and now deserted Gowrie House, in the grip of a fever that seemed likely to quench his life.

Chapter Twenty-four

Davy Rose had inherited his cousin's house in Potter's Close, that same cousin whose sickness and sudden death had been the reason for his disappearance from Falkland. Now his future seemed assured, a man who could write a fine hand had little difficulty in finding employment in the city of Perth. Davy had other skills too but not one of them, he realised in desperation, was of any use in keeping Tam Eildor alive.

That task fell to Tansy and Jane who sat endlessly at his bedside, applying cold compresses and herbs in an endeavour to break the fever, the result of John Ramsay's stab wound to his arm having become infected.

Davy came into the bedchamber often, looked down on the sick man and considered the situation. 'If his life is in danger, there is a physician who would remove his arm.'

'No,' said Tansy in panic. 'We cannot do that.'

'Many who come back from wars or have accidents manage very well with only one arm,' Davy insisted. 'They get used to it and it is better than being dead – a young man like that. Why, I ken three fellows lost limbs – '

But Tansy was not listening. She refused to be persuaded. How could she ever make them believe that Tam did not belong in the year 1600, that he was on a time-quest from the future? If that was beyond their understanding how could they deal with that black triangle on the wrist of his injured arm, the guarantee of returning to his own time.

What was she to do? Watch him die?

And, praying for a miracle one day when all seemed lost, Davy brought in an old crone.

Tansy was not impressed. The woman looked like a witch, but she was told on the best authority by Davy that she was kin to the innkeeper and well-known and respected as a wise woman.

'Leave him to me, lassie. I will soon have him on his feet again.' Giving Tansy a toothless grin, she produced a bundle and shook out a quantity of strange objects and ill-smelling herbs on to the table.

Observing Tansy's look of astonishment, she said reassuringly, 'Never fails, lass. Brought many a man, aye, and wives and bairns back from the very brink.'

'Do you need my help?' Tansy asked nervously, hoping that she did not.

The wizened old face peered at her. 'Na, na, lassie. I will do fine on my own, thank ye kindly. Mebbe a mite to drink for my trouble.'

Tansy realised she had to have faith in someone, for there was little more she or anyone could do to save Tam now. He was dying anyway. She knew all the signs too well not to recognise them.

As if aware of her dilemma the old woman, already busy at the table, said gently, 'Bide if ye wish, lass.'

Tansy, anxious and curious, decided to do so. She sat down in a chair, tired out with days and nights of nursing Tam. Even with Jane's help she knew that Will was deeply concerned about her, but all he could do was sit by Tam's bedside and watch for an hour or two in case Tam recovered consciousness.

Eager to see, sceptical about what the so-called wise woman was doing, she found her eyelids growing heavy. Fighting against sleep, her last glimpse was the sight of the old crone laying a hand on Tam's forehead.

Tam had lost the world. He had wandered he knew not where and it was the touch of a soft hand carrying liquid to his lips that brought the dream.

Later he was never quite certain whether it was because of the fever that he had dreamed of Janet Beaton of whom he knew he had no memory, but from Tansy's description he

241

seemed to recognise immediately when she put her hand on his forehead and sat by his bedside.

'Tam Eildor,' she smiled. 'You came back as I promised Tansy you would. I am delighted to see you again and relieved to find that you are alive. A little longer and I fear I would have been too late.'

Her hand stroking his forehead was such a comfort. 'But you cannot stay here,' she said. 'You know you must return to your own time.'

'I have failed,' he whispered.

'No, you have not. You have what you came for, what lay behind the reasons for King James killing any who knew the truth he had at all costs to conceal.'

'The document?' Tam gasped.

'The document is not here. It is in Edinburgh and you must go forward again. But wait until you are stronger to get the final answer.'

He wanted to ask her how, and where, but the words would not form themselves.

She was smiling gently. 'You do not remember that we have met before.'

Faint memory stirred as once before when Will Hepburn had put the same question to him. But it was confused, a half-remembered dream.

Her smile was sad now. 'We were lovers once.' She shook her head, sighed and looked towards the sleeping Tansy. 'No matter. Before you go get her to tell you the rest – '

Tansy was stirring. Janet leaned over and kissed him gently on the lips. He closed his eyes trying to remember.

When he opened them again she had gone.

Two days later, claiming that it was thanks to Tansy and Jane's excellent nursing and his natural resilience that the fever had passed, Tam was up and about again. The inflammation had receded in his injured arm and although Tansy maintained that his recovery was due to the old wise woman from the inn, he made light of that.

'You must have seen her, Tam. She was not a sight one would readily forget. An old witch, if ever I saw one.'

But Tam shook his head. He had no memory of an old woman.

And while Tansy was not really surprised, considering his delirium, he retained, with a certain diffidence, his silence about discussing with anyone his vision of Janet Beaton.

Tam had decided that some things were best left unsaid and, wondering what to do next, while Tansy and Jane prepared food to tempt his ever-growing appetite, Will put before him the broadsheets containing the king's epistle and also that of the Reverend Galloway.

Watching him consume a large slice of game pie, Will looked at him and said, 'I can hardly believe that you were so ill. It is like a miracle.'

And the business of miracles was very much to the taste of the king's chaplain, Reverend Patrick Galloway in a sermon delivered at the Mercat Cross.

'On Tuesday last, Alexander Ruthven came to Falkland to his Majesty and found him at his pastime. And so he leads him from Falkland to Perth, as a most innocent lamb to the slaughterhouse. There he gets his dinner, a cold dinner, yea, a very cold dinner – as they know who were there.'

He then went on reiterate the king's account of an armed man with a drawn dagger and Alexander's accusation,

'"You were the death of my father; and here is a dagger to be avenged on you for that death." Judge, good people, what danger your David was in. An innocent lamb, he was closed in twixt two hungry lions thirsting for his blood, and locked doors between him and his friends.

'What sort of delivery got he? It was wholly miraculous. Five or six things which you will all call and acknowledge to be miracles. First of all, his Majesty standing between two armed men, he at his entry should have been astonished at the sight of an armed man to take his life. Yet on the contrary

243

this armed man was so astonished that he might neither move hand not foot. Was not this miraculous?

'Yet further when Alexander had taken him by the gorge and had held the dagger to his breast, so that there were scarce two inches between his death and his life, even then by his gracious Christian and most loving words, he overcame the traitor. The words so moved the heart of the traitor that he began to enter into conditions with the king.

'And so he went forth to his brother, from whom he received commission to despatch him hastily. He then coming up again brings a pair of silk garters in his hand. After he had locked the door he says, "You must die, therefore lay your hands together that I may bind thee", to the intent, no doubt, that the king being bound, they might then have strangled him and cast him in a cave or pit which they had prepared for that use.

'Now here is the third miracle. The King answers the traitor, "I was born a free prince, I shall never die bound." With this each grips the other's gorge till in wrestling the king overcomes and gets him under him.

'Now is this not miraculous? The Master of Gowrie, an able young man in comparison with the King, I am assured had strength double, yes threefold greater. And yet is overcome and cast under.

'Now yet another miracle. When they are thus wrestling up comes John Ramsay by the black turnpike and, at the King's command, gives the Master a death stroke.

'Now yet a miracle. Into the chamber with the King gather four. My Lord Gowrie comes up and eight with him. At first he drives all four into a corner and never rests. But John Ramsay chanced to cry "Fie, cruel traitor, have you not done evil enough? You have got the King's life, must you have ours?" At which he drew a little back, and in back going he got the stroke whereof he died.'

While preaching by royal command, the body of a man named Henry Younger was brought to Falkland Palace.

244

Suspected of being the man with the dagger and on his way to prove his alibi, but finding a party of armed searchers making their way towards him, he decided they might not be interested in his alibi after all and took to his heels.

They cornered him in a cornfield where one Henry Bruce put a rapier through him, for which he was made a colonel by royal command. As for Galloway, never wishing to lose a chance of drama, he had spread his arms above the human sacrifice and proclaimed to the King.

'Thank God. The traitor that should have slain you could not be taken alive, but there he lies dead.'

But they got the wrong man. This was a new candidate for the role of the quaking man who was given out in proclamation as a 'black grim man' where in fact Henderson who had rapidly removed himself from the scene, had a ruddy complexion and a brown beard.

Shortly after Galloway's recitation came a dramatic announcement that he had that very day received a letter from the missing witness to the miracles, none other than Henderson, the real quaking man with the dagger in the turret who was to have aided the king's dispatch.

There were some caustic remarks concerning Galloway when he repeated his performance in Glasgow, miracles and all, declaring to the sceptics, 'God forgive them that say the King cannot be believed.'

As an interesting postscript he brought in the powers of darkness. 'If the Earl of Gowrie had bidden still in Scotland he might perchance not have attempted such a treason. But when he went to Padua there he studied necromancy. His own tutor, Mr Rynd, testifies that he had those characters upon him that he loved so much that if he forgot to put them in his breeks he would run up and down like a madman.'

Reading the broadsheet distributed so widely containing the king's "Discourse on an Unnatural and Vile Conspiracy", Tam found it much as he remembered, except for the lie about the pot of gold coins which had been carefully substituted for the real reason of James's visit to Gowrie and the tragedy that followed.

The Casket Letters and the secret document.

Rumour was, according to Will and Davy, that not all ministers were convinced by the king's epistle, or Mr Galloway's miracles. Most brought reluctantly to heel only by the threat of permanent banishment and the loss of their livings, they had it on good authority that Robert Bruce remained firmly sceptical and defiant.

All was quiet in Perth. Danger and terror no longer stalked its streets and in Davy's house plans for a journey were being made. In Methlour, Martin and Simon appalled, like most honest folk, by the murder at Gowrie House understood Will and Tansy's decision to abandon their proposed visit to Edinburgh and Dirleton.

Tansy had received a message from her foster-mother that, while bringing no relief to bitter grief, brought joy that the two younger sons, William and Patrick, had escaped King James's vengeance. Warned in time, Lady Gowrie had seen them across the Border to England just hours before the king's men came to arrest them.

The plan was now to travel to Falkland Palace with Tam and once Tansy had retrieved her possessions, Will and she would return again to Kirktillo to pick up the threads of their life together.

There were tearful scenes when the time came to leave little Jane and Davy but promises were made of future visits to the Hepburns. It was harder for Tam to bid them farewell, knowing full well that he could give no such promise of any future meeting.

And so the three set off once again in Will's coach. The groom, disappointed at the cancelled jaunt to Edinburgh, had been compensated by a promising romance with the innkeeper's niece.

They avoided Gowrie House and at the end of their twelve mile journey found Falkland Palace similarly deserted since the court had returned to Edinburgh. The Keeper of the Gatehouse gave Tansy the keys to her lodging. Sad and strangely silent, she knew she would never return.

And neither would Tam. He need fear no more encounters with the amorous king. King James had no doubt forgotten all about the simple fisherman by now. But of one thing he was certain. The king who had taken so many lives had, by his intervention, spared him from John Ramsay's death-stroke. While Will and the groom carried out her possessions to the waiting coach, Tansy walked with Tam into the garden, both silent, absorbed by their own sadness. So much tragedy that had begun with the murder of Margaret Agnew. Even that would never be fully explained without the document for which Davy Rose's home, as well as Gowrie House, had been ransacked in vain.

At last they reached the seat where they had first met – oh, what seemed so long ago.

They sat down together. Tam's arm was still bandaged in a sling and saying, 'It is almost healed now, but you will take care,' she took his hand in hers.

'Before you go there is something you should know, Tam Eildor.'

He smiled. 'We are brother and sister, is that it?'

She shook her head, looked at him earnestly. 'No, Tam. I believe I am your daughter.'

'How can that be?'

'Janet Beaton was not my granddam. She was my mother, well past fifty. My aunt, her daughter, died in childbirth so she passed me off as hers.'

'Surely no woman in this age can have a child so old,' said Tam.

'What about the Bible?' asked Tansy wryly. 'And sometimes they didn't count very well. But Janet had extraordinary powers. She told me that I was her daughter and that one day my father would come back.'

She paused. 'She told me his name. And if I hadn't guessed

that very first day we met, then my mirror would have told me and everyone else – except you – the truth.'

Tam sat up sharply. So that was what Janet Beaton meant. He thought rapidly. Will claimed that they had met when he was four years old – thirty-four years ago. That would be 1566, the year before Tansy was born.

'She wanted you to tell me,' he said.

Tansy looked bewildered so he told her about the wise woman and his dream vision of Janet Beaton.

At last she smiled. 'I am glad you met again. I think she loved you very much. Maybe we – '

'Tansy!' Will was calling.

'Say goodbye to him for me,' said Tam. 'Explain if you can, what you think he might understand.'

They embraced and Tansy whispered, 'One minute of our own out of time. Is that all we will ever have together, Tam Eildor?'

Kissing her, he said gently, 'Who knows, Tansy, who knows.'

And turning swiftly, fighting back the tears, she ran back down the path to where her love and her life, Will Hepburn, awaited her, leaving Tam Eildor to travel on that next journey through time.

Not quite The End ...

SENSATIONAL HISTORIC DISCOVERY

Two workmen, engaged on renovating the royal apartments at Edinburgh Castle after a fire, have made the gruesome discovery of a tiny coffin. Nearly in line with the Crown Room and about six feet from the pavement of the quadrangle, the wall was observed to return a hollow sound when struck.

On removing a block of stone, a recess was discovered measuring about 2 feet 6 by 1 foot, containing the remains of a child enclosed in an oak coffin, evidently of great antiquity and very much decayed. Wrapped in a shroud, a cloth believed to be woollen, very thick and somewhat resembling leather, and within this the remains of a shroud of a richly embroidered silk and cloth which suggested some portion of a priest's vestment, most likely used in the Masses secretly held in Queen Mary's oratory. Such a sanctified garment would be approved as suitable for the interment of one of royal blood, a little prince, born and baptised in the Popish faith, rather than for the hasty disposal of some Court lady's indiscretion. Further evidence being two initials wrought upon the shroud, one alas, was indecipherable, but the other, the letter 'J' was distinctly visible.

From the coffin's concealment in the wall, secrecy of the closest character was evidently the object, and being wainscoted thereafter, no trace remained.

By order of the Castle officials the remains were restored to the coffin and the aperture closed up.

To the two workmen who made the discovery, dragging out a box immediately gave rise to exciting thoughts of hidden treasure. When its true identity became apparent, however, the apprentice, an Irish lad and a devout Roman Catholic, was in such a panic at the sight of a coffin that, crossing himself, he let it fall to the floor.

Cursing the lad, gibbering with terror, for his clumsiness, the older man in charge of the renovation work scrambled about trying to put it together again. The results were not very encouraging and he decided they had better break off their work and inform the Castle authorities of their find.

There was some argument as to whether the coffin should

be carried with them, but considering its now fragile condition the man in charge decided that wasn't a good idea and that it had better be left where it was.

The clumsy apprentice, quaking, swore by the Mother of God that he wasn't going to be left alone with any coffin. There might be ghosts. The other workman laughed. A big strong fellow, he could fight anything or anyone. No ghost would bother him. Besides it was just a wee bairn's bones. What harm could they do anyone?

Telling the lad to go with the message instead, and be quick about it, he would stay and watch the coffin. Truth to tell, he'd be glad of a wee break and taking his clay pipe from his pocket, cursing, he realised the lad had gone off with the matches.

No matter, since they had needed extra light for the job in the dim recess, there was a candle on the box beside the wall.

But what to light his pipe with?

Looking round he saw on the floor a piece of rolled paper, yellowed with age, stained and torn.

Picking it up, it crumbled in his fingers and as he tried to unroll it, spread it on the table, he saw there were some words written on it, but he had never learned to read.

Besides he was dying for a smoke.

So he held it to the candle and used its bright flame to light his clay pipe.

Puffing away happily he became aware through the smoke of a tall man standing near the entrance.

Someone in authority. That was quick. About to spring to his feet, footsteps announced the return of his clumsy apprentice.

The officials were on their way to inspect the coffin.

'Who was that then?' asked the pipe-smoker.

The lad looked blank.

'You must have passed him coming in, he was standing by the door. Daft-like clothes, an old-fashioned white shirt and his arm in a sling.'

The lad shook his head. He had seen no one.

But Tam Eildor had seen enough. When the workman so obligingly spread the faded document on the table, the almost illegible signatures of Janet Beaton and Margaret Agnew were for a moment faintly visible.

From his talk long ago with Martin Hailes at Kirktillo, Tam knew the identity of the baby who had lain in the castle wall near Mary Queen of Scots apartments since 16 June 1566, and the reason for the ruthless search throughout King James's reign that had cost so many innocent lives, including the slaughter of the Earl and Master of Gowrie.

Now, seeing the workman so leisurely using the crumbling document to light his clay pipe and watching its charred fragments drift away into the Edinburgh skies, Tam saw that the irony was complete.

The king's secret was safe at last. The contents of the documents that had haunted him destroyed forever by 'that vile custom', the subject of his treatise, "A Counterblast to Tobacco".

He decided that King James would have approved.

Author's Note

Four hundred years ago today, Queen Elizabeth died and James VI of Scotland became James I of England, his great ambition fulfilled in the Union of the Crowns. He reigned for twenty-two years and returned only once to Scotland in 1617 to attend the General Assembly.

Perth County Council Chambers, with a commemorative plaque, marks the site of Gowrie House, demolished in 1807.

After the terrible deeds within its walls on 5 August 1600, the name and arms of Ruthven were extinguished and their estates forfeited. Ruthven Castle became known as Huntingtower, the name it bears to this day. Property of HM Office of Works it is open to the public.

Regarding the fate of the two younger Ruthvens. William made his escape to France where he remained in exile and was to distinguish himself by his knowledge of chemistry.

His younger brother was not so fortunate in escaping the king's vengeance. As soon as James was crowned king of England and Scotland in 1603, he immediately had Patrick Ruthven hunted down and imprisoned in the Tower of London. There he remained for 19 years after which he was released and became a noted surgeon.

By Queen Anne's intervention, the Ruthven sisters Beatrix and Barbara were returned to her service.

Meanwhile the key historical players in the slaughter at Gowrie House were suitably rewarded. Sir John Erskine of Mar who delivered the wounded Master of Ruthven's death-blow received the Lordship of Dirleton Castle and lands. John Ramsay who first daggered Alexander and then killed the Earl received a knighthood and was created Lord Haddington. Even Henderson, the armed man in the turret, was not forgotten. The king gave him a lifetime pension and his son was raised to the peerage as Lord Dunkeld.

The heir to two kingdoms, Prince Henry died in 1612, aged 16. Ironically, on 15 November 1600 the day of the posthumous trial of the corpses of the Ruthven brothers, Queen Anne gave birth to a son, the future Charles the First who succeeded his father and was fated to die under the executioner's axe.

The king who became known as 'The Wisest Fool in Christendom' was a prolific author, scholar and poet. Despite his dubious reputation and the many scandals associated with his reign, his name was to be remembered with due reverence by generations for the King James Version of the Holy Bible.

Tam Eildor and Tansy Scott are fictional. William Hepburn, illegitimate son of James Hepburn, Earl of Bothwell by Anna Throndsen, lived as a child with Bothwell's mother Lady Morham who mentioned him in her will.

In this second fictionalised reconstruction of an unsolved historic mystery, the key issues are as depicted in contemporary documents with letters and actual speech used where recorded. Tam Eildor's first time-quest (Mary Queen of Scots and the Murder of Darnley) wherein he met William Hepburn and Janet Beaton is *The Dagger in the Crown* (Macmillan 2001).

ALANNA KNIGHT

Edinburgh, 24 March 2003